DIANE CULVER

Love on the Run

Hampton Thoroughbreds

The saga begins
Diane Culver

LOVE ON THE RUN

COPYRIGHT 2013 by Laurie Bumpus

Cover design Jessica Lewis www.authorslifesaver.com

Editor - Gina Ardito www.excellenceediting.com

Disclaimer

This book is a work of fiction. Names, characters, incidents, and places are a product of the author's imagination or used fictitiously. Any resemblance to persons, (living or dead), business establishments, and actual events are entirely coincidental, except for the use of Eckart's Luncheonette, which has been done with permission of the owner. The unauthorized reproduction or distribution of this copyrighted work is illegal. No part of this book can be scanned, published, or distributed in any manner without the express written consent of the author, Laurie Bumpus, writing as Diane Culver, except when quotations are embodied in articles or reviews. Thank you for respecting the author's work.

All rights reserved.

ISBN-13: 978-1475085266

DEDICATION

This book is dedicated to my aunt,
Virginia Gilmore
My mentor, my friend and my port in the storm.

She is the glue that has held the Culver family together
And has taught us all the true meaning of family.

PROLOGUE

Three weeks earlier

The memory of the dark, filthy five-foot by eight-foot cell was still with her. But payback for the incarceration endured was within reach. Zoya Stalinski's hands tightened on the steering wheel as her thoughts flashed back to her six-month imprisonment at the hands of the United States government. The images and wounds of torture and humiliation were fresh. Plans to extract revenge had taken too much time, in her opinion, but were now precisely mapped out. Her contacts were in place. She had to get to her destination as soon as possible. She was the focal point of the mission. And she was late.

Zoya's small black Toyota Camry rolled forward behind the line of cars creeping towards the border checkpoint. Her heart hammered in her chest. Stay calm, she willed herself. Don't give the agent any reason to be suspicious. Zoya glanced down at the watch on her wrist. In order to meet her contact by nightfall, she needed to be on her way to Washington, D.C.

"Hand me your passport," Zoya forcefully said to her male companion. He did as she asked. "Look at me." The man turned; his blue eyes pierced hers. "Stavros, don't you dare say a word, not unless you have to. Do you understand me?" The man silently nodded his assent. "You could very well jeopardize everything. Your English is good, yes. But you haven't totally mastered disguising your Russian accent when you speak quickly."

The young man pointed out the windshield. "Look over there." Cars lined up in a cordoned-off section, waiting to be searched by agents. K-9 patrol dogs sniffed in and around the cars' wheels and hubcaps. One dog stopped, his nose on the bumper of a white Mercedes. "I don't like this. I'm nervous, Zoya."

"Put your hands down, you fool!" Her own accent escaped in the terse retort. "We don't need to draw attention to ourselves. Security cameras are well hidden." Zoya chastised her brother. "If only you'd done as directed last week, we'd be in New York. Your misguided sense of judgment cost me valuable time. Our contact moved on. He couldn't wait. Now we have to be sure we're constantly on the move." She glared at Stavros. "Act as if we're just patiently waiting. Everyone is being watched closely. Pretend we're having a civil conversation."

Stavros slightly reclined his seat, smiled, and gave the semblance of a laugh. "If we pull this off, Zoya, you will have evened—"

"If?" Zoya interrupted. "There is no if. I have my job, and you have yours."

Her brother nodded. "I know. I do this for you, Zoya."

"Just stick to what we rehearsed if the guard questions us."

The border patrol agent waved her forward. Zoya abruptly stopped talking. The agent motioned for her to roll down the car's window.

Placing the vehicle in park, she pressed the button to open the window, saying in flawless English, "Good morning."

"Enhanced drivers' licenses or passports, please."

Zoya handed the agent the requested documents.

The guard read the information before him, looking through the car's window when he'd finished. "Your destination and length of stay?"

"New York City," Zoya replied. "We plan on being there for one week."

"You, sir." Zoya stiffened, noting the guard was taking a closer look at Stavros's passport and then leaned slightly in the window. She held her breath, praying the exchange between her brother and the guard would be brief. "Where were you born, sir?"

"Quebec," Stavros spoke, his words kept to a minimum.

"Ma'am, your place of birth?"

"Toronto." The agent nodded and closed the passports, handing the documents back to her.

"Enjoy your trip. The Peace Bridge exit is up ahead on the right if you're taking the Thruway." The officer signaled to his partner to open the white barrier to allow their car to pass through from Canada to the States. Within minutes, the Toyota was cruising down the highway.

Zoya turned to Stavros, this time with a wide grin on her face. "Well done. Now, we make up for time lost." With Canada behind them, she'd reverted to her native tongue.

Stavros reached into the glove compartment and pulled out a manila envelope. Zoya knew it contained the important information needed to conduct their mission. Their Canadian contact had passed it to her that morning at the coffee kiosk outside the Toronto Zoo. "May I?"

"Yes. Read it to me as I drive. But, before you do, set the GPS with our final destination."

Stavros typed in the address. "We've a long drive ahead of us. At least ten hours."

"We'll make it." Tapping her fingers on the steering wheel, she frowned. Zoya's main concern was that things wouldn't go as planned. "Stavros, you know we've only one chance to make this right."

She felt a reassuring squeeze on her right knee as her eyes scanned the highway for the sign for their exit.

A very confident voice spoke up from the seat beside her. "Zoya, never doubt your ability to do your job. We know where they are. Revenge will be ours when we've killed them."

CHAPTER ONE

Hallock Farm
Hampton Beach, Long Island

Katherine Hallock knew from the look on Hannah's face she was in for a tongue-lashing. Katherine's duties as head veterinarian at the farm had made her late for supper for the third time that week. And she had to have a pretty damn good excuse if she missed dinner at the estate house.

"Your mother's in a snit over you missing that meeting today, Miss Kate." Hannah, the Hallocks' housekeeper for forty years, wiped her hands on her apron and proceeded to admonish Kate as if she was twelve and not twenty-nine. "You forgot all about that wedding planner on purpose." Hannah paused and looked at her sternly. "Didn't you?"

Trying to ready herself for the showdown, Kate stopped, sniffed the air and took in the aroma of her favorite meal - Yankee pot roast. Then, crossing her fingers behind her back, she replied, "No, I didn't." *Although it did cross my mind.* "I called Mother twice to tell her I wasn't going to make it, but got her voicemail." Kate held up two fingers to make her point. "Can I help it if she never answers that phone? We had some issues with one of the colts down at the stables. Mother should know by now not to make my appointments for me."

Hannah motioned to the door leading to the hallway. In her thick Irish brogue, she replied, "You'd best hurry. You're late. Get in there and face the dragon lady. Supper's ready."

Kate leaned her hip against the butcher-block island, grinning as she imagined her prim and proper mother breathing fire. But her voice took on a more serious tone given the topic at hand. "Hannah, why doesn't Mother just plan the wedding all by herself? She doesn't need me. The other day I tried to talk to her about what *I* wanted and I got 'the look.' You know the one. She and Mrs. Bennington booked the church and hired the best wedding planner in the Hamptons before Ty officially put the ring on my finger. Maybe it would be better if Ty and I just show up."

Kate paused to take in the stunned look on the housekeeper's face. "Better yet, maybe we should just elope?" The expression on Hannah's face was priceless. Kate loved the fact she could push the right buttons to get Hannah's Irish temper so easily riled up.

Hannah stood on the opposite side of the kitchen island, her hands on her hips. "There's not a lot of time left, Katherine. Your mother needs you. The wedding is only three months away. You've got to meet your mother halfway, dear. Think of it from her point of view. She's the mother of the bride, and you're her *only* daughter." Hannah shook her finger at Kate. "You, missy, are creating a monster. And the rest of us have to deal with her while you're out in the paddocks. She's on the warpath tonight, thanks to you."

"But, I don't want—"

"No." Hannah put up her hand to ward off any more talk. "No buts tonight. Get cleaned up. Dinner's on its way to getting overdone." Hannah sniffed the air. "*That* odor is not my pot roast! You smell like horse manure. Go take a shower. You've got five minutes before dinner's on the table."

"Can't you stretch it to ten?" Kate had Hannah wrapped around her little finger. The woman practically raised Kate and her four brothers. The woman had read and tucked the five siblings into bed every night while Robert and Helen Hallock were out socializing at various Hampton society galas. Their housekeeper was a saint, and Kate loved her dearly.

"Ten minutes is all you'll be getting from me tonight, and no more. Your father will have my head because his meal wasn't on the table 'at the stroke of six.' I'm warning you. Play nice tonight. Your brothers are here."

Katherine took the back staircase, bypassing the dining room where everyone had already convened. She took a whiff of her denim shirt. Hannah was right. She smelled like one of the groomsmen.

Being the head veterinarian of the family business, Hallock Farm, one of the largest thoroughbred farms on the eastern seaboard, had its perks, but the sixteen-hour days were wearing her down. The training schedule heated up this past week for Torch's Thunder, Hallock Farm's entrant in this year's Belmont Stakes. Kate had been late because the horse's time trials had exceeded her and the trainer's wildest expectations. But Mother wouldn't care that Kate needed to take time to discuss tomorrow's workout.

Mindful that she was keeping everyone waiting, she ducked into the shower. Thoughts of the wedding danced through her mind for the first time in weeks. Time. Time was the issue that brought Kate and her mother to butt heads. There weren't enough hours in a day to balance her job at the farm, the wedding planner's demands, and the multitude of engagement festivities. Add to that her patience with Ty Bennington, her fiancé, was stretched thin. Where the hell was he when she needed him? MIA for the past three weeks, Ty claimed there were too many cases coming to trial at his father's law firm in New York City. He'd insisted there would be plenty of time to rest and relax on their honeymoon.

Upon hearing someone pounding on her bedroom door, Kate turned off the shower. She called out, "I'm coming!" A loud fist banged again. "Who is it?"

A deep voice growled from the other side. It was Thomas, her eldest brother and CFO of Hallock Farm. "Mother's in one of her royal snits, thanks to you, Katie. Get your butt out of that shower and downstairs. I, for one, am sick of dealing with her ranting and raving all because of your damn wedding plans."

Kate tugged a red knit dress over her head and reached for her black heels. "Judas Priest! I'll be there in a minute! Tell Mother I'm just throwing on a change of clothes. God forbid we shouldn't dress for dinner. I'll be down in a few minutes. Fix her another gin and tonic, Tom. Coupled with what she's probably had, she'll be more mellow."

Kate grinned inwardly when she heard what sounded like a laughing snort, followed by receding footsteps on the wooden floorboards in the hall. She liberally sprayed on her favorite perfume to be sure the smell of the horses had truly dissipated. Following closely behind her brother, Kate headed for the stairs leading to the main foyer off the dining room.

Knowing she was headed into the dragon's den, Kate attempted to put herself into a positive frame of mind. She was twenty-nine years old. She'd accomplished her life's goal of becoming an equine veterinarian. As a Hallock, her life in the Hamptons gave her opportunities most people could only dream of. And she'd fallen head over heels in love with the perfect man – one who was just as ambitious as she was and supported what she was aiming to do for Hallock Farm. Kate would be marrying Ty on what would, if she didn't kill her mother tonight, be the most perfect day.

CHAPTER TWO

Kate adjusted the black belt of her dress as she descended the main staircase to the foyer. She muttered under her breath that she had better things to do than sit through another of her mother's mandatory formal dinners. Stepping off the bottom stair onto the marble floor, a loud boom reverberated against the wall, shaking the antique mirror hanging to her left. Taken by surprise, Kate gasped, grabbing for the valuable item, which looked as if it were about to fall, and secured it back on its hook. An argument was in progress within the confines of her father's study.

"Let go of me, you fool! Take your hands off me!" Kate heard her father bellow. "You've got no right to talk to me like that. Don't forget whose house you're in."

"Oh, I know where I am. I'm here to remind you what you agreed to. The people you contracted to do business with have a unique way of being sure they get what they want. I've been sent here to deliver their message. Your farm's new business associates want their money and the merchandise you promised, Robert."

It wasn't news to Kate, hearing her father displeased with someone in his office, but upon recognizing the voice that barked back, Kate grasped the knobs of the French doors of the study for support. The voice was that of Ty Bennington – her fiancé. Whatever was he doing here? Three days ago, he'd informed her he had to travel to a law conference in Washington, D.C. That was after he'd finally returned the fifteen plus messages she'd left on his voicemail.

Ty continued, "You have one week…*one week* to make good. I warned you not to make promises you couldn't keep or offer to pay money you didn't have."

Katherine's ear was as close to the door as she could possibly get as she heard the Hallock patriarch retort, "Wait just one minute! *You're* the one who advised me to sign that deal on the dotted line. *You* assured me we'd have the capital to expand Hallock Farm faster if I took their offer. Don't you recall the challenge from Thomas? How irate he was that we were going behind the board's back. *You* got me into this mess, Ty. You're in as deep as I am."

Kate heard a thud as if a chair toppled over inside her father's inner sanctum. The guilt she felt from eavesdropping flew out the window the minute she heard the farm's finances were involved. For the past six years, she'd worked night and day to bring Hallock Farm to the forefront in equine care and develop the full potential of the thoroughbred breeding program. Her ability to restrain herself from confronting her father and Ty disappeared.

Kate flung open the doors of the office with such force they crashed into the wood-paneled walls inside. Her father's treasured picture of his first Belmont Stakes winner, Golden Rod, fell to the floor, the glass smashing to pieces, the frame askew. The commotion of her entrance shocked the room's occupants.

Kate knew from dealing with her father in regards to the farm she had to get the upper hand in an argument as quickly as possible.

"What the hell is this?" Now, it was Kate's turn to bellow at both men. Kate looked from her father, who sat behind his desk rubbing his neck, to Ty, who stood adjacent to him, fingers flexing at his side. It became evident to Kate that Ty had physically threatened the elder man. She shook her head to clear that unbelievable thought from her mind. But the evidence stared her in the face.

Ty rounded the desk, heading for her. He righted the wing chair that had fallen over during the heated argument.

Kate put her hand up to halt him, and he stopped dead in his tracks. "Stop right where you are. Tell me what's going on." Kate stood ramrod straight, her hands on her hips. "I want the truth. I want the whole story…from both of you." Moving into the room, Kate diverted her gaze from her fiancé and glared at her father. "Have you done something illegal we'd all better know about, Father?"

Robert sat up in his leather chair as if nothing was amiss. But Kate knew better. "Ty and I are involved in a business deal that has hit a few snags. Nothing major. Nothing for you or anyone else to worry about. You just keep things running smoothly as you always do."

Kate would not be summarily dismissed. "Don't placate me, Father. I could hear you through the wall. Somebody in here got a bit physical." She warily eyed Ty, who again tried to move closer. Her hand went up, and he halted. "To *whom* do you owe money? And what's this about merchandise? You better not be referring to my horses. What have you done?"

Ty stood nearby, his arms crossed over his chest. "Contrary to his attorney's advice, your father entered into a business contract with men with unsavory connections."

Kate wanted to smack the smug look off Ty's face. But he'd captured her attention with the comment he'd made. Out of the corner of her eye, Kate saw her father blanch. "What kind of connections?"

"Several of the men have ties to Brooklyn's Russian mafia."

Feeling as if she'd been sucker-punched, Kate dropped into the Windsor chair just inside the doorway. She eyed the two men warily. To say she was speechless was an understatement.

As if Kate wasn't even in the room, her father continued, "You, of all people, Ty, know I don't have access to that kind of ready cash."

Kate cringed. This must have been what Thomas had been so adamant to talk to her about on Wednesday. But she'd just brushed him off, busy with the horses. He was always on her case regarding their father's business dealings. Her father and brother argued continually over what was happening within the financial end of the family business, and Kate had tuned Thomas out. She had enough on her plate. God, she could kick herself now.

Her father's quivering voice brought her back from her musings. "Hell, Ty. Can't you buy me some leverage? You must be able to broker a deal? You and your father both know them well."

Kate's head snapped up. Ty's family associated with people with ties to the mob? Had she met them at some of the Hampton society events the two attended this past year?

The increasing harshness and untypical threatening tone in Ty's voice started to frighten Kate.

"Listen to me, old man. You and I both know you don't have enough money in your personal accounts to pay what you owe. But you're going to find it from somewhere, somehow, or things will happen around here you hadn't planned on. How much does your precious business and family mean to you?"

"Ty!" Kate cried out. "How can you possibly—"

"Why, you son of a bitch!" Kate's father cut her off as he rose from his chair and pounded his fist on the desk.

Ty retorted, pointing his finger at her father. "You are playing with fire."

"Get out!" her father roared, his face red from anger.

Kate stood rooted in place, knowing she should move but unable.

Her father was vehement. "I didn't drag *you* into anything *you* didn't want to be part of either, *son*." Robert spat out the last word. "You wanted in and signed on. And need I remind you in all of this…*you* wanted Katie. You know full well I can't deliver what they want from Hallock Farm…legally."

"I'm telling you if you don't come across with what they want, what you value most will disappear." Ty turned to lock his dark, smoking eyes on hers.

A chill ran down her spine. Kate knew exactly what he meant. The man didn't need to spell it out. Panic set in. She could hear her heart beating like a drum in her ears. Her chest tightened. Everything she believed in was imploding around her. Suddenly, Kate was aware Ty was coming across the room…for her.

"Kate, I—"

Kate didn't give Ty time to explain. She twisted the diamond ring off her finger and flung it through the air, hitting him squarely in the chest. She was beyond hurt. Beyond angry. Kate exploded in rage. "How dare you not look out for me, my family and, most importantly, our future! You selfish son-of–a bitch! For years we've treated you as if you would be one of us. And this…*this* is where you take us? We were going to be married! Raise a family together. There's nothing left to say. We're finished!"

Ty bent over to retrieve the ring that lay on the oriental carpet. If he got too close to her, Kate didn't know what she would do to him. Turning to look at her father, Kate was at a loss for words. He had slumped back in his chair. The worst feeling she'd ever felt in her life washed over her – betrayal. She'd been tossed to the wolves by the two men she loved most.

Realizing that neither man would be more forthcoming with information or show any concern for her well- being left Kate with only one thing to do. Run. But to run was against every fiber of who she was. Katherine Hallock never ran from her problems. She met difficulties head on and solved them. But based on what she'd discovered in the few brief moments in the study, she had no choice. Kate had to get far as away from Hampton Beach as she possibly could. Now.

Kate bolted from the study, ignoring her father's calls to come back. A nauseous feeling swept over her as she heard Ty threaten her father one more time.

Teetering on her black high heels, Kate ran down the hall and through the kitchen door, bypassing a shocked Hannah without so much as a goodbye. Leaping into her Jeep parked where she'd left it when she'd arrived back at the house for dinner, Kate reached for the keys hidden under the driver's seat and gunned the engine. As she took off, the Jeep's tires squealed on the pavement. Turning down the tree-lined drive that led up to the front of the main estate, Kate felt like a modern day Scarlett O'Hara running from Rhett Butler and Tara.

Bringing the Jeep to a screeching halt at the estate's main entrance on Apaucapoint Road, Kate took one last look out over the glistening water of Moriches Bay, knowing she wouldn't see this view for quite some time. Kate's peaceful, perfect life was gone. Vanished.

With no oncoming traffic in sight, Kate wrenched the steering wheel to the right and headed for the main highway. Suddenly, it dawned on her. She'd left without food or cash. With her comings and goings around the farm and the errands she ran, she always stashed the farm's debit card in the glove compartment. Her cell phone was, at that moment, clipped to the belt of her dirty jeans lying on the floor of her bedroom.

Assessing her situation, she glanced down at the dashboard and breathed a sigh of relief, seeing the full tank of gas. Knowing she would not need to stop at the Valero gas station on Montauk Highway, Kate made a u-turn and headed for the Eastport grocery with the ATM. She needed to be quick. There wasn't a doubt in her mind that Ty and her father would spin a tale to the family within a half-hour. Her father's security detail would be searching for her soon.

Fearful of being tracked, Kate yanked the GPS off the windshield, tossing it into the brush at the entrance ramp to Sunrise Highway. There was only one place to go, and she would have to drive all night to get there. But on her arrival, Kate would be welcomed with open arms, and her safety would be guaranteed around the clock.

Robert Hallock often quoted that he'd never visit her intended destination unless "Hell froze over."

Kate set the cruise control on seventy and, barring any sort of major traffic, she'd be in the nation's Capitol by sunrise.

CHAPTER THREE

The sky lit up as flashes of lightning arced across the sky. Rain pelted the windshield of Kate's Jeep with such intensity she thought she'd be pulling off the interstate for the second time that night. Her windshield wipers barely kept the water off the window, making travel difficult. She was forced to slow down every time a tractor-trailer passed for fear of going off the road, due to lack of visibility. She eyed the clock on the dashboard. Four-thirty. If she hadn't been forced to pull into a rest area south of Philadelphia when the rain started, Kate would be within miles of her destination.

With the radio announcing the impending storm several hours earlier, Kate realized the need to secure the vehicle's top. Also needing to fill her tank with gas, she had pulled into a rest stop just north of Baltimore. By the time Kate locked down the roof, the rain was coming down in torrents. She was soaking wet from the top of her head to the shoes on her feet. Her shoes were ruined from standing in water up to her ankles, and her red knit dress clung to her body, outlining every feminine curve, weighing her down.

Thankful for always being prepared for any emergency that might have occurred at the farm, Kate pulled a small duffle bag from the storage locker located behind the front seats. Looking about, she spotted the sign for the women's bathroom. Deciding to make a run for it, she placed the bag over her head, although it was pointless in protecting her from the elements. The soaking rains had wrecked havoc with her hair and clothes by then. Struggling out of her dress in the small stall, Kate realized her body shivered not just from the cold rain. She was in shock and distressed her comfortable world had been turned upside-down.

Don't concentrate on the past ten hours. Place your energies into getting to Arlington by sunup. Stay focused. You're almost there.

When she exited the stall, she looked into a mirror by the washbasin for the first time since fleeing the farm. Kate didn't recognize the woman staring back. Wringing the water from her long hair, she rummaged through the bag she'd placed on the counter. Her hand finally located the spare brush she always carried with her. Trying to make herself look presentable was not an easy task. Her arms felt like lead weights as she went through the motions. After sweeping her auburn hair up into a ponytail, she drew a ratty baseball cap from the duffle bag, tugging it on her head. Satisfied she was dry and ready to roll, Kate left the bathroom.

In the foyer of the rest stop, she spied several travelers gathered near a stand offering free coffee. Knowing a good jolt of caffeine to keep her awake and alert on the highway was just what she needed, she walked towards it. Had she not been so motivated to get to her destination by sunrise, she'd have placed the Jeep's seat in the horizontal position, grabbed the horse blanket from the storage bin and gone to sleep for a few hours. But time was of the essence. Kate had to get to where she'd be safe, where no one would harm her. A place she knew she'd find help rationalizing the jumbled, mixed-up puzzle that lay at her feet. She was one hundred percent positive she was headed to a place where there would be help putting the pieces of her imploded life back together.

Kate thanked the volunteer manning the coffee booth and walked away from the table, breathing in the scent of the hot liquid. Taking a few quick sips, she spied a vending machine. Her stomach growled as if on cue. Carefully eyeing the contents, she saw exactly what the doctor would prescribe for her present situation. Chocolate. Dark chocolate. What else better to add to the caffeine jolt? Fishing in the pocket of her riding pants, she was lucky to find four quarters. Making her selection, it dawned on Kate she possessed no identification but the ATM card she had stowed in the glove compartment. For now, she considered that the least of her problems. Inserting the coins, she pulled the lever. Kate reached down and retrieved the candy bar from the bottom of the bin.

Looking out the door into the dark night, Kate saw the storm had increased in intensity. She'd stopped just in time. The ride would be slow, but she knew she would be in Arlington just in time to beat the morning rush.

Making a mad dash for the Jeep, she unlocked the car and hopped in. The sky lit up again, making the area look as if morning had come. Kate hated thunderstorms ever since she and Matthew, the youngest male heir to the Hallock fortune, had been caught out in their Sunfish sailboat on the bay one summer afternoon. She and her younger brother hadn't made it in to shore before the storm hit. The waves had toppled the boat, but Matt had secured a life preserver around her neck and brought her safely to shore.

How she needed the TEAM and their wisdom, given her present predicament - Thomas, Ethan, Adam and Matthew. What would they think about her running away? Were they even aware of the dynamics of what transpired in her father's study? Other than Thomas, there was little interaction about the farm's daily business with the other three.

Stop. Concentrate on getting through the storm, she muttered under her breath. There'd be time to worry about the family she had left behind when she reached D.C.

Another streak of lightning crossed the sky as Kate put the key into the ignition. She pulled out of her parking space and drove onto the interstate.

Gripping the steering wheel with her left hand, Kate took a sip of the coffee, sighing as the warm liquid hit her stomach, the chill now gone from her body. Taking a bite from the candy bar was as if she'd tasted a small piece of heaven. Keeping her eyes on the road and the cars around her, she chewed slowly, savoring every mouthful. A sudden smile lit up her face as she recalled her recent conversation with Sarah Adams. Sarah worked for the Sunfish Beach Club owned by her brother, Matt. Both women, who were constantly commiserating about their love lives, agreed there were times when chocolate was better than sex. When eaten properly, it actually could be classified as orgasmic.

Looking through the windshield, Kate's eyes locked onto a bright green neon mileage sign – Washington, D.C. – 92 miles. Checking the clock in her dashboard, she estimated she'd pull into the compound around six.

Hunkering down for the rest of the ride, her eyes on the road, Kate tuned the radio to a local country music channel. Tammy Wynette was in the middle of singing her classic song, "Stand By Your Man." Kate choked as the remnants of the candy bar slid down her throat. Giving the knob a good twist, Kate found another station, one with a talk show, and concentrated on the road ahead.

* * *

Arlington, Virginia

Kate could drive to the compound with her eyes closed. Dawn had broken. Taking in the familiar landmarks, she slowly made her way down Madison Road. The farther she drove, the larger the houses became. Within a few blocks, the houses exponentially grew in size, the edifices hidden behind large brick walls with keyed entry gates. Some even had armed guards posted. It was here diplomats and Congressional representatives lived, as well as other key figures in the president's administration.

Kate's mind had been awhirl for hours. She was faced with two dilemmas. Fleeing as she did, she hadn't time to follow compound protocol. She was in need of the daily numeric password code for the keypad should there be no one in the gatehouse. Given the job of the person she had come to see left open the possibility that, if absent, the grounds would be secured against visitors. Kate mentally kicked herself. She should have checked the status in D.C. before leaving Hampton Beach. But her cell phone was on the floor of her bedroom, leaving her with no way to communicate with anyone at the compound. Stupid. Stupid. Stupid.

It had been two years since her last visit to Arlington. Big changes were made in security details and personnel. The home's occupant was known only to a few of the residents of the other houses along Madison Road, and she mentally tried to configure a way in without causing suspicion.

Kate drove past the address just as the sun broke the horizon. How odd. There was usually one or two black SUVs parked at the entrance, whether its occupant was present or not. Maybe Kate was correct in thinking the person had been called away. Was it worth the risk to circle the block one more time as she tried to come up with a plan to enter the premises? Surveillance cameras were mounted in the climbing vines on the brick walls. Of that she was certain. The last thing Kate needed was someone calling the Metro police and becoming part of a public police blotter.

Stopping the Jeep at the end of the property line, she studied the neighborhood. Devoid of the usual cars and traffic given the time of day, an odd feeling crept over her. She'd been hell bent on arriving under the cover of darkness so as not to be seen, but at this time of day, Kate expected the street to be busy with the hustle and bustle of another Washington workday. Her eyes darted to the few driveways on the other side of the street. Nothing. It certainly was not a government holiday of some sort. Had there been a lockdown? No, definitely not. The place would be teeming with SWAT teams and other forms of law enforcement. What was going on?

For the first time in twelve hours, Kate had a smile on her face. Of course! The old brick wall! Still vine-covered, even more so than years ago, she'd played "Hide the Spy" with Adam one summer many years ago in their youth, using it to enter and exit the property.

She knew the compound had undergone a major overhaul since 9/11. Praying the gods would be on her side and what she sought hidden behind the vines was still there, she surveyed her surroundings. Kate had only one try to get in. And she was well aware she didn't have much time to execute her plan to gain entrance before someone else's security camera picked her up and alarm buttons rang out.

The distance to the wall wasn't far from where she sat in her Jeep. But what would she find on the other side? Counting off the brick columns from the telephone pole, Kate hoped she remembered how to find what she sought. With the seconds ticking by and her heart hammering in her chest, Kate opened the driver's side door and made a mad dash to a section of wall between the third and fourth column. Placing her hand up under the vine at eye level, Kate searched for the brick that would slide to the right when activated.

She panicked when her fingers found no outcropping. No! It had to be there. No one else had known of its existence. Well, Kate took that back. Sam Tanner caught her and her brother using it to play their game, but after a stern lecture about security, promised to not tattle. But how could she not think that in all these years someone would not have done away with the hidden door? She slid her hand once more over the rough surface, hoping to trigger the brick. Nothing.

Now, her only recourse was to climb up and over the ten-foot wall. Kate knew security cameras were mounted everywhere, catching her for sure. But it was the only way in and her last resort. Kate had no doubt she could get up and over the wall. She'd beaten her brothers time and again to the top of the old oak tree in the backyard of the estate house.

Testing the vines, she wound a few around her hands. Her riding boots offered her the traction she needed. Within minutes, Kate had scaled the wall, landing softly on the other side. As she scanned the grounds, the well-landscaped lawns, gardens and pool were showing signs of the Virginia summer heat. The backyard was as beautiful as she remembered.

Listening for the sounds of people chattering and moving around given the hour of the morning, she found the compound eerily quiet. Kate knew the drill. Sam and his team always roamed the grounds well before sunup after getting a briefing from the night shift. Kate recalled what she'd learned about his special ops training - the man rarely slept. It was Sam's mission to always be by *her* side.

Spying the mudroom doorway, Kate took one last look. Seeing no one, she decided this was her chance. Staying low to the ground, she made a run for the door, trying her best to hide behind any small bush or tree. Kate was so tired she accidentally let out a hysterical giggle. She clapped her hand over her mouth to stifle the small squeak that came out of her mouth. It took only seconds to arrive safely at the kitchen door. Kate slowly opened it, letting herself inside.

CHAPTER FOUR

Katherine Hallock was safe. And she intended to remain that way.

As Kate stealthily entered the large kitchen, she noticed nothing had changed since her last visit. Cherry cabinets lined the walls, and a long butcher-block island stood prominently in its center. Beams taken from an old plantation estate crossed the ceiling, adding an antique flair to the décor. It was early. She could see the sun barely peeking through the kitchen's bay window. Taking in her surroundings, Katherine took a deep breath and sighed in relief.

Kate recognized the symptoms of being beyond exhausted. The events of the previous day left her emotionally and physically drained. Food, a soft bed and a good hot bath were her first order of business, not necessarily in that order. Spying the ever-present pot of coffee percolating on the counter, Kate walked to the cabinet directly above the dishwasher. Knowing its contents by heart, she opened the door and fished around in the glassware for one particularly special mug. She smiled as her hand came to rest on it. It was still there! The very one she'd used since she was six years old. After pouring herself a steaming cup of coffee, she wrapped her hands around it.

Raising it to her lips, she blew on the liquid and sipped the contents slowly. The hot liquid hit her stomach. A soothing tingle of warmth shot through her taut body.

Kate grew suspicious of the empty kitchen…and even more the empty grounds of the estate. Where in the world was everybody? At this time of day, the compound was crawling with employees running to do the bidding of the mistress of the house. Had something happened in world events overnight to force *her* into a secure location? There'd still be someone here to guard the home.

Kate was one of the very few in the family who knew the drill. Becoming more apprehensive by the minute, Kate placed her half-finished cup on the counter. She leaned forward, bracing her hands on the granite countertop. Trying to calm herself and erase the panic that was beginning to invade her thoughts, she took several deep, cleansing breaths. In… Out… In… Out. It wasn't helping. Her mind went into overdrive, reeling from everything. Everything was too much to take in, given her present state. But she'd find her answers here…she hoped.

Feeling a feather-like tickle near her earlobe, Kate's hand reached up to brush the errant strand of hair behind her ear. It was then she heard the sound of a gun cocking. Startled, she froze.

"Lock your hands above your head," a feminine voice commanded. "Turn around…slowly now. If you so much as move the wrong way, this baby will blow your head and your socks off at the same time."

Kate did as she was told. The lady meant business. She'd witnessed the woman's marksmanship firsthand. Hands on her head, Kate rotated slowly to face the voice behind her and came to a halt. Anticipation, not fear, had her heart pounding and adrenaline pumping. She wasn't surprised to be staring down the barrel of a thirty-eight revolver; she'd seen it often enough. Nor was she alarmed to be looking directly into a face that resembled her own.

Seeing the shock of recognition register on the older woman's face, Kate gave in to a cocky grin. Knowing she, not the gun, now had the upper hand, Kate said calmly, "Sure glad to see you still have it, Aunt Elizabeth. I'm happy to see you, too."

* * *

"Katherine Elizabeth! What…? Where…?" Elizabeth Hallock was taken aback by the identity of her intruder. Her hand shook as she reset the safety on her revolver. "Whatever are you doing here?" Her previously commanding tone had been replaced by a soft southern drawl. "Why didn't you call?" With her gun safely stowed away in the holster under her left arm, Elizabeth grabbed her niece into a bear hug. "Love a duck, dearie. You scared the hell out of me! Don't you know I could have shot you?"

She stepped back, grabbing Katherine's upper arms, taking in the sight of her surprise visitor.

Kate answered sheepishly, "Ah…that's dawning on me now, Auntie. But, quite frankly, when I realized I couldn't call, all I could think of doing was to climb up and over the back wall." Kate paused, then smiled. "Let's just say I haven't had anything, much less a gun, licking my ear as of late."

Elizabeth grinned and laughed. "Not even Ty?"

Kate shook her head. Her niece's smile rapidly disappeared from her face.

"Everything's okay, Sam." Elizabeth released Katherine and called to a man with his gun still drawn, standing off to her right just inside the kitchen door. "Check the perimeter along the back wall. Find out who was supposed to be stationed there this morning. And I want a report about the security monitors. I've got a feeling we should expect some unwanted company very soon." She eyed Katherine questioningly, but received nothing more than a blank stare in return.

Katherine's silence had Elizabeth's radar pinging. Why this sudden visit? Since a child, Katherine never turned up unannounced. Katherine was well versed with the operating rules and protocol when visiting the Arlington estate.

Scrutinizing Katherine from head to toe, Elizabeth noted Katherine's puffy eyes. Had she been crying? The wrinkled condition of her clothing, added to the state of her hair tucked under her ratty baseball cap, led Elizabeth to deduce Katherine drove all night. The vibrant, happy woman Elizabeth always entertained in the past was not the same one who stood before her. Elizabeth was excellent at reading people's body language. The dejection and defeat she witnessed had her worried.

Determined to get at the cause, she asked probingly, "Why are you here? Have you any idea what time it is?" Elizabeth's eyes scanned the kitchen floor. "And where is your luggage?"

As an operative for the United States government for forty years, and now the Director of the CIA, she'd conducted her fair share of interrogations. Fearing the worst, Elizabeth needed answers. Her instincts told her to proceed with caution. Katherine would tell her what happened in her own time. But how much time did Elizabeth have to get at the truth?

"Don't you think you owe me some sort of an explanation, Katherine? You just can't waltz in here looking like death warmed over. You're trying to act as if nothing is wrong, but I know perfectly well something is."

Katherine stared at her feet. She kicked at the wood floor with the heel of her dusty riding boot.

Seeing her niece clam up, Elizabeth knew she'd pressed too hard. Taking a more soothing approach, she asked, "Katherine, *why* are you here? The timing doesn't make any sense, dearie. Isn't it the height of the racing season?" Elizabeth placed her hand on Katherine's chin, raising it up so she could directly look into the dark eyes so like her own. "Why aren't you home, readying the thoroughbreds for the Belmont Stakes?"

Tears welled up in Katherine's eyes. Her chin trembled. Elizabeth had a feeling she wasn't going to like what she was going to hear.

"I'm so sorry for showing up like I did. But, it was the only place I could come." Katherine's hands swiped at the tears running down her cheeks. Elizabeth's heart ached. She was awash with a helpless feeling. Her instinct had served her well. Something was horribly wrong.

Suddenly, Katherine spurted out in no particular order why she'd left Hampton Beach. Elizabeth tried her best to follow Katherine's jumbled ramblings. It was hard to make out what Katherine was trying to convey as her words spewed out. "I chucked my GPS on the way out of town. The first thing I thought of was its tracking device. Then, there's the farm. *Everything* blew up at the house." There was a hitch in Katherine's voice. "Things have been building with Mother and Father for a while, but *yesterday*…Oh, yesterday, when Father…" Elizabeth watched Katherine grab for her stomach, sucking in air, but she seemed to need to catch her breath to continue.

At the mention of her estranged brother, Elizabeth stiffened. Robert Hallock still made her blood boil, and she hadn't laid eyes on him in twenty years. But she needed to maintain a calm exterior.

"Katherine, *what* has your father done?"

Had Robert put his daughter in harm's way? Had Katherine stumbled onto something from Robert's past? What had impacted Hallock Farm to make Katherine drive hours through the kind of storm that had battered the seaboard last night?

Knowing her brother was capable of a wealth of possibilities swirled through Elizabeth's head. Even with the demands of her job with the CIA, she was always briefed about the goings on of Robert and the farm. But, it wasn't always possible to follow or react to his every move. Thomas called her on occasion to keep her informed on the activities taking place and the financial rifts he was having with his father, but most of the time they'd discussed what were the best moves he could make for the sake of the family business.

Elizabeth was roused from her musing by the sounds of sobs, as if a dam had burst. More words tumbled from Katherine's lips. "And it wasn't just Father." Katherine paused. Removing her hands from her stomach, she stood straight, her hands clenching and unclenching at her sides. "Ty was involved."

Elizabeth's radar went on high alert at the mention of Katherine's fiancé. Elizabeth hadn't liked Ty Bennington from the moment she'd met him. Call it her sixth sense. And with good cause, based on the background check Sam ran on her niece's future husband.

Katherine's tone of voice rose, almost as if she was shouting. "I had to get away! I was being hit with too much at once. I couldn't absorb it all. I couldn't stay any longer!"

Elizabeth stepped forward and wrapped Katherine in a loving embrace. As she hugged Katherine tightly to her, she let her niece cry her heart out. The shoulder of her white starched blouse grew wet, and still, the tears flowed. Patting Katherine on her back, as a mother would a newborn baby, she whispered soothing words of comfort. "Shush, Katherine. You're safe now. I'm here. We'll get to the bottom of whatever this is. But first, you need to rest. I'm going to have Juanita cook you up a good breakfast. Then, you will tell me what you've gotten me into, and we'll put our heads together and see what I can do to help." She tried to reassure her niece with an encouraging smile.

Katherine broke away and leaned back against the kitchen counter. She glanced down at the floor and up again, her eyes locking on Elizabeth's.

"What is it, Katherine? Elizabeth was certain there was something important Katherine needed to tell her, but was trying to figure out a way to do so.

"Auntie, I need a favor. I know I don't have any right to ask. It will break the rules and put you in a bad position. But I had a lot of time to think my plan through while I drove through the night."

"Think what plan through? We haven't had a chance to brainstorm yet, and I don't know your predicament. You know I'll try to do whatever I can."

Katherine pushed herself away from the counter, standing straight and tall, eye level with Elizabeth. "I need you to hide me."

Trying to mask the shock she felt, Elizabeth stared back, dumbfounded. Stepping back, she braced her hands on the island behind her. "*You want me to do what?*"

"It's only temporary. Just until things get sorted out. You're the secret agent in the family. Can't you put me in a safe house?" Elizabeth stood speechless as Katherine talked on. "I don't see why you can't. After all, *you're* the Director."

"Katherine, I can't hide you. It doesn't work that way. You know that. You're not involved in some covert operation. I have people to answer to." Katherine's shoulder slumped dejectedly. "Whatever happened, I can't imagine your father and Ty being a serious threat. No. You're going to stay right here. We'll work out whatever needs to be taken care of. Your father will never come within a hundred miles of D.C., but he may send people to bring you back."

Katherine crossed her arms and defiantly shook her head. "No. Staying here isn't an option. God knows you've got a mini-army surrounding you at every turn, but it won't work. Not this time."

"And you deduced this from what?" Elizabeth arched her eyebrows.

"I overheard something I shouldn't have."

"And because of that, this compound isn't good enough?" Elizabeth's mind whirled with possible dangerous scenarios, especially given the Hallock family history.

"No, it's not." Katherine stated firmly.

Elizabeth knew there was no stopping Katherine when she had an idea in her mind. She was headstrong, determined. She wouldn't back down until she had her way. Inwardly, Elizabeth swelled with pride. The apple didn't fall far from the tree.

Needing to be moving on making plans, Elizabeth sighed, placing her hands on her hips. "All right. I'll bite. But you better give me a damn good reason why I have to hide you."

The look Katherine leveled at Elizabeth was one she'd never seen before. Having been through hell and back on her missions for the CIA, she was a seasoned veteran of drama and suspense. The expression on her niece's face sent a chill down her spine.

Katherine replied, "Ty and Father somehow are involved with some not so nice business associates. They have connections to the Russian mob."

The air rushed from Elizabeth's lungs. She stood up straight, taking a more defensive stance, waiting to hear the rest.

"I heard their argument, Auntie. Ty told Father he was a fool. That Father didn't have assets to pay his debt. Then, I confronted the two by bursting in on them in the study." Katherine drew in a deep breath and said, "Something's going to happen to Hallock Farm…and somehow it involves me."

CHAPTER FIVE

Istanbul, Turkey
One year earlier

It had taken six months of preparation and planning, but Special Agent John Clinton's men had successfully infiltrated a cell of buyers from Iran, looking to get their hands on American-made weapons to pursue their cause. This particular mission had been a hard sell to the Agency, which was spread thin by events occurring in other parts of the world. When the cell of terrorists was finally identified, it hadn't taken long to convince the Director to put her stamp of approval on the operation.

The previous evening Elizabeth Hallock had sent an encrypted message giving orders for the team to strike the target at ten o'clock the next night.

The day had passed swiftly. John and his team planned out the final details, going over and over their options should something go awry. The special ops' final meeting in the cellar of the dingy, incense-filled café in Istanbul had gone well. During a mock-up of the evening's agenda, his agents had rehearsed their positions. John was confident with every man under his command. His crew was well trained: some former Navy SEALs and two Army Rangers.

Now, time had ticked down to the bewitching hour. John had done his due diligence in the set-up and planning and felt assured the targeted cell would be apprehended.

Crouched low, hiding behind the fence in the alley that led to the warehouse, John waited in position. He wiped the perspiration from his brow with his black bandana. Dark clouds of an impending storm passed over the moon, leaving him with no other recourse but to rely heavily on his night vision goggles. Other than the cackling of a few birds from the nearby trees, the grounds were eerily quiet. The parking lot was empty. Even the loading dock of the warehouse was devoid of vehicles.

John's senses heightened to high alert when he glanced down and saw the hour hand of his watch tick past the appointed start time. For the last few minutes, chatter in his earpiece had been non-existent. His sixth sense served him well during his tenure with the Agency. According to reliable sources, the warehouse was supposed to be crawling with activity. His men should be stationed around the warehouse in their respective positions and checked in.

"Base to Jonah. Over." Nothing. Securing his rifle over his shoulder, John reached for his pistol and moved in for a closer look. What he saw solidified his fears. Where was the semi-truck loaded with weapons? The building seemed empty, with no sign of guards of any kind. All John saw was a deserted parking lot.

He whispered again into his mouthpiece, "Base to Jonah. Do you copy?" No reply.

"Base to Tiger. Do you read me? Over." The silence set John on edge.

The team's plan called for a small window of time to make

the move into, what they had been led to believe by trusted intelligence, a heavily-guarded warehouse. John made one final attempt to contact his team, but his effort was futile. Deciding to back away from a possible trap, he headed down the alley to locate Mike Stanton, his second-in-command, who would have fallen back into his secondary position for Plan B. Every minute was precious. As he turned to fall back, the first thought was their frequency had been jammed. If so, the team had big problems.

He ran out of the alleyway, checking over his shoulder to ascertain whether or not he was being followed. Like the others, John had no choice but to make for the pre-arranged rendezvous point.

Within minutes, John stood behind the café where the team had met previously, pistol still drawn, his eyes darting everywhere. A small light glowed in the window of the building, but it was closed for the night. The street market was devoid of the hustle and bustle of the people who moved about during the day, bartering and selling their wares. Watching for any signs of movement and seeing none, he slipped down the path between the café and the market next door.

An unusual sound stopped him in his tracks. Straining to hear if the noise would recur, he flattened his back against the wall. The sound came again, only this time, as a moan, but more pronounced. John spied a dumpster at the end of the passageway. Placing his pistol in his holster and readying his rifle, he edged closer. Seeing nothing but a few rats nibbling at the trash on the ground, he stepped around the large, dark obstacle. Taking a defensive stance, he pointed his rifle at the object on the ground in front of him.

John had seen a lot in his years as an agent, but nothing prepared him for what lay at his feet. Bile rose in his throat. Recognizing the man lying on the ground, John knelt beside

Mike Stanton. The man bled profusely from all areas of his body. John hurriedly ripped his backpack from his shoulder, searching in vain for a cloth of any kind to stem the flow of blood from Mike's severed hand. But his effort was futile. A quick assessment told him Mike had sustained mortal wounds with a shot to the major artery of his leg. There was nothing John could do. Mike was bleeding out. He was losing his best friend.

Gasping for air, Mike tried to speak.

"Don't, Mike!" John placed a comforting hand on his comrade's shoulder. "Save your strength."

Mike's face grimaced. His last breaths came in deep gasps. "Warehouse…a set-up…go now…" Mike's voice trailed off as his eyes rolled back, his body lifeless.

With shaking hands, John closed Mike's eyes. He willed away the tears forming behind his own eyelids. His training instantly made him leave his emotions on the ground with Mike's body.

John looked up and down the alleyway. Where were the others? The other six men should have been back to the cafe by now. Had they found Mike and decided to make for the warehouse? With communications down, John prayed they'd seen Mike and would follow through and head back to reconnaissance. John repositioned his night vision goggles and checked his weapon. Deciding to high-tail it back to his assigned spot at the warehouse, he took off on a run.

Back in position, having had no contact with the men in the operation, John stopped to catch his breath. There was only one thing to do. Making the decision to move forward, he lunged up and over the chain link fence, landing softly on his feet on the pavement on the other side. He listened for the sound of anyone moving about as he squatted in the dark. Had he been followed? His gut told him no. He closed his eyes and let his sense of hearing take over. It was too eerily quiet. With no backup, he prayed his men had dispersed to the safe house. John tried one final time to make a connection, but failed. But as the man who always saw a mission through to completion, John had no choice. The Director had made the call. The mission was a go under any circumstances. He hadn't planned on being alone, but he was.

It took only seconds to get inside the building. Hearing what sounded like a cacophony of voices at the end of the tunnel, John slowly moved forward. Hiding behind a large wooden barrel, he observed the four Iranian buyers he'd met several weeks earlier. The top of a large box had been propped open. One of the buyers held a grenade launcher in the air. He grinned broadly, yelling to his friends who smiled in return. They, too, were opening boxes of ammunitions that had been supplied by the US government.

Taking several deep breaths, John blocked out the vision of Mike lying dead on the ground. He needed to focus, be steady and calm. His team had been given orders to bring the terrorists back alive. But alone, he deemed it an impossible task. With one swipe of his machine gun, it would be over. At least, the Agency would have bodies to identify. There would be consequences for the Director, and at some point, for him as well, because of his actions. John swallowed hard, realizing the ramifications, but he had no choice.

When he raised his AK-47 to take aim, it was then he felt the cold barrel of steel come to rest on the side of his temple.

A woman's soft, sultry voice demanded he face her. "Well, it took you long enough, my friend." There was a touch of sarcasm in her tone. John's head reeled with the knowledge that the woman who stood before him, her gun pointed at his chest, was his contact in Istanbul. Crap. Zoya had turned on him. How could he not have seen the signs of her being a double agent?

Zoya laughed mockingly. "You are such a fool, Clinton. You've been wrapped around my little finger since we met at Yale, no? You men are all alike! You think with only one part of your body. But that friend of yours?" She spat on the ground at his feet. "Puh!"

John had all he could do to restrain himself. To make a scene might call attention to the men who were well within hearing distance. He could spin this. He had to get the drop on her. He knew her mind inside and out.

It was then Zoya poked the gun into his chest. Sliding the Glock up and under his chin, she said, "You, my friend. *You are valuable to us!*" She waved the gun in front of his face. John didn't flinch. "We need you for bigger and better things. You are valuable to your government. Yes? But first… I think you must feel a little of what your comrade went through tonight." Zoya glared directly at him, her hazel eyes piercing his. "Don't worry too much, my *love*. You are no good to us… dead."

John saw the flash and felt the searing pain tear through his abdomen.

Zoya had shot him.

CHAPTER SIX

Alexandria, Virginia
Present Day

"No!" John Clinton shouted out as he bolted up in bed, clenching his stomach. In the dark, his hands felt for the blood that had vividly poured out moments ago. But there was no liquid, no hurting, burning feeling. His head ached. A light sheen of perspiration covered his upper body. Panting from the dream induced anxiety attack, he breathed in and out deeply, counting from one to ten as his counselor had taught him to do. Groping in the air, he finally located the light switch to turn on the bedside lamp. The Agency shrink warned him of the fallout of PTSD – post-traumatic stress disorder. The memories of what had befallen his team still played out as if it were happening today, though he was not plagued by the nightmares that occurred as frequently as when he'd first come home. The therapy helped, although he wouldn't admit it to anyone.

The lighted dial on his iPhone sitting on his nightstand read five o'clock. John reasoned he could try to catch another half hour of sleep, but decided it would be better to get up and head to his desk job at Langley. Its sudden vibration denoting an incoming call took him by surprise.

His eyebrows arched at the number that registered on the screen. He pressed the button to answer. "Clinton."

A woman's authoritative voice came through loud and clear. "John, did I wake you?"

"No, Madam Director. I was just getting ready to head into the office." Why was Elizabeth Hallock calling him at this hour of the morning? Since he'd returned to the States and had been debriefed she'd paid little attention to him, other than to assign him menial tasks to complete. He believed it was her way of making him serve penance for creating an international incident. "What can I do for you?"

"I want to see you as soon as you arrive at Langley. Meet me in the debriefing conference room on the D deck."

The location of the meeting had John sitting on the edge of his bed, fully awake, his curiosity piqued. The D deck? No one had used it since the Agency underwent a major renovation. Some new employees didn't know of its existence since it was buried under the new construction. Only certain people knew how to gain access. It was where he and his ops team had spent their time planning the Istanbul mission, out of the prying eyes of other agents.

"All right. Would you care to tell me why we're meeting in the old cellar office wing?"

"No," came the abrupt reply. "Tell no one where you'll be."

The line went dead, leaving John to stare at the screen that said, "Call ended."

Standing up, John stretched and rolled his neck to relieve the kinks of tension. He saw his reflection in the mirror on his dresser. He looked gaunt and tired. The scars from the weeks spent in captivity had healed, but the emotional wounds were still with him, as was evident from the nightmare.

The phone call had John wondering about Elizabeth Hallock. Was he finally going to be allowed back to carry out the only job he'd been born to do? Or was the Director finally going to dismiss him for his failure to follow mission protocol? Word around the office was the jury was still out.

Glancing back at the clock, John realized with disgust he'd be fighting Beltway traffic. He made a beeline for the shower. He had two hours to pray his mentor would give him his second chance.

* * *

Waiting in the bleak, semi-dark interrogation room on D deck reminded John of his debriefing upon his return from Istanbul. Was the Director standing behind the glass window, watching his every move, reading his body language, trying to make a determination of whether or not he was ready for a new assignment?

Aroused from his thoughts, he heard the door open. Seeing who entered, John stood as a sign of respect, his metal chair scraping the concrete floor. Director Elizabeth Hallock, his mentor of ten years, walked in and closed the heavy steel door behind her. Her high heels clicked on the cement floor. She came forward and took her place on the opposite side of the long rectangular table. She was carrying her ever-present Agency-issued briefcase.

Dressed in her traditional black suit, her trademark glasses sitting on the top of her graying hair, she addressed John. "Agent Clinton."

"Madam Director."

She motioned to his chair. "Sit. My secretary will be here momentarily with coffee. We've a great deal to discuss. Time is getting away from us."

Not knowing the who, what, where, when or why to what she was referring, John simply nodded, took his seat and waited.

Elizabeth sat in her seat as well and spun the combination lock on her briefcase. As it sprung open, John spied a .38 revolver sitting on the top of the papers within. Even with the security that surrounded her on a daily basis, it came as no surprise to him that she packed a weapon. She was old school. He'd learned that in his training.

"You've been working hard, from what I hear."

John was a bit startled at the casual start to their conversation. "Yes. I put together those reports you requested. And the data for the field agents' expenses will be on your desk by noon."

Elizabeth eyed him up and down. To John, it seemed she had a purpose for scrutinizing him. And it made him nervous, as if something monumental was about to go down. Was she having doubts?

"Good. I'm glad to hear it. You're probably wondering why we're meeting in this dungeon of all places, but—"

"Director, with all due respect," John interrupted, knowing full well it wasn't a wise thing to do. But he was edgy, and his nerves got the best of him. "Exactly what am I doing *here*?" John looked about, taking in the starkness of the cement block room. He inwardly shuddered, the reminders of Istanbul and what had transpired on his return reeling through his mind. "What's going on? Why all the secrecy?"

The Director's eyes flared as she drummed her fingers on the metal table in response. His interruption was a bad move on his part.

"You are *here*, John Clinton, because I need you *here*." Her words were clipped. As she tapped her finger on the table to make her point, John's legs shook under the table, but the woman had his undivided attention. "We had to meet without the prying eyes of the remainder of the Agency staff who'd try to imagine what we were discussing behind closed doors."

Just as she finished her explanation, the door opened.

Elizabeth's secretary carried in a tray of coffee and tea. She placed it on the table, turned and exited without saying a word.

"Coffee?" Elizabeth eyed him closely as she pointed to the silver vessel. She reached for the pot of tea. Everyone at the Agency knew her penchant for drinking Earl Grey tea.

"Yes. Thank you. I could use a jolt of caffeine." John poured himself a cup of black coffee, but only watched the steam rise from his cup where he'd placed it on the table. If he picked it up, he was sure his nerves would show. There was no doubt from the way she was looking at him that she knew he was wondering where his purpose at the Agency would lead. After all, she had said she needed him.

The international incident had been more than a small blemish on his record. It had affected the Director's as well. Not only had it taken her contacts, but also the influence of a former United States President, to free his team from the terrorist organization that held them captive. Multiple diplomatic avenues had been attempted before a covert rescue operation was approved to put boots on the ground to free him and his ops team from the torture chambers of one of the largest terrorist groups operating in Eastern Europe.

"John!" The Director's fingers were snapping in front of his face.

John's thoughts were back in the D deck in D.C. with the Director sitting across from him.

With her glasses perched on the tip of her nose, she read the papers taken from her briefcase. Once perused, she placed the pages on the table beside her. Tapping her index fingers together, she pressed them to her lips. "I've received the necessary confirmations you've done what was required of you during your probation. You've been cleared by the Agency shrink for active duty. My sources tell me you believe you're fit to take on another assignment. Is that correct?"

Before answering, John gripped the cup, brought it to his lips and swallowed, hoping he wouldn't choke. *Choose your words carefully. There may never be another chance.*

Just as he was about to respond, Elizabeth held up her hand. "Being the Director has certain perks. I think you know I have the final say on the status of all jobs here at Langley. There are few people up *there* who think you're not ready." She pointed her finger towards the ceiling.

John knew the offices of the higher powers were located six floors above. John's shoulders slumped forward, his head downcast. Here it was. His career ended because of the stupidity of not following Agency protocol. At the top of the checklist Elizabeth had rattled off during the time he'd been debriefed was the violation of the number one rule regarding employees of the Agency. He'd allowed a personal relationship with his partner to compromise his objectivity.

Zoya Stalinski had been a stunning, redheaded Russian beauty on a student visa to the United States. They'd met at Yale while John was studying for his Master's degree in criminal profiling. She was obtaining her doctorate in art history. Upon graduation, both were recruited by the CIA. Much to John's dismay, Zoya opted to move back to her native Russia while he made the choice to set up shop in D.C. Two years ago, Zoya showed up working for MI6. John was a bit skeptical at first, seeing her working in London, but was delighted.

But Zoya was dead, killed in the raid on the terrorist compound when he'd been freed. Nothing dug in his craw more than knowing he'd been played, duped by a double agent. It was a valuable lesson learned, and one he would never repeat, if given that coveted second chance.

"I have a proposition for you." John's head snapped up to see Elizabeth twirling her half-specs in her hand. "But before I brief you, I have a need to get something off my chest." Placing her glasses on the top of her head, she stared him down. "You *owe* me, John Clinton...big time." She then sat back in her chair, waiting for his reply.

John tried his best to stem his nervousness. He cautiously asked, "Am I headed back into the field?" Her sober reaction made him hesitant to ask anything else, but he continued wanting to know what awaited him. "Or does your proposition involve some other duty with the agents here inside Langley?"

An unusual gleam crept into Elizabeth's eyes. What did the woman have planned for him? "Oh, it's in the field...in a manner of speaking." Hearing the word "field" which equated in his mind to "mission," John tried to mask his enthusiasm. Elizabeth drummed her fingers on the table. "Your farm... the one near Mount Vernon? Do you still own that broken down old rat trap?"

His farm? John shook his head perplexed. What did his horse farm have to do with anything? Erring on the side of caution, John pointed at the file she had opened, its content lying on the table. "You know very well I live on F Street. *And* that I still have that farm." Elizabeth was after something. "It doesn't look like much on the outside. But, I've spent the majority of my spare time working and hiring contractors to make the inside habitable. I've been using the inheritance money from selling my parents' ranch in Montana. It's all documented in that file in front of you." Leaning forward in his chair, his eyes locked on Elizabeth's. John had to be direct. He wanted answers now that his instinct told him he wasn't going to be let go. "Why do you ask?"

"Perfect." Too familiar with the devious look she sent his way, John swallowed hard. Her dark eyes were locked on her target. John braced himself.

"I want you to hide someone. Someone important. Call up your team. We'll meet tomorrow morning at 0800 sharp. Right here. No one is to know. No one. Consider this 'Classified' for now. You report only to me. Do I make myself clear?"

"Yes, ma'am." John enunciated both words, dying to jump up and salute. He rose from his chair.

"Sit down. I'm not done with you yet." Gulping, John parked himself back in the stiff chair. Elizabeth had his undivided attention. "One last thing. You screw this operation up, John Clinton, and I will personally escort you out the door of this Agency myself." Her fist landed with a thud on the table. The sound of her hand making contact echoed loudly throughout the room. "The repercussions from Istanbul will look like a walk in the park compared to what will happen to you if you botch *this* job."

John knew the Director meant business. She'd called in all her favors to save him last time. This time he'd be out on the street.

"Have I made myself clear?"

"Yes, Madam Director. Perfectly." John was impatient to get to work. "May I be dismissed? My team is scattered all over. I need to make calls. Get some on planes back to D.C."

Elizabeth waved him away. "Go. Get ready. I'll see you in the morning. And remember. *No one* is to know. Absolutely *no one*."

John rose and opened the door, trying to hide the small grin on his face. Closing the door behind him, he walked the corridors in the bowels of D deck to the hidden elevator.

His mind whirled with what she would give his team as an assignment. The Director was hiding someone "important." He entered the old, dingy elevator and pushed the button for the fourth level where it would open in the Director's library. As the doors shut, John pumped his fist into the air. Special Agent John Clinton was back on duty!

CHAPTER SEVEN

"You're back!" A beaming face met Elizabeth as she took off her shoes at the mudroom door and entered the large country kitchen. She'd lived in many places in her career as an agent, but this was the only place where she could let her guard down long enough to relax. The smell of freshly brewed coffee wafted in the air. "I thought you'd gone MIA on me." Katherine laughed.

Elizabeth felt like she'd been missing in action. She'd spent the last forty-eight hours brainstorming with John and his team on Operation Hide and Seek.

"I shouldn't say this, Auntie, but you look like hell."

Elizabeth managed a semblance of a smile. "Well, isn't that a lovely compliment? I can't wait to get a good look at myself in a mirror. A dip in the pool should perk me up. Laps would relax me. However, I'm not sure if I'd make it from one end to the other at this point." She hugged her niece, who'd come to her side to welcome her home. "Katherine, you'd probably have to play lifeguard and save me. Come to think of it, why aren't you out at the pool yourself, resting and getting some sun like I told you to?"

"I'm too keyed up. Resting by the

pool and taking naps didn't help." "So you went for the good stuff?" Elizabeth indicated the coffee pot sitting on the kitchen counter.

Kate moved to it and picked up a cup off the counter. "Absolutely. Although I know you wouldn't be caught dead drinking anything but Earl Grey tea." Katherine winked, but grimaced. "Nasty habit you picked up in London after all those years, if you ask me. Can I make you a pot?"

"Oh, Katherine, would you? That would be heavenly! I know Juanita is busy with her chores." Elizabeth parked her backside on one of the barstools at the kitchen's center island. "I need to unwind for a few minutes." Pausing briefly, she cleared her throat. "You and I need to clarify some things."

"You've got news?" Katherine asked, her eyes lighting up with the possibility.

"Not exactly. During my meeting with Agent Tanner this morning, I discovered you neglected to tell me a few important details when we talked the other morning."

Katherine had moved to place the kettle on the stove, but deliberately turned her back on Elizabeth to gaze out the window overlooking the pool and the gardens. "I haven't the faintest idea what you're referring to."

"Honey, of all people, you know I can find out what no one else can."

Katherine glanced over her shoulder, and then returned to the view of the backyard's landscape.

Elizabeth's brow furrowed. She was truly puzzled. It wasn't at all like Katherine to be evasive. She was always forthright and straightforward when it came to discussing her home. Something triggered the change in her demeanor. Aunt and niece always shared everything. The good and the bad.

Still facing out the window, Katherine ended her stony silence. "It works both ways, you know."

Elizabeth's heart lurched, her deepest fear surfacing. No, Katherine couldn't possibly know the truth. Trying to maintain a calm, level voice, she asked, "Whatever do you mean by that comment?"

But the question came out more sharply than she intended since she was operating on little to no sleep for the last two days. She regretted the way she replied. In her younger days as an operative, she never gave sleep a second thought. In the twilight of her career, her body shouted out for it. There was a necessity to stay sharp and focused if Operation Hide and Seek was to succeed as planned.

Katherine turned around to face her. "I think you've known something's been going on at Hallock Farm for some time."

Elizabeth prayed her face masked the alarm she felt. What had Katherine discovered?

"Why did you stay away all these years? I've racked my brain these past few days trying to come up with some sort of explanation. Personally, I think it's linked to what happened several days ago. I told you what I overheard and why I ran - but I think there's more." Katherine issued the challenge. "Is there?"

Katherine's doubts and question had hit the mark. There *was* more. Sam Tanner confirmed the current status of everyone at Hallock Farm, as well as the history of several unsavory members of a well-known mafia family who'd taken up residence nearby in Hampton Beach over the past months.

Elizabeth's gut instinct had her brother's history coming back to repeat itself. In her book, a leopard never changed his spots. Her brother Robert's dubious past would always trail behind and haunt him. She'd thought she'd rectified his issues years ago. But apparently, her brother hadn't learned anything from the past. How much did her niece been able to piece together, now that she'd had time to think and mull over the events that brought her to Arlington?

The time had come to share with Katherine a few of the deeply buried family secrets. But Elizabeth felt the timing wasn't right and her niece's emotions were too raw. She glanced at the clock on the kitchen wall. Elizabeth needed a few more hours to clear her mind. She needed to rest and think of what needed to be said. It was critical how she framed what she must share. The last thing Elizabeth wanted was to have her niece running from the safe harbor of the compound.

Elizabeth rose from the bar stool, placing her cup of tea in the kitchen sink. "You're right. I do know what's going on. But, I'm bushed. I haven't slept in two days. I need to regroup. Why don't you meet me in the library around six? That will give me the time to check in with the agents assigned to your case. Then, I promise to fill you in on the details – those you know and those you don't. Juanita can bring us some supper as we work."

Elizabeth walked up behind Katherine. She turned her niece around by the shoulders to face her, framing Katherine's face in her hands. "Look at me." A pair of teary brown eyes met her own. "In all these years, I've *never* lied to you. You must know that. I admit I've buried some of our sordid family secrets, but only to protect you and your brothers. I did what was best for the family. And if need be…I would do it all over again." Katherine's gaze fell to the floor. Elizabeth took her finger and raised Katherine's chin. It was imperative they be able to see eye to eye. "The time has come, Katherine, for you to know what's going on and what's transpired in the past."

"I know you have my back, Auntie. You always have. But I'm scared for everyone I left behind. Thomas, Ethan, Matt, and Mother. Adam, thank God, is here in Washington. I've been able to run. But I hope my leaving the farm didn't place the family in further danger."

Elizabeth shook her head. "No, dear. You did the right thing."

Katherine gave her a peck on the cheek, returned to the kitchen counter and picked up her cup of coffee. "Then go. Get some rest. I'll meet you in your library later."

Elizabeth made her way to the back staircase. She watched Katherine grab the daily newspaper from the island and head out to the patio. Elizabeth felt as if the weight of the world had been placed onto her shoulders. Her niece had no idea the ends to which Elizabeth would go to protect her. Or why.

* * *

Although the door to the wood-paneled library was open, Kate knocked anyway. Her aunt sat in a black Windsor chair behind a large desk in front of three arched windows. She typed diligently on the keyboard of a laptop in front of her. The sun was setting, which added to the soft pale glow from the several hurricane lamps strategically placed about the room.

Kate stood at the doorway and awaited permission to enter her aunt's private sanctum. Elizabeth looked up from what Kate knew was an encrypted computer, given the nature of her job.

"Sorry, Auntie. If you're busy, I can come back when you're ready."

"No. No. Come in." Elizabeth rose and strode to the overstuffed sofa in the sitting area side of the library. "Sit by me." She patted the area of the couch beside her. Kate sank into the deep plush cushions of the white sofa. "We've a lot to discuss and very little time left."

An uneasy feeling swept over Kate, but her inquisitiveness got the best of her. "What's the plan? When do I leave? Will I have a team of agents to guard me? What did you decide?"

Kate was used to being in control. She wanted answers. Yesterday. Not being able to plan out her life on a daily basis had her nerves on edge. That came with being a Type A personality.

Elizabeth poured a cup of tea from the pot on the tray sitting on the marble-topped coffee table. Kate eyed her aunt cautiously, pouring herself a cup of coffee from the carafe.

"Easy, Katherine. You'll have your answers soon enough. I need some clarification. What *really* made you run from Hampton Beach? Take me through the conversation in the study once more. With some of the things Sam was able to uncover, something's missing."

Puzzled and a tad shocked, Katherine took a moment to think. She took a sip of coffee musing over her aunt's comment. What she wouldn't give for a good shot of Baileys just for added courage. As much as she and her aunt shared everything and had a mutual respect for one another, she did find her aunt a bit intimidating at times.

"I told you everything Father and Ty argued about that I heard. The Russian partners, the money, something about handing over valuable farm merchandise. I've wracked my brain trying to connect the dots. I have a feeling you're about to tell me you think you can."

A knock at the door drew the attention of both women. Juanita entered, carrying a tray with two turkey sandwiches on ironstone plates and a small of bowl of fruit. With a brief nod to her employer, Juanita placed the blue tray on the table and left the room.

Her aunt reached for a napkin and one of the sandwiches. "Katherine, as an operative, I've shared some of the training I've had over the years. One of the most important lessons is when our emotions are engaged, our brain intakes things subconsciously. We think we don't remember insignificant details, but we really do."

"You're not going to give me truth serum, are you?" Kate asked facetiously.

Elizabeth chuckled. "For heaven's sake. You've read too many of those spy novels. Besides, the Agency has other avenues for information gathering. Much more fun." Katherine knew her aunt was serious, but caught the twinkle in Elizabeth's eyes and laughed. The tension in the room evaporated. "Seriously now, break the day down." Her aunt bit into her sandwich, chewed, swallowed and wiped her mouth. "When did everything start to come apart?"

Katherine leaned back and closed her eyes, trying her best to see the events play out in her mind. "I'd been at the stables since sunup. As usual, I was running late for dinner so I ran upstairs, changed, and was on my way to the dining room when I heard the argument. I eavesdropped for a few minutes, not believing what I was hearing. But when Ty threatened Father, I barged in. Then, all hell broke loose."

"How so?" Elizabeth probed.

"Well, they certainly weren't expecting to see me. Ty especially. From the looks on their faces, it was clear they knew I'd heard part of their argument. Suddenly, Ty was trying to talk his way out of his involvement. From the look on his face, I knew better."

Her aunt shook her head. Kate knew the look. Elizabeth wasn't pleased with Kate's recap of that night.

"What? That's how it went down." Kate grew exasperated. How many times did she have to relay the details? Every time she'd gone over what had happened, she felt as if she was repeating her story verbatim. Nothing had changed.

If was as if her aunt had read her mind. Speaking more forcefully, Elizabeth said, "Tell me *again*. Think, Katherine. I need very, very specific chronological details. You know the drill."

Katherine got up and began to pace back and forth across the oriental carpet. Finally, she came to a halt. "Father and Ty were arguing over money. The context of their conversation had to do with Father not coming through with assets he'd promised to the new business associates. Apparently, it included money and farm merchandise. Father was enraged that Ty made him sign what he thought were perfectly legal documents. I got the feeling Ty had misled him. Neither one of them would explain the situation. They clammed right up. Father did tell me it was nothing to worry about. Can you believe that? However, Ty threatened if Father didn't do what was asked of him, there'd be grave consequences for both he and the farm. But no one identified the specifics of who, what, where, when or why." She looked at her aunt. Kate knew she wasn't done being interrogated.

"Keep going, dear. Talk it out."

"I was getting nowhere with both of them. Ty had me so furious at how he'd treated Father and getting the farm mixed up in some sordid deal. I was irate. I knew then he wasn't the man I agreed to marry. I took off my ring and flung it at him. I was sick to my stomach, knowing I had worked so hard and everything was going to disappear. I didn't give a thought to anything but getting away from Hampton Beach. And here I am."

Katherine's nerves got the better of her. Reliving the conversation pushed her anxiety level to the limit. She lowered herself into a club chair nearby. Kate was aware her aunt heard every word, although she spied her doodling on the paper sitting in her lap.

"You're still not helping me." Her aunt tapped her pen on the yellow legal pad.

Kate meant to rant to herself, but spoke out harshly instead. "What else could there be? I've told you all I know."

If Kate thought her aunt was satisfied with her recounting of the events at Hallock Farm she was mistaken. Director Hallock was readying for another round. Her aunt turned the page of the pad in her lap, clicking her pen. "Take a deep breath. You're talking so fast you're making my head spin."

Kate curled up in the chair and tucked her knees beneath her. She eyed her aunt warily. They had *never* squared off before. For the first time in her life, she felt as if they were on opposing sides. But Kate knew it was a strategy to get her to remember.

Elizabeth moved on, the tip of her glasses now perched on the end of her nose. "There's more to all this than the argument. My experience tells me you've blocked something out. And it's significantly related to the confrontation. It happened during that day. You've buried it in your subconscious."

Kate fidgeted.

"Sit back and close your eyes."

Kate did as she was told.

"Now, run through the events of the day. From the time you got up until you…"

Her aunt hadn't quite finished directing her when the image of a man's face flashed through Kate's mind. Her hands gripped the arms of the chair so tight her knuckles turned white. No! Why hadn't she remembered?

"Katherine! Are you all right, child? Tell me." Her aunt reached across the space between them. She took Kate's hands in hers and massaged them. Her soft southern drawl as she spoke was soothing. But it didn't tamper the panic welling up within her.

Kate's hands became clammy. She began to perspire as the memory of the morning flooded back.

"When I drove from the birthing barn headed to the office, I thought it strange to see a Mercedes and an Audi parked outside the fence near the office so early in the morning. Father stood alongside the training pen with the trainer and several of the quarter horses we'd planned on entering in the upcoming races. Two other men were there. One man was very burly and muscular. The other extremely tall and lean. He had a thick graying head of hair and a well-kept beard. You know that brief moment when you think you've recognized someone, but it passes?"

Her aunt nodded, but there was an odd look on her face, as if she was thinking the same thing.

"The burly man was a Savorski rep. The Savorskis had been to the club with Mother and Father on several occasions."

"And the other?" Elizabeth dragged out the question as if she knew the answer.

"Yes, Auntie. It was him! You have that file."

Her aunt had the best poker face in the business. Elizabeth rose from the sofa and took her cell phone out of her pocket and walked to her desk. Kate watched her pick up the encrypted phone line she used in case of an Agency emergency. She had two phones activated at once. From what Katherine could ascertain the National Security Association, the NSA, was on one phone and a man named Clinton on the other.

Elizabeth stopped talking and called to her. "Katherine, you're absolutely one hundred percent sure?"

"I'm positive. What's wrong?" Her aunt waved away her question. A short, succinct conversation ensued. Her aunt hung up the phones and returned to the sofa.

"Katherine, my contacts at the FBI briefed me this morning. Recently, there's been a significant amount of money laundering in the Hampton area. People within your parents' social circle have been under surveillance. But adding *my* Russian into the mix has massive ramifications for the FBI, the Agency and the NSA."

Elizabeth reached for the papers on the coffee table. "You'll leave in two days. My agents are readying the safe house. You'll go there while I deal with this. Don't worry. Everything's just become a tad more complicated than we originally thought."

Kate said a silent prayer, hoping all would be as her aunt promised. Her natural instinct for survival had brought her to the one woman who would keep her safe. Kate would get through this crisis. And then she would go back. Her father had met his match, a woman with a team of agents in her pocket – his own sister.

CHAPTER EIGHT

A cool breeze blew in from the east off the Potomac River. The sky was a robin's egg blue. To most people, the view from the top of the hill was spectacular and worth every dollar they plunked down to get in to see the national historic site.

A couple wandered the path from the main house at Mount Vernon to the gardens, not caring about the scenery or the tour they'd just taken. It was all for show. They cared only about the man walking up the dirt path from the where the boat from Alexandria had dropped off its daily run of tourists for the day. He was the man they had traveled all night and day to meet.

"Stavros, stop taking pictures!" Zoya batted at the digital camera her brother held in his hands.

"What is your problem? You said to act like we are tourists. I'm doing that." Stavros pushed her hand away.

In a hushed, but direct tone, Zoya said, "Demetrie is here."

A tall, slim but muscular man dressed in white linen pants and a white shirt came towards them. He had his hands in his pockets as he strolled along the path leading up from the boat's drop off point. Acting as a tourist as well, he viewed the glorious setting around him. Zoya stewed as he seemed to be taking his time to reach them.

Hopefully, she would finally know how long she had to set her plan in motion. She'd become increasingly impatient in the brief time she and Stavros had been in Washington, worried someone would recognize them. They'd made every effort to stay on the fringe of the nation's Capitol and its prying cameras.

The call to come to Mount Vernon had come very early that morning. She wasn't happy about meeting in a public place, but she came as requested. The border had been surprisingly easy to enter. But here, there were too many security cameras and checkpoints to go through, especially since 9/11. She'd worn a golf cap to shield her face as much as possible, and she cringed when her bag was checked at the entrance even though they'd found nothing in it to hold her. She'd been smart to leave their passports at home, traveling only with their drivers' licenses and cash.

Zoya was extremely puzzled Demetrie chose this iconic place. It felt wrong. But who was she to question the people helping her obtain the revenge she so desperately sought?

"Good afternoon. I hope I haven't kept you waiting. The boat from Alexandria was delayed." Demetrie spoke flawless English. He'd been trained by the best. That was why she'd requested he be the point man.

"No, not at all," she responded, hoping her voice did not reflect the tension she felt.

"I take it your trip went well?" Demetrie smiled down at her, his large frame overpowering her more diminutive one. "You made good time. All is ready."

Zoya wanted to get right to the matter of why they were at Mount Vernon. "Demetrie, I want to talk about…"

Demetrie cut her off. "Let us enjoy the gardens. You know the side garden was a particular favorite of Martha Washington's. There's many a rose that's been bred and named after her from here." He mumbled under his breath, "We need to move away from the house and larger trees and bushes. Trust me. There are too many cameras and hidden microphones. We must be careful."

Demetrie tucked Zoya's arm through his and walked leisurely down the path, headed in the direction of Washington's tomb and the riverfront. The thought of being overheard had been on her mind since she and Stavros arrived at Mount Vernon.

Zoya spied a bench close to the river, shaded by a large tree, and made for it. Demetrie immediately sat down beside her. He rested his arm across her shoulder. Stavros walked on along the path to the tomb, seemingly content to take more pictures of the house and gardens. Stavros knew his place. There was business to be discussed, and she would inform him later of his role.

Demetrie whispered in her ear, "It is done."

"You are sure?"

Demetrie drew back to look at her. His blue eyes pierced hers. "You question my contacts, my resources? Zoya, don't say you underestimate my abilities. My contacts here in Washington go deep into the Agency. You will be pleased at what I found out. It is better than we could ever imagine." Removing his arm, the man rubbed his hands together. "Plus, I will be doing a favor for a friend."

Zoya looked at him, a puzzled frown on her face. "A favor for a friend is not part of my attack on John Clinton."

Demetrie patted her knee. "What is it the Americans say? Something about two birds, one stone."

Zoya sighed. "All I care about is what I need. That is in place? Yes?"

The man sitting next to her nodded and squeezed her knee. Demetrie was known to have a reputation with the ladies. Zoya personally didn't care for him in that way. But if she had to put up with his advances to get what she needed done, so be it. He was expendable as far as she was concerned. But it was necessary to tread cautiously around him. Demetrie had friends in high places in the intelligence community.

"Yes. Yes. All is set." He slipped a piece of paper into the palm of her hand. She glanced down to see an address on the note page. "You and Stavros will meet me here tonight. Don't be late."

Zoya smiled inwardly. Finally. "You must have done intensive research. I'm impressed with the contacts you've made since you came to America, my friend." Zoya rested her head on his shoulder. "Clinton has no idea, has he?"

"No. It is clean - one of my better jobs, if I do say so. I was in and out before anyone noticed. My contact worked well to maintain our cover."

"Good. And Elizabeth? Where is the woman who made my life a living hell?" Zoya needed to know her enemies' every move.

"It's strange, Zoya. Elizabeth's not been following her regular routine. Something doesn't add up. My contact says in the last week she's acted more like an operative than the Director."

"Our plan will work, won't it?" Zoya asked, needing reassurance. "I can't fail."

"Did I not ask you to leave everything to me? We'll extract our revenge. But *you* need to be patient. Clinton will make a mistake. Rumor has it he's not ready to go back out into the field. He'll let down his guard. The call will come when the timing is right. Then, we will make our move."

Satisfied with the future of the operation, Zoya stood up, searching for the third member of their party.

"Stavros. Stavros!" Zoya called out. Where the hell was he? It hadn't been her idea to bring him to the briefing. But he'd suffered as much as she had in Istanbul and deserved the right to be there.

Demetrie stood and walked away from the bench, striding down the path that led away from the grassy area by the tree to the out buildings by the main estate house. Zoya followed at a brisk pace and ventured up the hillside, halting on the steps of the piazza. Sitting in one of the many chairs lined up on the front porch was her brother, lazily taking photos of the grounds and the view of the Potomac.

"You idiot!" She marched up on the porch and wrenched him by the arm. She tried to pull him out of the black chair. "What did I tell you?"

"Let go of me!" Stavros yanked his arm from her grasp. "I'm playing tourist," he spoke softly in a thick Russian accent. "You didn't need me for your planning. I know what my job is when the time comes."

Zoya shook her head in disbelief. How could he not realize? He may have jeopardized the entire operation by sitting on the porch of the house.

"Think! Where are you?" She gestured as if to point out the view. Stavros's head swiveled in the same direction. Clipped to the corner of the white siding, about twelve feet up from the piazza's floor, a surveillance camera was mounted. It swiveled, flashed and captured both their faces.

CHAPTER NINE

John Clinton hit his muddied, navy blue Agency-issued baseball cap on the dilapidated fence in frustration. He stood ankle-deep in wet tractor tracks. Picking up the high-powered binoculars that hung around his neck, he surveyed the outlying paddocks at Clinton Stables.

"Gives new meaning to being in the field doesn't it, Chief?" Jake Martin, one of the members of his Ops team, came up on his right side and slapped him on the back. By the look on Jake's face, John could tell the man was trying his best to keep from laughing as he leaned on the rail beside John. "Always did think the Director had a sick sense of humor. What'd you do to piss her off this time?"

"Very funny, Martin. You're in this muck as deep as I am." John pointed to Jake's boots. John should have been leery when Elizabeth said he was returning to the field "in a manner of speaking." Hell, Operation Hide and Seek was starting to be his worst nightmare in more ways than one.

"Listen, Chief." Jake's laughter was gone, replaced by a more serious tone. "The team's wary about the details of this mission. We're international espionage experts. The FBI should be heading up this operation, given the scenario. They're the experts in organized crime."

"I thought the same thing. But we're back to dealing with the Russians." He and Jake exchanged subtle glances. "You thinking what I'm thinking?"

Jake replied, "Yeah, I am. When the Director told us there was chatter about some Russian agents in the mix, the hairs on the back of my neck went up. It's been almost a year since Istanbul. I've been to see the shrink more times than I care to admit, but I can't stop thinking about what happened."

"Me, either." John leaned against the fence. "But the Agency wouldn't have allowed us out here if there'd been any doubts of our ability to carry out what needs to be done."

Jake nodded. "True. But, why aren't we in a safe house somewhere in DC? This territory is too wide an area to cover."

"I hear you. I don't like using the farm. But after the briefing, I realized our main mission is to hide the woman. It's my understanding Elizabeth utilized her contacts and is handling what needs to be done." John slapped Jake on the shoulder with his hat. "Hey, we're not pushing papers anymore. We're out where we belong, doing what we're trained to do."

"When's Lizzie O'Brien's ETA?" Jake asked.

"I'm waiting for final confirmation. Probably sometime tomorrow morning." John turned from surveying the paddocks and scanned the barnyard. "We've got a lot to do to lock this place down. I'm still trying to make sense of the Director's rationale for bringing Ms. O'Brien here. For some reason, she was adamant the lady would fit more comfortably here than anywhere else. I couldn't get her to budge."

"Well, our visitor's got quite a resumè. But I must admit, I don't think anyone will look for her in a rundown farmhouse. And honestly, she'll definitely have a lot to do around here, being a vet doc and all. You hadn't planned on bringing in your mares and stock from the look of the place."

John shook his head. "You're right. It's a mess, but we'll survive."

"So where do we go from here?" Jake looked out over the yard and jerked his head toward the farmhouse. "There's not much time. Tim and Chuck are testing the motion detectors and setting up the hidden security cameras. I don't like having the south meadow and main gate so far from base camp. I have Wade and Bob checking for possible blind spots. We don't want the monitors to miss anything."

"Good. We're ahead of schedule. Did Wade and Bob lock down the perimeter and place their men in position?" His team was efficient. John tapped Jake Martin to take over as his second-in-command. Tim Thomas, Chuck Raymond, Bob Taylor and Wade Houghton had been in Istanbul. His team was the best of the best and they, like him, had not seen the signs that Zoya was playing both sides of the fence. But the past was the past. Each man was ready and grateful for the new assignment.

"The security cameras are being installed in the places you and the Director mapped out. The men should be down in the secure room, tweaking the surveillance equipment. Everything will be operational by late afternoon."

Jake reminded John of Mike Stanton. He was detail-oriented, the consummate professional. John knew if things went down, Jake would have his back, no questions asked. John thought how fast Operation Hide and Seek had been put together. He'd spent long hours into last night, making sure no one had overlooked any important details.

John and Jake walked gingerly through the mud back to the farmhouse. Hearing the creaking porch door open, John looked up to see Wade and Bob coming out to talk to him.

Before either one could distract him, John directed a question at Wade, who leaned against the porch railing. "How tight is the perimeter? Are the cameras angles set right?"

"Chill. Everything's as it's should be. This job's a walk in the park."

John stopped, put his hands on hips and barked, "Wipe that smug smile off your face, Wade. Have you any idea what's on the line? We screw up this job and we can kiss our careers good-bye. I've worked with Elizabeth Hallock since I started. She'll hang us out to dry if we don't get the job done right. Get it? Everyone has to be vigilant."

Out of the corner of his eye, John spotted Bob waving to someone over his shoulder. He turned to see Tim and Chuck headed in their direction from the barns.

"Everything all set?" John called out.

"Done." Tim was the more serious member of the team. "What's next?"

John looked at the group gathered around him. "You're each in charge of your unit on the property. When Lizzie O'Brien gets here, we watch her every move. Never let her out of your sight. Pass off her from one to the other, as instructed. The Director says the woman's got a mind of her own. That will end as soon as she arrives. Ms. O'Brien will do what we tell her to do."

"And if she doesn't?" Chuck asked.

John said, "If she wants to be safe, she won't have a choice. Contact with the Director will be through the encrypted cell. I want Ms. O'Brien contained to the main floors. I'd prefer she not be near the secure room." It felt good to be back at the head of the team, putting the plan together, making it happen. "Secure your weapons. Report anything unusual as soon as you see it." He looked at the group. "Any questions or concerns?" The five men shook their heads. "All right, then. Let's get ready to welcome our company."

John had to complete the last item on his personal checklist.

A call needed to be placed to Langley. The safe house was ready for Lizzie O'Brien.

* * *

"Aunt Elizabeth?" Katherine poked her head around the door of her aunt's private office. "Juanita insisted I come and find you right away." Her aunt sat on the sofa, surrounded by mountains of paperwork piled on the sofa, floor and coffee table.

She motioned for Kate to enter. "Come in. Close the door behind you."

As Kate entered the small chamber, she remembered back to the several times she'd been caught playing here. Her imagination got the best of her as a child, and she'd thought the room was a part of a secret castle where spies trained. As a grown-up, she'd known it to be true. When she visited over the years, her aunt had allowed her to discover a very different world that existed outside the walls of the compound.

"…contacts in Washington as soon as he could. Katherine, I need you to pay attention!" Her aunt's voice was sharp.

Kate snapped out of her childhood daydream. "I'm sorry. You're right. My mind was miles away. Could you repeat what you just said?"

Exasperated, Elizabeth sighed, the tone in her aunt's voice taking her by surprise. "We don't have much time to get this right. I knew your father's associates would try to locate you at some point. My sources say there've been inquiries into your whereabouts in Washington. I need to get you out of here ASAP. Looks like you're about to get your wish."

Katherine tamped down the lump forming in her throat. She wasn't sure whether it came from the thought of what she'd ask for coming to fruition or sheer panic of the unknown. "All right. What's the next move?"

Her aunt patted the cushion beside her. Katherine circled

the oval table and sat, seeing a large map on the table, marked with various colors and Post-It notes. She glanced at her aunt whose ever-present glasses sat on the edge of her nose. She looked tired and weary. Kate knew she'd been in meetings all morning.

"Your name will be Lizzie O'Brien. Here are the necessary documents for the change in your identity."

Her aunt handed her a long, white envelope. Peeking inside, Kate saw a driver's license and a new Social Security card, as well as a license to practice veterinary medicine in Virginia. "My agents have been briefed, but they do *not* know you as Katherine Hallock of Hallock Farm. *No one* can know that you are my niece. I pulled in a big favor to make this happen, Katherine. The agents were briefed as to what you do, why you are running, and from whom, but as Lizzie O'Brien. It's imperative you maintain your cover.

"The lead agent on the case is John Clinton. Coincidentally, he owns a horse farm on the outskirts of Mount Vernon. His breeding farm will be used as the safe house. Agent Clinton has informed me his team is in place and the safe house is ready for you."

Her aunt pointed to the manila folder lying on the table. "Open it and look at the contents." Kate pulled out the photographs inside. "The faces of those six people are the lead team members. There are other agents who will be at the farm, as well. The territory is wide, and I had to hire private security to cover my tracks. Just do your best to blend into the everyday workings of the farm."

"Who's he?" Kate pulled out John Clinton's photo first. The picture was a simple black and white Agency-issued ID headshot.

"John Clinton, lead agent and owner of Clinton Stables. You'll be working as his vet as your cover."

Kate's felt a bit of tension ease from the pit of her stomach. "At least I'll be doing something I'm trained to do. I know me. If I don't keep busy, I'll go crazy until this mess is put to rest."

Her aunt looked over the rim of her glasses. "We couldn't have picked a more perfect cover. Sheer luck, if you ask me. But, Katherine, you must make me a promise. It's important to your safety and those at the safe house who are putting their lives on the line to protect you."

Kate stared at her aunt intently and asked, "What do you need me to do?"

"You must do what you are told to do, when you are told to do it. *And* by whoever tells you to. You know the drill. I don't need to remind you." Katherine nodded, understanding perfectly the implications. "If you can't abide by those terms, I can't promise to keep you safe."

Kate knew the danger had grown exponentially when she'd overheard her aunt talking on the phone about her father's Russian business partners. "I'll do whatever you need me to do. I'll be ready bright and early."

Kate bent over and kissed her aunt's rosy cheek, inhaling a jasmine scent. Grabbing the envelope containing the documents and the photos from the table, she walked to the door, turning back for one last look.

Aunt Elizabeth sat on the sofa, a contemplative expression on her face. Had Kate been able to read her aunt's mind at that very instant, Kate would be shocked by her aunt's train of thought – even though it was against all the rules, could two people, one who placed duty to country above personal relationships and the other whose life revolved around family and responsibilities, heal from the realities of their painful pasts – together?

CHAPTER TEN

The knock on her bedroom door came at three o'clock in the morning. Kate had been ready for hours. Unable to fall asleep, she lay on the top of the bed, fully dressed and ready to go. Work clothes provided by her aunt were packed in a brown duffle bag and sat alongside her vet bag on the white shag carpet.

After a quick cup of coffee and a tearful goodbye to her aunt and Juanita, Kate was ushered out the back door of the compound into a waiting black SUV with tinted windows. There was a lead and follow car in place to carry Kate to her final destination. An agent, dressed head to toe in black, opened the car door for her. She piled herself and her gear into the back seat, buckling in for the ride ahead.

In three hours, if all went as planned, Kate would be at Clinton Stables. With one last look at the shadowy outline of the brick mansion, Kate watched the gate swing shut as the SUV caravan rolled out onto Madison Street.

* * *

Kate was jarred awake as the SUV took a sharp turn down a narrow dirt lane. Within minutes, after hitting every possible pothole on the rutted road, Kate detected the beginning of broken fences marking off the paddocks of a farm. The entourage must be nearing Clinton Stables.

"Are we almost there?" Kate asked Agent Howard in the front seat.

"Yes. Just a bit farther, Ms. O'Brien. You'll be able to see the farmhouse around the next bend."

Kate strained to see out the tinted windows, taking in the lush green farmland around her. She pointed through the front window to a large dilapidated building coming up on her right.

"Is that it?" she asked. No reply was forthcoming from the two agents in the car with her.

The three SUVs swung into the asphalt turnaround. The minute the cars stopped, five agents swarmed her vehicle. Feeling a bit intimidated, she slowly exited the car, her eyes darting from man to man to man.

"Miss O'Brien?" a tall, dark skinned, burly agent asked.

A face she had memorized. "That's me. Agent Martin?" Kate had done her homework. She recognized the man from his photo. But Agent Martin wasn't the lead agent.

"Yes, ma'am. You've met the official welcoming committee."

"But I'm supposed to report to Agent Clinton."

Jake Martin scratched his head. "Yeah, you were." He turned to the agents who had driven her from Arlington. "We've got it from here. Inform the Director her package arrived."

Within moments, the cars were gone and she was left behind in the most godforsaken-looking place she'd ever seen. This was a working horse farm? The paddocks and buildings were in total disrepair. One of the barns looked as if a tornado had touched down, knocking down one wall and caving in part of the roof. She shuddered as she focused on the farmhouse off to the right side of the property. Coupled with the yard and gardens, the place was in total disarray.

"So where is he?" Kate questioned Agent Martin. "I think

I'd better do as I was instructed and report in."

Kate detected a small snicker of laughter from behind, but when she turned the agents standing there stood at attention, awaiting their instructions to proceed.

"Ms. O'Brien. I'm Wade Houghton." A younger man with a brown beard stepped forward. "I'll take you up to the main barn. I think time got away from John. He's been there for over a half an hour."

"Great. I'd appreciate it. And then, if it's okay, I'll get settled in."

"Follow me." Agent Houghton motioned in the direction of the largest building on the property.

By force of habit, Kate picked up her vet bag and carried it with her as she trailed along next to him.

"This is some place." Kate tried not to sound sarcastic, given the surprise of the condition of the so called "safe house."

"Yes, ma'am. The Director said this was just the best place for you." He stopped in front the barn. "John should be in there… somewhere." The agent pointed to the interior of the barn. "Do you want me to go in with you?"

"No, I've got it from here." Walking up to the open barn door, she looked back to see the agent take up his position as a guard, his weapon at the ready, by the fence near the paddock. She ventured into the dark tunnel before her. "Hello? Agent Clinton?" Her voice echoed through the long, dark corridor. It took a few seconds for her eyes to grow accustomed to the dark. The stench of rancid manure hit her nostrils. Reaching for the bandana she always carried in her back pocket, Kate held it up to her nose. Glancing down at the filthy, mud-caked walkway, Kate knew it had been quite some time since anyone cleaned or washed the stalls and cement floor.

Sidestepping the dirt and grime, she called out once more. "Agent Clinton? Are you in here?"

Walking on, Kate took in the sorry state of the stalls. Bridles, saddles and bits lay strewn all over, covered with dirt. Peeking inside the tack room made her cringe. Kate briefly thought her idea of hiding away given these circumstances was now a very bad idea, an emotional reaction to what she'd been through. She should call her aunt and return to the compound. But she immediately changed her mind upon hearing the painful whinnying of a horse from an area near the far back stall.

"Agent Clinton! It's Lizzie O'Brien!" The clamor of noise piqued Kate's curiosity as she inched closer. She wasn't sure what she would find on the other side of the stall door. "Are you in there?"

A gruff, commanding male voice came from behind the box stall's door. "Yes, I'm here! Goddamn it! Get in here and help me! This mare isn't going to give birth by herself!"

Kate's veterinary instincts kicked into high gear. Rounding the gate, she stopped dead in her tracks when she spotted the man kneeling before her. No way could this handsome man possibly be the person whose bland mug shot she'd been given in her aunt's office. John Clinton's picture hadn't done him justice. A green flannel shirt outlined an extremely muscled upper torso. Worn work jeans fit snuggly over his backside and hugged tightly to his thighs. Although he was squatting down on one knee, Katherine made him out to be at least six-four. His tan, angular face was framed by wavy brown hair. The deepest pair of sea green eyes she'd ever seen, like those of the waters off the beaches of the Bahamas, gave hers a piercing look.

"Well, are you just going to stand there gawking at my ass? Or are you going to help me, Miss Veterinarian?" Kate sprung to attention. "My boss told me you're one of the best, and this here's my prize mare. So get your damn rear in gear and grab that vet bag!"

Kate jumped to do his bidding and was beside him in seconds. "What's her name?"

"Wild Flame. She's not about to give us much more time from what I can tell. Is she?"

Kate shook her head, fumbling in her bag for her rubber gloves. "No, she's not. Get out of my way." She squatted down beside Agent Clinton and shoved him with her knee to make a space so she could work and do her job. From the panicked look on John Clinton's face, Kate wasn't going to count on him to be of much help.

"You sure you know what you're doing? I can't afford to lose her. She's my meal ticket to start my breeding farm." With one eye on Wild Flame, she glanced up, seeing deep concern etched across John Clinton's forehead.

As she slid her hands within the mare to grab the foal's hooves, she turned to him, smiled and winked. In her best imitation of a southern drawl, she said, "Why, Mr. Clinton. I know nothin' about birthin' horses!"

* * *

When did veterinarians come off looking like Lizzie O'Brien? She was stunning! Her long, auburn hair was drawn up into a baseball cap. Her shirt and jeans hugged voluptuous curves. John stared into a pair of dark, smoky brown eyes. Lizzie O'Brien possessed a natural beauty. She was tall, tan and wore no makeup. Her body was sleek and athletic. And Ms. O'Brien was totally oblivious to the effect she had on him as she nudged him for a closer view of the horse.

John kicked himself for the direction his thoughts were headed. Hadn't the last mission ended with Zoya because he put his interest in a beautiful woman before his sense of duty?

A small strand of Lizzie's hair escaped her cap and lay on his shoulder. John smelled the scent of lavender. With their thighs touching, an electric bolt rocketed up his thigh and into his groin; his jeans grew tight.

The stern face of his mentor flashed before him, bringing John back to reality. Even though he swore to follow Agency protocol to the letter on this mission, John wasn't dead. Any man would take a long look at the woman by his side. Twice. Hell, even three times.

"Well, are you going to get your rear in gear and help me?" the voice beside him countermanded. "The mare's in trouble. Can't you tell?"

John's knowledge of ranching lay primarily with cattle, not horses. When he worked his parents' ranch in Montana as a young boy, horses were for riding the range. Changing Clinton Stables into a thoroughbred breeding farm was a lofty goal.

"Ah…" he stuttered, trying to rein in his errant thoughts. Resigned, knowing time was of the essence, he said, "No, I can't. What's wrong with her?" The woman's hand snaked out from out of nowhere and connected with his arm. Lizzie shoved him out of the way so hard that John landed on his backside with a thud.

"The mare's too tired, Agent Clinton. She doesn't have enough strength left to push the foal through the birth canal. The foal's stuck." Lizzie nodded to her bag behind them. "Grab me that rope in my vet bag."

John did her bidding. The lady was all business. Now he knew what Elizabeth meant when she'd said he'd have his hands full keeping Lizzie O'Brien in line.

Turning, he found her half-standing, half-kneeling behind the mare. He eyed her questioningly. "What the hell do you think you're going to do?"

"I'm going to pull the foal out, cowboy. Here. Give - me - that." Lizzie wrenched the rope from John's hands, tied it around the hooves, took a deep breath and pulled. When John tried to help, she pushed him away with her hips. "Watch out! You don't have protective gear on. You'll get your hand or fingers sliced off. The foal's hooves are too sharp. I can do it."

"You? You think you can do this all by yourself?" John stared at his charge in disbelief.

"Listen, I don't have time to argue. Just stay the hell out of my way for a minute, and your mare and foal will be fine."

With one last pull that any normal man would struggle with, Lizzie gave one hard tug and birthed the foal. John watched as a smile of accomplishment radiated across her face. Who was this woman? Lizzie O'Brien had just proved she was strong and stubborn as hell. And *she* was running from members of the Russian mob. Why? The team understood the basics of the case they'd been handed, but at the moment, they operated on a need-to-know basis, with Elizabeth handling point. Protection wasn't new to them. But operating in the woods of Virginia was far different than the bazaars and streets of Eastern Europe.

"Hey!" Lizzie was trying to get his attention.

John's attention circled back to the woman who'd saved his prize mare. He watched as she cleaned herself up.

"Isn't she a beautiful sight?" A smile broke out on the woman's face as she put her utensils back into her vet bag.

The wobbly-legged chestnut colt suckled quietly at Wild Flame's underbelly. John watched, fascinated, as the woman came to stand by his side to take in the scene, as well. Gone were the bloodied work gloves. Instead he saw rough, work-hardened hands. Her rugged, scuffed riding boots confirmed his theory she'd spent many hours in a barn. However, John knew boots. And the ones on her feet cost a pretty penny. She wasn't any two-bit vet doctor, scraping by to make a living.

"You've got yourself quite the colt, Agent Clinton. I sincerely hope Wild Flame has good bloodlines if you plan on making a go of this place." Lizzie chattered as if she'd known him for years. "You didn't answer my question."

"Sorry, I got a bit distracted." *By you*, John thought. "What was it you asked?"

"I said, isn't *that* a beautiful sight?" She pointed to the colt, nuzzling at the mare's underbelly.

John didn't need to look at the mare and the newborn colt to answer. He drew in a deep breath and stared down into the eyes of the woman by his side. "It surely is, Lizzie O'Brien. It sure is."

Judas Priest, John said to himself. *Lizzie O'Brien's already trouble with a capital T and Operation Hide and Seek has only begun.*

CHAPTER ELEVEN

Kate wiped away the sweat on her brow. She wasn't acclimated yet to the humidity and heat of a Virginia morning. Leaning over the stall door with John Clinton at her side, she said, "You can't leave them like this, even for one night."

"Why not?" John asked. "Where the hell am I going to put them? You can't tell me you didn't notice the condition of this place when you drove up."

Although this wasn't her farm, Kate felt responsible for the horses she'd just birthed and cared for. "Look…Your barn's filthy. There's rancid manure. The mare is eating bad straw and hay. I know her feed is okay, but if you're not careful, infection will set in. In no time, it will spread to her milk. You'll have two sick horses before you know it."

John sighed in resignation. "You're right. Given my time frame, I never gave any thought to the animals I brought to the farm. Some of the other horses I own aren't here. I board them at a local stable about five miles away. Got any ideas?"

"First, you need to sanitize the barn as soon as possible and be quick about it."

The sounds of voices suddenly came from the open barn

door. A deep voice boomed down the corridor, "Hey, Chief! You still in here?"

Another voice with more of a Texas twang followed suit. "Everything okay in here, boss?"

Kate stepped behind John Clinton. Since she left the compound, her nerves were on edge.

John spoke in a low, reassuring tone. "Everything's okay, Lizzie. It's just my team. You met them when you got here."

"Back here, guys!" The shuffling of boots along the concrete came closer, and five men emerge from the dark recesses of the shadows. "Lizzie, let me acquaint you with the best there is." He first pointed to the man she'd met when she'd stepped out of the black SUV. "Jake Martin, my second-in-command. This tall Texan is Tim Thomas. Wade Houghton, Bob Taylor and Chuck Raymond." The last three men tipped their hats to her.

Kate acknowledged all five with a brief nod.

She was grateful John took control of the conversation. "Lizzie's just informed me this barn needs to be cleaned ASAP. Take a look at my new colt. Ain't she a beauty?"

Wade spoke up. "Chief, I hate to break into your enthusiasm, but you have a secure call to make."

Lizzie glanced at the men assessing her. From her aunt's photographs, she knew them only as agents armed to protect her, nothing more. "Well, I'm here." she interjected, trying her best to sound upbeat. Turning to John, she said, "Got any fresh straw?"

"In the back of my truck. I brought it with me this morning when I brought several of the other horses. My men here would be happy to help you clean up the barn." Lizzie couldn't help but notice the shocked expressions on their faces. Obviously, mucking out stalls was not on the agenda in Agent Boot Camp 101. "But, I can only give you two hours. We've got more important things to tend to now that you're here. My men and

I need to brief you on what's going to happen."

Kate semi-saluted. "Then, I'll be sure to make it quick. Right now, we need to find a place for Wild Flame and the colt to stay while we try to wash out the stalls and walkway." She yawned then considered assigning particular tasks to each man.

Agent Clinton started to walk away, but came back. "You've had an early morning. Can I get you a cup of coffee?"

Out of the corner of her eye, Kate once more caught more amazed looks on the faces of the men who'd be helping her. John Clinton did not have to treat her with kid gloves.

"No, thanks. The Director's cook packed me a Thermos. I need to get to work. And it sounds like you do, too. But, Agent Clinton, I'm a tad confused."

"Confused? About what?"

Kate glanced around and asked, "Where exactly is your safe house?"

All six men pointed in unison down the corridor. Kate could see the back porch of the rundown farmhouse she'd passed on her way into the barn. Her jaw sagged. Her aunt had been right. She'd been reading too many spy novels where the victim was protected in an out of the way in a Georgetown townhome. That dilapidated shack was going to be home?

"You're can't be serious!" All six heads nodded in the affirmative. "I can't possibly stay in that rat trap."

A grim look passed across Agent Clinton's face. "We'll be living there for however long it takes to complete the mission." John spoke in a more authoritative tone. "Believe it or not, it's very deceiving to the eye from the outside. Perfect cover. Director Hallock wanted to use it. If you have a problem, you can take it up with her."

Kate, wanting desperately to retort, bit her tongue. John motioned to Jake Martin. "Jake, come with me. Lizzie, Jake's our cook. When you're done with my men, head over to the house and you can sample some of his southern cooking."

John had set the tone for moving forward. Who was she to question him?

"Yes, sir. Got it. Two hours. Everything will be set by then." Kate grabbed two shovels from the wall and handed them to Wade and Bob. "Didn't think you'd be pulling horse dung duty, did you?" She watched in amusement as the two men woefully glanced at each other. "I'm fine here, Agent Clinton."

"Good. Come on, Jake." Lizzie watched John stride to the barn door. He stopped apparently deep in thought and abruptly did a u-turn and marched back to stand in front of her. "For the record, this is my *home*, Ms. O'Brien. For whatever reason, Director Hallock deemed it necessary to be yours for the ensuing weeks. I don't know what you're accustomed to. It could be the Ritz for all I care. But as long as you're here, you'll treat it with respect. This is no rat trap! Got that?" As John raised his voice, Lizzie's eyebrows arched in surprise, his comrades-in-arms doing likewise.

Having four older brothers, Kate never backed down from any kind of dare. She knew she had to follow his rules to be safe, but she hoped he had a good horse. He didn't know it, but he was in for one hell of a ride. She never backed down from a challenge.

"Well then, *su casa es mi casa*, cowboy."

* * *

"Come on, John. Dinner's been ready for twenty minutes," Tim complained as the team sat around the long rectangular table in the newly remodeled kitchen, waiting to eat. "Maybe Lizzie fell asleep. She worked her ass off today."

"Have you seen that woman sit a horse?" Chuck chimed in. "But she pushed the rules by taking a ride out to the back trail. She was gone before we even realized it."

"She what? This is the first I'm hearing about it. One of you…"

Tim interjected, trying to change the subject. "Lizzie likes to be in charge, in case you hadn't noticed."

Everyone at the table nodded in unison.

"Yes, I noticed!" John barked. It wasn't his team's fault. He slammed his hand down on the table, rattling the plates and glassware. "We really didn't get a chance to put her through the full briefing of what's at stake. I'm well aware in the short time she's been here she's determined to show us she's got a mind of her own. And if we're not careful, we'll all be up that creek without the paddle. The Director informed us Lizzie knows the stables are her safe haven. Please, just remember to keep an eye on her 24/7."

Jake chuckled. "Well, we're doing a hell of a job on that score so far." John glared at his friend. "Look, John. We know this is high priority. But, understand we're operating outside our normal mode of operation."

Tim interrupted, "Well, I, for one, am hungry. And I'm sick and tired of waiting. Are you going up and get her, or do you want one of us to do the honors?"

"I'll go." John mumbled under his breath and reluctantly pushed back from the table. What the hell took a woman so long to grab a shower and change her clothes? Hell, normally on assignment, they'd go days without bathing. He took the back kitchen stairs two at a time and knocked at her door at the top of the landing. No answer. Great. Just great. Maybe she had fallen asleep.

He pounded again. "Lizzie! Supper's ready and it's getting cold." John spoke louder. No response. This time, he balled his hand into a fist and knocked loudly. "Lizzie?" Trying the doorknob and realizing the door wasn't locked, he opened it, poking his head inside the room. It was empty. His heart jumped in his chest, visualizing her disappearing out the open window. But hearing the shower running set his mind at ease.

His eyes dropped to the floor, immediately seeing a trail of clothes strewn along the length of the braided runner that led to the bathroom door. John swallowed at the mental image forming in his mind of his charge stripping out of her work clothes. Dirty denim jeans, a shirt, socks and one pair of very sexy black lace panties and bra only made his groin hard.

Lizzie had left the door wide open. John's pulse sped up. He licked his lips as his thoughts ran wild. He tried to steel himself against the feelings she conjured up. What was wrong with him? Had he not learned from the past? John couldn't blow this assignment. Keeping Lizzie O'Brien safe and maintaining his objectivity were now his primary two goals.

The open bathroom door was an invitation. Knowing it was unprofessional and he'd catch hell if the Director ever found out, he convinced himself it was his duty to check to be sure she was safe. Besides, his crew was hungry and they'd assigned him the task of bringing her to the kitchen for dinner. From the song she was singing, it was apparent she had lost track of time.

Standing in the doorway of the small steamy room, John saw Lizzie through the glass shower door. Her well-proportioned body stood naked in the confines of the tiled walls. Beads of water ran across her freckled shoulders and down her back, trickling down her buttocks and long, sleek tan legs.

An image of Elizabeth Hallock flashed through his mind for the second time that day. What was the rationale behind his reaction to this stranger whom he'd never met? He'd been without a woman in his life for a year. A self-imposed punishment for what transpired. In that time, John thought he had done a good job training his mind to not bend to the pressures of outside relationships.

John quickly grabbed the towel he spied hanging on the hook by the shower. Holding it up to block his view of her nakedness, he shouted over the sound of the rushing water, "Lizzie! Supper's been ready for fifteen minutes. You coming or not?"

A deafening shriek echoed in the small enclosure. Lizzie slammed the knob of the shower off. John raised the towel higher to block his view. The last thing he needed was to be cited for sexual harassment.

"What the hell do you think you're looking at, cowboy? And what are you doing in my bathroom?"

Opening the shower door, she reached for the proffered towel, quickly wrapping it around her body. "I repeat, Agent Clinton. Why are standing in *my* bathroom?"

John's temper got the best of him. "My men and I are hungry. We're not waiting all night for you to eat. They've had a long day. Tim's had supper ready for twenty minutes! And, besides, there's business to take care of when we're finished. Get your ass moving and head down for chow!" John stormed out, slamming the bedroom door behind him.

CHAPTER TWELVE

Hallock Farm
Hampton Beach

Helen Hallock stood in the hallway outside the living room, eavesdropping on a very heated conversation between her husband and the head of the farm's security detail. Katherine's disappearance had taken a major emotional toll on her, her sons, and Hannah, as well as those in her daughter's employ. From the little Helen was able to confirm, Katherine ran because Ty and Robert had manipulated some business dealings, placing both her daughter and the farm in jeopardy. Helen feared for her daughter's safety. She was frightened for everyone within the Hallock Farm complex, employees and family members alike.

Since he was standing near the slightly ajar French doors, Robert's deep voice resonated throughout the room and out into the hall.

"No, Geoff. That's all I can tell you. Katherine took our conversation *totally* out of context. Before Ty or I could explain otherwise, she turned and ran. No one here has heard from her since."

Liar, Helen thought. Her husband didn't know the meaning of the word "truth."

Geoff Daniels replied in a clipped tone, "Robert, with all due respect, I don't believe you. I've known Kate since she was a child. There's something you're not telling me. For one, why didn't you make any attempt to contact us the minute she left? Hell, Robert. What were you thinking, keeping her disappearance covered up? She's been missing for more than three days! Don't tell me you didn't think to file a missing person's report. I don't buy any of this."

The room was silent. Helen knew her husband well enough to know he'd never answer when backed into a corner.

But, from the tone in his voice, Geoff Daniels was determined to get to the bottom of Katherine's disappearance. "Her friends in New York. Would she have gone there?"

"No." Robert's voice rose in response. "Thomas called Janine. No one has seen her."

"What about Washington?"

Helen tensed and leaned closer. She couldn't wait to hear Robert's response to *that* question. Thank goodness it was Geoff pushing Robert hard about Katherine's possible whereabouts. He was the only person who could do it and not suffer repercussions.

With no forthcoming reply from her husband, their chief of security continued on. "Do *you* think she may have headed to DC? She'd be safe at the compound."

Helen took that as her cue to enter. She opened the doors and walked in. Geoff looked surprised to see her, but Robert glared at her audacity to enter into his private conversation. He knew precisely what was on her mind and what she was thinking.

It was Helen's turn to reply. "I believe that's exactly where she is."

In forty years of marriage, Robert Hallock had shown his wife all facets of his personality, some of which she wished never to see again. Helen had gone along with his facade. She had her reasons. There were secrets, long buried in the past. If discovered, the fabric of their family would be broken forever. Robert Hallock was a master of masking his true persona and hiding anything he didn't want anyone on the outside to know.

"So, you think she's gone to Virginia, Helen?" Geoff queried. He began writing in his small notepad. "You think, like I do, she's at the compound?"

"It's the only place I know where Katherine would go to feel safe, given the circumstances." Out of the corner of her eye, she saw Robert's face redden as he tried to hold his temper in check. Inwardly, Helen was pleased he was uncomfortable and put in his place.

Robert interjected harshly, "Helen, you're interfering in matters that shouldn't concern you. Geoff and I will work through the details of locating Katie."

How typical, Helen thought. A perfect example of her husband's self-serving attitude rearing its ugly head. One thing the family had learned over the years was that Robert hated his authority being usurped. Helen had news for him this time. She intended on being involved from now on. She expected to be notified of every aspect of Geoff's investigation. Helen wasn't going to allow Robert to control her any longer.

Geoff cleared his throat. "I don't have time to waste. As it is, we've lost valuable time. If you two will excuse me, I'll head back to my office and get my contacts activated. I'm going to ramp up security for everyone here at the farm, as well as setting up details down by the barns. We need to be cautious. I'll get back to you both when I have more to go on."

After Geoff left, Helen sat in the white wingback chair by the fireplace and watched Robert pace. She cleared her throat, and he stopped. The tension between them could be sliced with a sharp knife.

"Well, what is it?" Robert said, irritated. "I don't have all day. Say what you came to say and get out. I have work to do."

Helen took a deep breath to strengthen her resolve. "I can clearly see you backed yourself into a corner again." She vowed not to be intimidated by the angry glare the man sent her way. "Don't stare at me like that. You know exactly what I'm talking about. I don't know where I would rank *this* debacle among those you've been involved in through the years. But it's certainly near the top of the list."

She pinned him with a dagger-like glare of her own. Helen had lived with the man too long not to know his fuse was about to ignite. But for once, she wasn't going to let him override her or their conversation.

In a threatening tone, she said, "I warned you… *I told you*, the next time you involved this family or farm in something improper or illegal, I wouldn't stand for it. You obviously didn't think I meant what I said, did you?" Helen stood up, her left hand on her hip and her right index finger pointing at him. "If you don't find some way to get out of this mess and bring Katherine home, it will be the last you see of me…and my money." Robert's face blanched. "You heard me. *My* money. I'll walk out that door and never come back."

"You don't have the guts to leave all this!" Robert taunted her.

Helen took a step towards him. "You don't think so? Well, you don't know me as well as you think you do, *husband*. I'm not the prim and proper Hampton society matron you married forty years ago." Robert's shocked look built up her courage to continue. "You forget it was Elizabeth and I who bailed you out twenty years ago."

"Helen!"

Helen raised her hand to silence him. "I have a suspicion your dirty little secret has something to do with what happened between you and Katherine the other day. You can deny it to Geoff, but you know damn well where she is. Don't tell me you don't. You just won't admit it." Piercing him with a cold, stony glare, she continued, "I think she's gone to the only sanctuary she's ever known in her life."

Helen's comments hit their intended target. Robert began to shake as his face lost some of the redness from anger. He sank into the matching wingchair.

Trembling, Helen still stood, her arms crossed over her breasts in a defiant stance. "You can't help but be thinking the same thing I am. Elizabeth will be forced to tell her *everything*… due to your stupidity. The glory days you've enjoyed at Hallock Farm and being atop the Hampton social scene will be over. You'll be lucky if you're not sitting in some jail cell…"

"Helen! Enough!" Robert leaned over and picked up a glass from the table in front of him. His hands shaking, he poured a brandy from the decanter.

"I haven't finished."

Robert downed the liquid in one gulp. "Yes, you have. You let me handle this. I don't need you interfering in affairs you know nothing about."

Helen promptly sat in the chair opposite him and leaned closer. "You don't think I didn't know something had to be amiss with the business dealings of the farm for the last month?"

Her husband's eyebrows arched in surprise.

"Those men didn't pay you a visit simply to buy a horse. Whatever shady business deal you've cooked up with Ty has finally caught up with you. And this time, you're not raking the family name over the coals and through the tabloids. I've had enough of you screwing this family over financially with your scheming and plotting."

"Don't you go dictating to me—"

"I'll dictate all I want!" she exclaimed and drew in another deep breath. "I'm done. Whatever it takes, whatever it costs, you find my daughter. I don't care what personal humiliation you have to suffer in the process. I'm sick and tired of living with secrets and lies."

Helen stood, brushing the wrinkles out of the front of her linen skirt. But as she looked at Robert's face she knew something was dreadfully wrong. Someone must be at the door. How long had they been there? What had they heard? She had no choice but to turn and follow his gaze. Her heart hammered, and her hands trembled as she, too, looked to see who had arrived unannounced.

"Robert… Helen…" Just inside the French doors stood Elizabeth and two hulking men in dark black suits. "I think we need to talk."

Helen sighed in relief upon seeing her sister-in-law, bursting into tears. "Oh, Elizabeth! Katherine? Where's my baby? Have you seen her?"

"She's safe." Elizabeth moved farther into the room and paused. "For now. I came to find out what's going on for myself. I have her version. Now I want Robert's."

Helen noted Elizabeth looked at her, but didn't glance at her estranged brother.

Robert's drink had given him the courage to stand up. He snarled, "I'll tell you about the details when hell freezes over, Lizzie."

Helen couldn't believe her ears. She shook her head. It was happening again. History was repeating itself, just as it had twenty years ago. But this time, the outcome would be different. Helen marveled at how, considering the past, Elizabeth could stand there so cool, calm and collected.

It was then Elizabeth's eyes pierced Robert's. "It just did, dear brother. It just did."

CHAPTER THIRTEEN

Washington, D.C.

The door opened to the small studio apartment the trio had lived in since their initial meeting on the grounds of Mount Vernon. Demetrie and Stavros walked in, talking quietly to each other.

Zoya's temper flared upon finally seeing them. "Where the hell have the two of you been all day?"

Demetrie arched his eyebrows at the tone in her voice. By the expression on his face, she'd crossed the line.

Needing to remember who was in charge, she spoke less harshly to both men. "You were gone so long. I was beginning to worry," Zoya said. Left in the seedy part of the northeast section of Washington, she was out of the loop of any communication among the three of them that day. It irked her to no end that there could be no phone contact amongst them in case their pictures were put through a database for facial recognition at Washington's estate. But she understood. "I was beginning to think something had happened since it's so late."

The two men left at the crack of dawn to scout the area where Demetrie's inside contact told them John Clinton had been assigned. She'd spent the better part of the day pacing the wood floor and checking the cache of weapons they'd procured while she waited for word in some form.

"You know where we went." Demetrie entered the small galley kitchen and took two beers from the refrigerator. "The setting was as we envisioned it would be, even better. But… we ran into a few issues coordinating with our inside man. My contact's choice of the double agent inside the Clinton camp has me a bit worried. Nothing I can't remedy if we need to."

Returning to the small living area, Demetrie sat down on the small couch, which doubled as a bed. He handed a beer to Stavros, who sat down beside him. Zoya could tell from one look that they'd had a rough day in the hot Virginia countryside. Their clothes were muddied and grass stained; the two men looked exhausted from their excursion into the hilly terrain.

As Zoya stood by the breakfast bar, she saw Demetrie eyeing her carefully. "You must have patience, Zoya. I'm disappointed in you."

"Disappointed?" Zoya was shocked. "I've done everything you've asked."

"No, my contacts and I have done what *you* have asked for… and more," he retorted. "Remember our mission is to avenge what happened in Istanbul. You were not the only person affected. Many fellow comrades got caught up in Elizabeth Hallock's trap when Clinton was taken hostage and then extracted. Five of our best double agents died at the hands of the American government. We are here for them, as well, not just for you."

Zoya knew better than to lash out. She could voice her dismay if she were dealing with others in their organization, but not with this man. She didn't care that she was being selfish. She felt she had a right to be. But there were repercussions she didn't want to face if she wasn't careful with her words around

Demetrie.

Plastering a smile on her face, she attempted to placate him. "You're right. You shouldn't need to remind me. I'm truly grateful for the opportunity to have the honor to have been chosen to get the job done."

Her personal goal was to eliminate John Clinton. Elizabeth Hallock would be an added bonus, one that would be a coup for the cell that had infiltrated their way into D.C.

"I smell something cooking, sister. When are we eating?" Stavros's mind was always on the here and now. Zoya had her doubts he'd be able to hold up his end of the assignment. He'd been distracted, by what she didn't know. He was an excellent marksman, and the mission's outcome was relying on him to take out the enemy when the time came.

"Now, Stavros. Come. Eat. Demetrie…" Zoya saw the man was sitting on the small sofa, deeply engrossed, talking with someone on his cell phone.

"He'll come as soon as he's finished," Stavros said, sitting on the bar stool at the counter. He reached for a plate. "We ran into some unexpected issues when we made it to Clinton's farm. Demetrie needs to check with his contact. We almost walked into a trap."

Zoya stopped dishing out the food onto her brother's plate. "Please tell me the plans we made haven't been compromised."

Stavros shook his head. "*Nyet*. But I wouldn't want to be on the other end of that phone right now. Demetrie's angry. Madder than I've ever seen him."

Zoya gave her brother his plate full of food. She was impatient to hear the details. Glancing to see that Demetrie was still on the phone, she whispered, "What happened?"

"His contact told us there was an old road which would access the farm from the north. We parked up near the meadow and slowly worked our way in. It was rough going. We hadn't prepared for the mountain-like terrain, the massive boulders and the trees. It took time, but we found the meadow."

Zoya stopped eating. Puzzled, she asked, "What happened? He isn't pleased. Look at him."

Her brother looked over his shoulder and returned to the food on his plate. "We had reached the section of the woods by the edge of the path where we needed to be. I was about to move forward when Demetrie shoved me to the ground."

"What? Why? Did you come across guards on the perimeter?"

"We couldn't get close enough to tell. That's one of the things he's mad about. It seems the intelligence information he's getting is constantly changing, and the contact is having trouble finding a way to make consistent contact." Stavros cleaned his plate and handed it to his sister. "Demetrie signaled for me to stay put while he shimmied through the grass. He returned moments later still on his belly."

Zoya mulled over what she was hearing. "What was the problem?" Zoya was afraid to ask, not liking where this was going. The mission had a timeline. They couldn't afford to slow down.

"Demetrie spotted a security camera mounted in a nest in a tree above us. Apparently his contact at the farm hadn't deactivated it. He's pissed. We don't think we were made. But he had us out of there within minutes. Then, coming back, we hit the Beltway traffic."

Zoya nibbled on her food. "You couldn't call?"

"Zoya, you know perfectly well we can't give the enemy the chance to hear chatter anywhere. Silence is the best route. Demetrie's on a throw-away phone, trying to find out if there's any trace of us on the farm's security tapes."

Zoya laid her hand on the counter, three fingers showing their signal to stop talking. Finished with his conversation,

Demetrie came to stand behind Stavros.

Trying to sound as normal as possible, Zoya put a smile on her face. "Demetrie. Come. You must eat. You look tired and troubled, my friend. A vodka instead of the beer, yes?"

Zoya knew his weakness. He was a typical Russian who loved his vodka, a good woman and his native food. She would ply him with all three tonight to get the information she wanted. Zoya walked around the counter and came to stand beside him, linking her arm through his. She murmured a few things in Russian in his ear that made his eyes light up. Good. It was safe to ask questions. But she'd pay for it later.

"Sit." She nudged him onto the stool next to Stavros and walked to the stove to fill his plate. Pouring a tumbler full of ice and vodka, Zoya placed it on the counter in front of him. "Is there something I can do to help?"

Demetrie sipped the vodka and dug into the stroganoff. He shrugged. "There is nothing on our end to be done. The fool at the safe house didn't deactivate the camera for the timeframe we needed. However, we were lucky, he was able to edit and splice the small section of tape of us in the meadow. My source tells me we have to get creative. If we're going to get close, we're going to need to start creating diversions, small ones, slowly. I believe if we can do that, we might even be able to draw Elizabeth to the compound. Two for one."

Stavros spoke up. "One good thing came of today."

Demetrie stopped eating. "And that would be?"

"The north meadow area is not what we thought. It's not flat. The hillside creates a perfect place for me to set up my sniper shot. If you can come up with a way to draw Clinton and Elizabeth to the outer building, I'll be able to take them down."

Demetrie swallowed the last of the vodka from his glass and slapped her brother on the shoulder. "You know you're not as dumb as I thought you were."

Stavros's eyes flared at the derogatory comment. Zoya knew her brother didn't care for Demetrie, either. However he was the leader of the team, and Stavros had no choice but to respect his position. Stavros was grateful he had his freedom, thanks to the man's contacts within the Istanbul police department. But he had shared with Zoya that there were many times when he didn't care for the way they both were treated.

"Zoya," Stavros waved his glass. "We need more vodka. Take one for yourself."

Zoya poured another round.

"A toast, my friends." Stavros stood, clinking his glass with Zoya and Demetrie. "To success and diversions."

Zoya, seeing the light at the end of the long tunnel in sight, tapped her glass to those of her comrades. "Let vengeance be ours."

CHAPTER FOURTEEN

Elizabeth stood by the sideboard and watched Hannah put the finishing touches on the table settings. She had fond memories of the housekeeper who'd been with the family since Robert and Helen were married.

"Oh, Elizabeth," Hannah said. "To have you home is like a dream come true. It's been far too long."

Elizabeth smiled and basked in the woman's warm welcome. "I can't deny it's good to be home, Hannah. But I'm sure Robert will be glad when I'm back in Washington."

The housekeeper stopped laying the dinner plates on the table and looked at her. "I know my job is to be seen and not heard. But, there are things afoot here. Thomas has been upset for weeks. He and Robert do nothing but yell and scream at each other in the study. And the way Robert has treated Helen these last few months. It's sickens me. You've got to do something."

Elizabeth came to stand at Hannah's side, placing a comforting arm about the woman's shoulder. "It's a small consolation, but Robert and I agreed to a temporary truce. I don't know how long it will last. Katherine's safe, as you well know, but she doesn't know the whole story yet. I'm going to have to tell her everything. Robert's given me no choice. He finally came to his senses last night after my agents shared the information we have on his new business partners. It didn't take long for him to agree to this family dinner meeting."

Hannah hugged Elizabeth. "You're always putting this family back together, aren't you? For me, just knowing Katherine is somewhere safe is good enough for now." Hannah brushed a tear away from the corner of her eye. "I've got to hurry along now. There's some whisky in the sideboard. You may need a drink before dinner starts." Hannah winked at Elizabeth and walked out the door that led to the kitchen.

As Elizabeth measured out two fingers of the liquid into the tumbler, she looked out the window. The sun was setting over Moriches Bay, its golden, reddish hues illuminating the horizon. Memories of standing at this very window and of growing up in the house came crashing over her. Although she'd spent the better part of forty years working for the Agency, mostly in the European theater as an agent, she'd never forgotten where her home truly was.

The house itself hadn't changed much in twenty years, but after being taken on a tour of the farm this morning by the head trainer, who was filling in for Katherine, Elizabeth was excited at the prospect of what Katherine had developed. The girl had an uncanny business sense and, coupled with the knowledge she'd gained working for an Olympic equestrian while in college, she'd managed to put into practice a new model of equine training and rehabilitation care. No wonder Robert's shady friends wanted in on the operation. It was the perfect place to launder money and the Hamptons was the perfect venue to gain access to the circle of rich and famous people and their pocketbooks.

"Looking out over your domain?" Elizabeth stood still at hearing the voice absent so long from her life. "You must be pleased by what you see. Why not? You taught her everything she knows." There was still a tinge of anger in Robert's voice. She knew she couldn't expect miracles overnight.

"Care to join me, Robert?" Elizabeth indicated the decanter on the tabletop. "We agreed to disagree when necessary last night."

"I didn't think you gave me any choice in the matter. Did you?" Robert walked over to her.

"You're right. I didn't." Elizabeth filled a second glass with the amber liquid and handed it to her brother. "Remember, you won't have any say in what goes on from this point. I'm done quarreling. Katherine and the financial stability of this farm are my primary concerns. Both should have been yours, as well. But you neglected to do your part." It was taking all of Elizabeth's willpower to keep her temper in check.

"I propose a toast then." Robert raised his glass. "To my daughter and her safe return."

"To Katherine." Elizabeth clinked her glass with her brother's.

A cacophony of voices turned Robert and Elizabeth's attention in the direction of the doorway.

A chorus of voices chimed out, "Aunt Elizabeth!"

Suddenly, Elizabeth was engulfed in hugs and kisses from her four nephews, Thomas, Ethan, Adam and Matthew. She noted Robert had taken a step back, allowing her access to the family. Helen stood beaming at the foot of the long dinner table.

Matthew stepped away from the group and went to stand by his mother's side. Elizabeth smiled when she heard him whisper, "Mother, you were right. Hell certainly did freeze over!"

* * *

Polite conversation reigned during dinner, but Elizabeth

knew the time had come to broach the subject of Katherine's disappearance. Robert pushed his dessert plate aside and stared at her. It was obvious by his posture that he was letting her handle the fallout of what was to come. Once again, he'd made a mess of things and she was there to clean it up.

She wiped her lips with her napkin and was about to speak when Thomas interjected, "We all know we're here to find out about Kate." He cleared his throat. Elizabeth noticed Thomas didn't look at his father, even though he was seated next to the man. "What the hell happened? If *you're* here, something's gone terribly wrong." Motioning to those who sat around the table, Thomas continued, "We've tried in vain to figure out what happened the other day."

Ethan spoke up next. "Katie has too much of a sense of personal responsibility to this place to leave it all behind without a very good reason." Elizabeth knew he chose his words carefully. "Ty's involved, isn't he? Hannah told us she heard Kate screaming at him. Mother told us the engagement is off." Sitting next to his mother, he nodded towards the other end of the table where his father sat. "What has *he* done now?"

Elizabeth watched her brother bristle at her nephew's comments. There was no love lost between father and son since Robert tried to interfere in Ethan's election to be president of the Hampton Beach Country Club. From the look on her brother's face, she prayed Robert would live up to their agreement of letting her take the lead in telling the family what had transpired years ago, not go off half-cocked. It would accomplish nothing.

Elizabeth addressed the group. "First, your sister is safe and being cared for by my agents. But more importantly, I came here because there's a history to Hallock Farm you and your sister have never been privy to. There was a decision made long ago by your father, mother and myself. I thought it in the family's best interest, once the matter was settled, not to open up Pandora's box and tell you all when you were old enough to understand." She laid her napkin on the table. The room was silent. Elizabeth reached for the crystal goblet of water, taking a long swallow before she proceeded.

"Aunt Elizabeth, are you all right?" Concern was etched across Adam's brow. "You look a bit pale."

She smiled to reassure him. "I'm fine, Adam."

Adam hadn't been involved in the farm since his graduation from George Washington University Law School. He currently worked for the legal counsel office at the White House. She never got the opportunity to get together with him, although the other day she was briefed he'd recently been seen dating the President's daughter.

Elizabeth sat back in her chair. "Well, best to begin at the beginning. Twenty years ago, I worked an assignment in London when a fellow operative informed me that my brother," Elizabeth glanced at Robert, "was a person of interest in a money laundering scheme working its way through the Hamptons. I took a leave of absence from my post and came home. Thank God I had the forethought to arrive with an attorney by my side." She saw several quizzical looks pass amongst the brothers.

"I don't get it. Why did you have to come home or have an attorney?" Matthew, the youngest, asked curiously.

"Yes…well, this is where things become a bit complicated." She rose from her chair and walked to the white marble fireplace on the wall behind where her brother sat. All eyes in the room followed her every move. "You see when your grandparents died, they left the farm to your father and me. Because of my field missions, I gave your father the power of attorney to act on my behalf while I was away, to do whatever was needed to be done financially for the good of the business."

"Let me guess," Adam interrupted. "Father decided to use your POA and act in *his* best interests."

The legal mind was always at work, she thought.

Adam's sea blue eyes pierced her own. "Would I be wrong if I ventured a guess to say he used your monies from the estate to do something illegal?"

Robert surprised Elizabeth by not erupting into a fit of rage when all eyes fell on him.

"Yes, Adam. Your father didn't possess any business acumen back then."

Thomas snorted. She'd known of Thomas's concerns about his father's involvement in the family business over the years. It was she who'd made sure he'd gone to the Wharton School and groomed him to take over as CFO.

"I'm sorry to say he was unwise in his investments and never investigated who he was doing business with."

Elizabeth paused, not sure whether or not to reveal the next piece of information. But it was relevant. "I also discovered your father had a gambling problem."

The four men gasped. Their eyes ping-ponged from one end of the table to the other. Helen sat stoically at the end of the table.

"And, you're right, Adam. Your father accessed monies by using my POA." She could tell she wasn't going to be in control of the situation much longer.

"To make a long story short, your father had no choice but to sell me his shares in the Hallock Farm to rectify matters. At that point, I took control."

Stunned, Ethan asked, "*You* own Hallock Farm?"

"Yes, I do." Elizabeth stated the fact as calmly as she could. "I am, legally, the CEO of Hallock Farm, not your father. To save face and the family's reputation, I let your father retain the title in name only."

Robert flinched as she leveled the final blow.

Looking at the faces watching her intently, Elizabeth could tell Thomas was dumbfounded and confused. She watched him grip the arms of the chair, his knuckles turning white. "I don't get it. Father and I have battled over his business dealings, especially during the last several years. All this time, I assumed he made the decisions. Some of which weren't in the best interest of the farm."

"I know that, Thomas. Your mother relayed what information she could and acted as a go-between. But there have been things at the farm I couldn't monitor, given my job. I've been using a business partner of mine, a former operative, on the more serious affairs. I let you down, Thomas. I know it hasn't been easy. But, things will be better in a few months. That is, if we can get Kate out of the predicament your father put her in." Heads perked up around the table.

Robert growled, "Now, see here, Lizzie!"

Elizabeth put her hand up to halt her brother, glancing at her nephews. "When your father took it upon himself twenty years ago to do what he did, with very little remorse I might add, I decided to change the family trust that had been established. The four of you sit on the board of directors, but Katherine..." Elizabeth choked up, tears welling in her eyes. "I changed Katherine's position. She will assume the position of CEO on her thirtieth birthday."

Forks and knives clattered on plates as the reality of Elizabeth's announcement sank in.

"I knew, by placing the farm in her very capable hands, your legacy, and all that comes with it, would be safe. Or at least I thought so at the time." She shot a glare to the far end of the table. Robert fidgeted in his seat.

Silent during the entire conversation, Helen finally spoke up, "You boys realize what *would* have happened on Katherine's birthday, don't you?" Her voice trailed off, and she reached for her napkin to dab her eyes.

The room grew eerily quiet as each of her nephews pondered what their mother proposed. Adam was the first to answer. "Her thirtieth birthday would have been her wedding day!"

"My God. To Ty!" Ethan spat out in disgust.

Nodding, Elizabeth set the record straight. "Your sister was nothing more than a pawn in a game for your father to gain financial control of Hallock Farm. He needed her to marry Ty Bennington. Your father even went so far as to arrange their initial meeting. Ty may be very well connected on Park Avenue, but his father's firm represents several members of a Russian mafia family, the Savorskis. And your father…" Elizabeth pinned her brother with another icy glare. "…once again managed to entangle Hallock Farm in a situation he couldn't get out of. This time, Ty was involved."

A shouting match ensued. The room went from silence to utter chaos. Elizabeth rapped on the table for quiet. "Now listen to me, all of you! You will promise me not to share this conversation with anyone. Is that understood? If you can't, Katherine's safety will be at risk. There will be a meeting of the staff of the farm tomorrow morning, and everyone will be briefed by the security detail. Those of you who remain here at the farm will be assigned a personal bodyguard. Our number one priority is to bring Katherine home. She is petrified not only for her own safety, but for all of yours, as well."

Helen began to sob. Elizabeth wished she could put a comforting hand on her sister-in-law's shoulder. "I don't know how long it will take to bring her home, but I pray she will be back soon. Thomas, I need to speak to you before I leave. I've brought a forensic accountant. We'll get to the bottom of this mess and find out where and how the Russians have infiltrated the books."

Elizabeth turned to her brother. "Robert, I can't predict how this will turn out for you this time. When I get back to D.C., I'm going to need to contact the FBI. I suggest you get yourself a good lawyer." She reached in the pocket of her suit coat and pulled out a business card. "Have Robert Sparks call me as soon as possible. We may be able to get you a deal, depending on when and if you crossed the line. I pray you were just a pawn in Ty's game, the same as Katherine."

She watched as her family took in the news. Elizabeth, in absentia, tried to protect and guide them for years. And she would continue to do so.

Hannah appeared at the doorway. "Elizabeth, there's an SUV waiting outside. A gentleman said he's ready if you are."

"Ah, that's Sam. I've got to go." She rose and walked to where Hannah stood waiting for her. She looked back at the group she left behind, who were still at the dining room table. "Do what I've instructed. Katherine's safety depends on it. I'll be back." Eyeing her brother, Elizabeth said, "Maybe, I'll even come for a long visit."

Elizabeth turned and walked out the door, wishing she could have seen the look on his face.

CHAPTER FIFTEEN

Clinton Stables

It didn't feel like Kate had been in hiding for three weeks. She worked tirelessly, night and day, readying the farm for the horses John had boarded at a local facility nearby. When Kate stopped and thought about it, she felt as if she'd spent another day on the job. Maybe that made dealing with the emotional highs and lows easier.

As the sun dipped below the horizon, Kate stood, admiring the newly-cleaned stalls. The smell of the fresh hay and leather was a stark contrast to what she encountered on her first day. It hadn't taken long to convert the filthy barn to a habitable environment. John Clinton's men had worked as hard as she had. Kate knew their first job was to protect her, but the men took an active role in the farm's revival and seemed to enjoy the diversion when their boss wasn't around. She still hadn't adjusted to knowing there were guns holstered and hidden from view beneath their denim work vests.

Night had always been her favorite time of day. She was alone, savoring the peace and quiet, or at least, she pretended to be. Agent Clinton was forever hovering close by. Kate strolled the grounds with instructions to go no farther than the training pen. Taking in the coolness of the night air after a day working in the hot, sizzling sun, Kate found herself in the large barn.

Listening to the neighing horses, and breathing in the aroma around her, allowed Kate the ability to relax and reflect. Closing her eyes, she pictured the sights and sounds of Hallock Farm getting ready for the Belmont Stakes. She was homesick.

Kate straightened the tack and bits strung up on the wall and patted the new saddles. She shook her head as she looked at the new equipment. Nothing surprised her more than John's revelation of his ultimate dream - to run a thoroughbred-breeding farm, not a boarding facility. She marveled that even in the countryside of Virginia, predominantly known for being horse country, the man had lofty dreams and goals.

The soft whinny of Wild Flame and her colt came to her as she walked the main corridor. Passing each newly cleaned stall, she peeked in. All was in order, as it should be. Ambling closer to Wild Flame and her colt, Kate flashed back to Chuck and Bob's riding lessons that afternoon. It had been a new experience for both men who had been game to take a turn. Chuck entertained her the most, reminding her of a bobble-head doll. He'd practically fallen out of his saddle when the cinch loosened. She laughed out loud, the sound echoing throughout the barn.

Wild Flame poked her head over the stall door, nuzzling Kate's pockets for the cubes of sugar she always carried with her.

"Hey, girl." Kate rubbed the mare's nose. "How's my favorite filly doing tonight?" Kate wistfully thought of home as she placed several cubes on her hand and leaned her head against the horse's neck.

"Penny for your thoughts, Lizzie?"

Caught off-guard, Kate twirled around. She knew he'd been close by, but the man made her nervous in a way she couldn't explain.

"Whoa! It's just me." John Clinton stood before her, two steaming mugs of coffee in his hands. He held one out to her. She gratefully accepted the hot brew.

"You have a nasty way of sneaking up on a body."

"It's part of the job. Next time I'll stomp my boots, okay?"

She nodded, looking him up and down as she sipped from her cup. She smacked her lips at the taste. Black and sweetened, just the way she liked it. How was it a man whom she'd been acquainted with for only three weeks knew how she liked her coffee while a man whom she'd known for five years, and had planned to marry, always had to ask?

"Thanks." Kate saluted John with the cup. "You have no idea how much I needed this. I was ready to go to sleep right next to Wild Flame."

John stood beside her, his hands curled around his mug. "Awful pretty out here tonight, Lizzie. Have you seen the sky?"

Taking a long swallow, she answered with a nod. "I was just watching the moon come up over the trees by the paddock. Virginia sure makes for some beautiful horse country. About the best I've ever seen anywhere."

"Spent a lot a time in Virginia, have you?" John probed. The man was eyeing her closely. Kate noticed he'd been assessing her a lot lately. She knew the drill. He was profiling her, waiting for clues. Of course, it was his job to watch her every move. She wasn't exactly sure how much John knew about her personally. She was brought out of her musings by John asking, "Lizzie? You in there?"

"Sorry. I'm way too tired. But I was just thinking…"

"Of what?"

"My job as an equine vet takes me to various horseraces up

and down the coast. I've passed through Virginia a number of times, but I've never worked way out in the country. The only places I've been to are large facilities and auction houses. This place is really coming into its own, isn't it, Agent Clinton?"

"Lizzie, I think it's time we dispense with formality. I know I work for Director Hallock, but just call me John. Okay? We're going to be spending a lot of time together."

Kate immediately thought calling him by his name sounded more…intimate. But she replied, "I suppose I could." When she glanced up into his green eyes, a weird sensation hit the pit of her stomach. "But you haven't answered my question… John."

"Oh, my farm. I'm amazed at the transformation. To be quite honest, if someone had told me two months ago the farm would look like this, I'd have told him he was crazy. Especially given my work schedule. You've certainly been a big motivator."

Lizzie blushed at the compliment and was surprised at the overwhelming sense of pride she felt hearing his words of praise. "Uh, thanks. But I really should be thanking you. You've no idea how working here has taken my mind off my situation. Well, most of the time."

The funny feeling in her stomach returned when John smiled down at her.

"According to the Director, you certainly do have a lot on your plate. But my men concur you've been a bit mum on giving us any details. Care to talk more about it?"

Kate placed her empty mug on the bench beside her and backed away from the stall and John. "No. I need more time to reason it out. I'm still racking my brain for clues I missed. I think about home every day." She saw John's left eyebrow arch questioningly. What had she said to make him react like that?

"Home?" John countered. "This happened at your *home*, not where you worked?"

Anxiety, tinged with the fear of accidentally giving out too much information, rushed through Kate's body. She had to remember what her aunt had told her to keep her identity as secret as possible. She simply stated, "I run the family business."

"And?" John probed further. Kate knew he was going to dig into her past in typical agent fashion, trying to stay on top of every clue that came his way.

"I overhead something I shouldn't have." Kate said.

John drew a thin piece of straw out of the bale of hay nearby. He chewed on the tip, eyeing her warily. "Lizzie, if I'm going to protect you properly, I need to hear your side of the story… just as you remember it happening. The Director gave me the mission's objective. But my team is no good to you if we don't know something lurking out there we should be aware of. You're not hiding something from the Director, are you?"

Kate squirmed uncomfortably and began to pace in front of John and Wild Flame's stall. "Look," she said forcefully, kicking the heels of her boots on the concrete as she walked back and forth. "I haven't hidden anything. You know what she knows."

"You know, Lizzie." John's eyes followed her as she walked before him. "When I needed to clear my mind, get my life in perspective, which I often did in Montana when my Dad was ill, I always felt the need to get on my horse and go for a ride. No one should knock fresh air. It makes a body think straight."

Kate's head snapped up, gazing directly at her protector. "Go riding? You're saying you'll let me get away from having an agent at my side for a few hours?"

John shook his head in denial. "No. This is the 'let's get away from prying eyes and have a good talk' ride. You've been working yourself day and night. I think you could use a break. We'll work the chores tomorrow morning. I need to check in with the Director and brief the team. Then, we'll head out to the meadow for a while. What do you say?"

Kate couldn't believe her good fortune. "Well, the horses do need to be exercised. I think that falls under the heading of 'list of chores' so it sounds legit." She let out a sigh. "Agent Clinton, you've just made my day."

John sent a serious look her way. "This isn't cut out to be fun and games, Lizzie. I meant it when I said I want your side of the story. I'm an expert in reading and profiling people. There's something you're afraid of."

A shiver ran down Kate's spine. He'd hit a nerve.

"It's nothing to worry about. You, Lizzie, have to trust in my team. We know what we're doing. We've got your back. Like the Secret Service guards the President, we are here to keep you safe…and, we agreed?" He winked at her. "The name's John."

That warm feeling whirled in her midsection again. The man did the strangest things to her libido. She'd convinced herself over the past weeks it was just his good looks and the fact she'd always been drawn to men who liked to be in charge. Ty, too, had those "wonderful" qualities. *And look where that got me*, she thought sarcastically.

"Well, I'd best be off to bed. Sunrise comes early." She turned to walk away from Wild Flame and his master.

"Tell me something."

Kate turned back and dreaded what he might ask. "I'll try."

"You ever take that ratty hat off, or is it glued to your head?" A hint of merriment danced in his eyes.

Kate countered. "Very funny. It's my lucky charm. I've had it since my internship in college. *You* ever think of getting rid of that muddied Agency-issued cap?" Touché.

John doffed his hat, a grin on his face, and headed for the barn door. "One o'clock, Lizzie. Be ready for the ride of your life."

Tense and anxious, Kate let out the breath she'd been holding. What was wrong with her? Yawning, she called over the stall to the colt, "Night, Shadow." Patting the mare on the nose, she whispered to Wild Flame, "Tomorrow, we'll take you out on a good run, girl. I've a feeling you're going to be one for the Roses."

CHAPTER SIXTEEN

Kate glanced up from digging the post-holes for the new south paddock fence. She pulled a red bandana out of her back pocket and dabbed it across her sweaty brow. "You guys ready to break for lunch?"

A few of the work crew nodded in assent.

Out in the open paddock, additional agents had been added for her protection, armed with automatic rifles. The sound of a horse's hooves riding towards them drew her attention. She spied John Clinton sitting on top of Dark Knight, his favorite mount, coming down the lane.

Kate called out, "I bet you're here to tell me I've been working your men too hard. We've just decided to break for lunch."

"You'd be right." John surveyed the positioning of his agents before he looked down. "I think you've accomplished a major dent in the chore list." He pointed to the farmhouse. "Wade, take the men and head into the house. Hydrate. Lunch is ready. Tim sent me out here to drag you in." John pulled the brim of his navy blue cap down over his eyes.

Wade leaned his shovel against the railing. "Fine by me, Chief. Sure is hot as hell out here. With such a demanding boss, we're lucky to get a break."

Kate saw the semblance of a quirky grin on his face and smiled back. "Hey, I'm just doing my job. Being the head vet usually doesn't afford me the luxury of a lunch break. I usually pull a sandwich and a bottle of water out of the cooler from my Jeep." Pulling her work gloves off, she eyed four sweat-streaked faces staring at her. "Sorry, guys. Didn't mean to be such a taskmaster. Agent Clinton's the boss. Go, get your lunch."

As the men placed their tools in the back of two trucks parked nearby, John Clinton climbed down from his horse. "Wade, when you finish up lunch, report to Jake. There's a briefing this afternoon."

Kate's stomach somersaulted. Had something happened? She couldn't stand not knowing what was going on beyond the perimeter of Clinton Stables. She'd hoped the tough physical labor would stop her from worrying over events back home. Last night, she lay awake for hours. And when she had finally drifted off to sleep, it was a restless night of tossing and turning, her mind mulling over everything that could possibly happen to her family. And the farm? Who had stepped in to take her place and set up the daily routines and training schedules?

"Lizzie!" Kate snapped back to the here and now to see Agent Clinton directly in front of her. "My God, where were you? I've tried to get your attention three times."

She gave him a sheepish look. She didn't notice the crew had left. But now she could see the dust kicked up from the trucks' tires headed down the rutted road.

"Sorry. Too much on my mind. I'll just finish up these last couple of holes..."

John wrenched the post-hole digger from her hands, throwing it to the ground. "You're taking a break. No more work."

"But, it will only take me..." She glanced up to see his sea green eyes sending a piercing glare that said "no way." The man meant business. He reached his hand out and tipped back her cap. She flinched as his touch sent a tingle through her. A surprised look registered on his face. Kate stepped back. She made a promise to herself when she lay in bed to keep her distance from the man when possible. But how, when he was assigned as her primary bodyguard?

"You forget about that ride I promised you?"

Now, he had her attention. Picking up her water bottle from the ground and pulling her hat over her forehead, Kate answered, "I thought you forgot."

"You thought I forgot? To be honest, I thought you've been avoiding *me* since I told you it's not going to be a normal joy ride. You and I need to talk. I think you'll feel more comfortable without a bunch of men carrying Glocks and rifles around you. You ready to ride?"

As much as Kate longed for a ride, she didn't want to be asked any more questions. "Sure. If it's okay with you, though, I'd really like some lunch. I had an early breakfast and was in the barn at four-thirty this morning."

"I know," John replied.

"You know what?"

"That you were with Wild Flame at the crack of dawn." Kate tensed. "How did you know that? No one was in there but me."

"Lizzie, I know every move you make and when you make it. Wherever you go and whatever you do, I know where you are."

There it was again. John's cocky smile made her knees feel weak. What was it about this man in particular after all she'd been through? She was visualizing all sorts of fantasies she shouldn't. A man had been the cause of her present predicament, and she certainly didn't need another to take his place. It was obvious. Her brain was fried.

John climbed back up on the horse, slid back in his saddle and reached down for her hand. Kate shied away. She shook her head. "I'll just get my things and walk back. I'll be there in a few minutes. It's not that far."

"Like hell you will."

Kate felt as if her arm was ripped from its socket when John pulled her up, nestling her between him and the pommel. She was thankful he couldn't see her face. She felt flush and it had reddened, but not from embarrassment or the heat of the day. Kate pulled the brim of her cap low over her brow, and as she did so, John jerked her body closer.

He whispered in her ear, "Bet you can't wait to go for that ride with me, can you?"

If she hadn't had a firm grip on the pommel, Kate would have toppled off, like a novice, as John kicked the horse's flanks into a trot. Good grief. What had she gotten into?

* * *

John Clinton had to admit he was impressed by the woman who rode beside him. He admonished himself on the ride back to the farmhouse that he'd let down his guard. He'd been on the border of crossing the line of professionalism with his innuendos. He mentally recanted his mantra – objectivity. The loss of it in his last job had cost him a hell of a lot. He wasn't about to lose his job because he was drawn to a woman of incredible strength and determination. However, there were times when Lizzie's wit, humor and intelligence got the better of him. The Director would have his gun and badge if she guessed the object of his dreams last night - a dark eyed beauty with auburn tresses lying naked in his bed. Lizzie.

"How far do you plan on riding, Agent Clinton?"

Kate's questions snapped John from his reflections of his life in the past and now.

"Aren't we too far from the yard?" She was looking up and

down the sides of the dirt path they traveled, as if danger lurked in the underbrush. "Haven't we gone too far from the house?" Her voice sounded panicked, and it rose in volume. "Shouldn't we have brought more agents? We're a bit too out in the open for my comfort level."

Knowing full well she was right, John said, "Let's just head to the tree line by the meadow." He pointed to the spot where the trail opened onto a wide expanse of grass and wildflowers. "We'll stop there. There's a small stream. The horses can rest and drink some water. Then, we can head back. But first…"

"I know. I know. We have to talk." As Lizzie rode along on Wild Flame, he watched in fascination as she wiped her bandana across her face and down her neck.

"Hot, isn't it?" John took his baseball cap off his head and wiped his brow on his denim shirt.

Lizzie's laugh was hearty. "Ah, yeah. You sure are one smart agent, cowboy. It's got to be close to one hundred degrees out here, shade or no shade." Without notice, Lizzie kicked Wild Flame's flanks and took off. What the hell was she thinking? John did the same to Dark Shadow, taking off after her. Lizzie was right. He shouldn't have brought her this far alone.

John saw her pull up at the edge of the tree line. By the time he'd caught up to the mare and rider, both were drinking from the stream. He jumped off Dark Knight, tied the reins around the nearest tree and strode to the water. He grabbed hold of her tee shirt, tugging her up and around to face him. Shock registered on her face. He'd given her a reason to be afraid, and he tried so hard to win her trust and keep her calm.

"What the hell do you think you're doing, O'Brien? Want to get yourself killed?" He kicked himself at his choice of words. Lizzie's ashen face spoke volumes. "Liz, I'm sorry. I need to take the lead when you move. Look out there." Her gaze followed to where he pointed to the meadow. "You're exposed to the elements and anyone who could possibly be hiding over there. Understand?"

Lizzie nodded her head in the affirmative. "I never gave it a second thought. I'm not used to being penned up. Can't you tell I'm going stir crazy?"

John felt like a heel for berating her, but it was for her own good. She had to remember the rules or she wouldn't be safe. "Let me grab the drinks I've got in my saddlebags. Find some shade." John pointed to the scrub pines. "We have to be sure we're not out in the open."

Lizzie's eyes widened.

"Not…that anything is going to happen," John reassured her. "Just being cautious. Go on. Find a spot without rocks so we can park for a bit. I'm bushed."

Lizzie didn't need to be told twice. John pulled the saddlebags and blanket from the back of Dark Knight and made his way to where she was picking up and tossing rocks aside.

"Here." John threw the Navajo blanket at her. Lizzie grabbed for it and helped to lay it on the ground before sitting down. One look told him she was as tired as he was. "Want something cold to drink?" She nodded as he sat down. He opened his bag and, taking out a Thermos, poured lemonade into two cups.

Lizzie took the drink he offered. "Thanks." She took a long, deep swallow. "Nice and cold. I needed it."

John reached again into the bag. "Cookie? Tim makes the best." As Lizzie reached out to accept the chocolate chip cookie, John snatched it back. "Ah…how badly do you want one?"

"Oh, I get it. You want something, don't you?" She eyed him questioningly.

"Yup. Time's up. No escaping me now." John gave her an intent look. "You *have* to trust me, Liz. I've been an agent long enough to know there are gaps in the information the Director gave me. The sooner you tell me, the sooner you can get back to the business of taking care of your horses." Was that a touch of wistfulness on her face?

"Okay." She sighed with resignation. "I don't know how much help I'm going to be." Without warning, Lizzie snatched the entire bag from his hand and squirreled all the cookies away where he couldn't reach them.

"What the…"

"You want the whole story. I get all the cookies." She poured more lemonade into her cup, took a long drink and licked her lips. Then pulling her ratty cap off her head, she shook her hair out. Twisting her auburn ponytail up and off the back of her neck, Lizzie reached into her pocket for her clip and secured her hair in place.

"Ahh…much cooler." She stretched and yawned. "Fire away, cowboy."

John watched Lizzie, fascinated by her every move. *Agent Clinton needed to keep his head in the game…not* on the tightening in his groin.

CHAPTER SEVENTEEN

Kate munched on a cookie, warily keeping her eyes on the man who sat propped up against a tree nearby. He chewed on a blade of grass, staring back, as if he were a cat watching a canary in a cage.

"I can wait all day," John stated, throwing the used blade off into a bed of pine needles. "Bet you didn't know I've been trained to stay in the same position for forty-hours at a time and never even have to pee." He wiggled his eyebrows.

Kate giggled at the absurdity of his statement. She sighed out loud. "All right. All right. Where do you want me to start?"

John reached into his pocket and laid a recorder on the blanket between them. "Start at the beginning. Don't leave out the part when you felt you had to run. I'll ask a question if I think there could be a piece of the puzzle missing."

Kate attempted to stand up to stretch her legs and work the kinks out of her backside, only to be pulled back down onto the blanket. "What? Come on. I have to move around! I think better on my feet!" She kicked her boot into the blanket in frustration.

"Well, you're not pacing where someone might be able to spot you. I can't tell if anyone can see us behind these pines.

Start talking." John glanced at the watch on his wrist.

Kate positioned herself with her back up against an old oak tree. She popped the last cookie in her mouth and contemplated where to start. She began by relaying the shouting match between her father and Ty. "It was when I heard Ty threaten Father to make good on some kind of payment that I crashed their party." She paused. "I can't put my finger on what Ty was referring to when he told Father there was an easy way to get out of the mess he was in. He said the people would want cash and merchandise. Every instinct told me that would be soon. When I ran from the room, Ty was screaming for my father to run after his meal ticket."

John crossed one leg over the other out in front of him. "So if I understand this right, your father and Ty have been doing business for quite some time? Could you clearly define their roles?"

Kate quenched her thirst again. How much should she divulge without breaking her promise to her aunt? She thought she'd given away too much when she told John she worked at her family's business. But dishonesty had brought her to Washington. Kate was convinced honesty would take her home—as long as she diluted some of the story. "Father is the CEO. Ty is a member of the firm that does legal work and…" Kate hesitated. She knew she had to choose her words carefully.

"And? Everything…" John tapped the recorder on the blanket.

Kate locked her eyes on John's to catch his reaction. "Ty is my fiancé."

John was stunned, just as she anticipated. Interesting for a man whose job required him to be master at masking emotions. Was that a flare of jealousy in those sea-green eyes? Had she imagined it?

"You have a fiancé?"

"Ah…" Kate paused. "Things aren't what they seem. Let me clear things up. I *had* a fiancé. He involved my father in business dealings with a Russian family. The Savorskis seemed to be a typical, wealthy society family wanting an introduction to Hampton society. Mother helped them make the rounds of galas and places to be seen. At least, that's what we thought."

"Did Ty ever allude to anything about the farm's financials?"

"Yes, that's what the argument was about. Father got in over his head and, from what I gathered, made promises of selling horses from our stables."

"What else?"

Kate closed her eyes, trying to recapture the scene. "I ran. Jumped in the Jeep and drove to Arlington." Kate stopped there not sure that she should tell him of her final conversation with the Director. He was inquisitive. He'd no doubt wonder why she'd run to the head of the CIA. "Look. That's about all I can tell you." There was no way she was about to bring up the Russian who'd shown up at the farm early that morning. *That* was classified. His appearance in Hampton Beach was solely between her and her aunt. If her aunt wanted to share that piece of info with John and his team, she may have already done so. "Father made his bed with the Russian mob. Plain and simple."

John sat upright and leaned towards her. She backed up, the bark of the tree biting through her shirt as he inched closer. "Look at me! Let's do this differently. This time, I ask, you answer."

She swallowed hard. His closeness made her uncomfortable. She was hot, sweaty and thirsty. Kate wanted the interrogation over and done with. Besides, hadn't her aunt filled his detail in on all the pertinent facts, other than who she really was? But they weren't going to leave unless she gave John some answers.

"All right. Play your version of twenty questions. Ask away, cowboy." She crossed her arms. "Make it quick. It's too damn hot out here."

She saw his eyes flare. Agent Clinton was used to agents always following his every command. Well, here, Kate would answer even if she had to skim over the truth.

"Cut to the basics. What were you doing that day?" John's voice was clipped and precise.

"I spent the morning going over the chore roster. We'd hired on a few new men, due to the fact I was pulling our best people to prepare for the Belmont Stakes."

"The business obviously performed background checks?"

"Absolutely. Resumés are thoroughly vetted, and references are not accepted at face value. We call every past employer on the list. Do you think someone is on the property who shouldn't be?"

John picked up another blade of grass and pondered her question as he twisted the blade between his fingers. "Possibly. What then?"

Kate rubbed her neck in an attempt to alleviate the tension she felt building. "I went to talk to my head trainer about our entry. We put the horse to a run on the track to clock…" Kate's eye caught a flash of light in the grove of trees across the meadow. Something shiny reflected in their direction. She froze.

"Lizzie!" John shook her shoulder. "Lizzie! What is it?"

"Over there!" She stammered as she lifted her index finger to point in the direction of the light. "There was a flash in those trees."

Before she could say more, John pulled out his semi-automatic pistol and tucked her securely behind him.

"Hide behind that rock and don't move!"

Kate immediately did as instructed, her heart racing. Panic

and anxiety set in.

"You wait here until I come back. You hear me?"

Kate nodded vigorously. She hunkered down behind the large boulder. Out of the corner of her eye, she saw John drop to the ground at the same time another flash broke through the leaves. Her breath caught in her throat. Who could it possibly be? John rose from his position, looked around and made for the shrubs along the stream. Before she knew it, he disappeared. Shaken, Kate sought out the biggest rock she could hold. Her hand shook as she latched onto a fist-sized stone. And she waited, alone, afraid the Russians had found her.

CHAPTER EIGHTEEN

Using the scrub pines as camouflage, John ran along the edge of the stream, gun drawn. He had seen the second flash from the patch of trees on the other side of the meadow. John grabbed the walkie-talkie on his belt. "Chief to base. Come in."

"Base camp one. Over." Jake's voice came over the radio.

"Check monitor and advise. Possibility there's someone on the north side of the meadow. Over."

Jake responded. "Nothing. Checking heat sensor. Over."

As John awaited Jake's response, he ducked down behind a small rock wall. He raised his gun in self-defense upon seeing the branch of a small oak tree broken and dangling. Was someone lying in wait, wanting to draw him out?

The radio crackled. "Nothing, Chief. No sign of motion or bodies. Over."

"Roger that. I'm moving in for a closer look. Over."

John moved nearer to the clump of trees. It was evident, even to an untrained eye, someone had recently been in the vicinity. Several of the live oak leaves were crumpled and lay on the ground, while two branches were snapped from the branch of the tree beside him. Sloppy work, John thought. Gun pointed forward, not knowing who or what he would encounter, John stepped forward. To his surprise, in the small cluster of trees he found a small clearing. Glancing down, he halted. He spotted one large footprint from a man's boot prominently embedded in the soft ground cover.

Assured he was alone, he radioed the farmhouse. "Jake, check the roads leading out from the north pastures and meadows. Send a forensics team up here. Over."

Bending down, John surveyed the ground. One very large person had stood in that spot. The footprint was fresh. He listened carefully for any movement in the brush. Nothing. Odd. How had the person managed to come in and out, undetected? And so quickly?

The crackle of Jake's voice interrupted his thoughts. "No sign of anyone on the roads. Over."

"I'm bringing Lizzie back to base camp. If we're not there in twenty minutes, head out to find us."

"Copy that."

John clipped the radio to his belt and stood up, taking in his surroundings. He peeked through the opening by the oak tree to scope out the perpetrator's line of sight. It would have been hard to see them from this vantage point, but not impossible.

The snap of a twig from behind had him ducking behind the pine tree, gun at the ready. Someone was there. John took aim at the entrance to the small path as he waited. Whoever it was didn't make any attempt to disguise the fact they were close by. He cocked his pistol.

A large stick lunged through the trees into the clearing, followed by none other than Lizzie. What the hell? John stepped into her line of sight, forgetting his gun was pointed in her direction.

"Didn't I tell you to stay put?" he barked. "Did you not understand the part that I would come and get you when the coast was clear?"

Lizzie jumped, swinging the stick in her hand. If he hadn't ducked, she would have clocked him upside his temple and he'd be out for the count.

"I..I..."

"Give me that!" John grabbed the large twig out of her hand, throwing it into the brush. "Just what the hell do you think you're doing?"

Lizzie's face, normally tan from the Virginia sun turned a pale shade of gray. "You took too long!" She looked around, her eyes taking in the open clearing, coming to rest on the boot print. "I knew it! Something happened. Someone *was* over here!" She wound up and punched him hard.

" Hey!" Rubbing his shoulder, John could only point out the obvious. "That flash?"

"Yeah?"

"Don't get alarmed. But we definitely had a visitor. At least one, from what I can surmise at this point. Jake's sending up the forensic unit." The minute he uttered the words, he knew he should have kept his suspicions to himself until he had more information.

"They found me? Here of all places?" Lizzie's voice shook, and her hands came up to wipe away the tears forming in the corners of her eyes.

John saw the mounting terror in her dark brown eyes. He grabbed hold of one of her hands, rubbing it gently, trying to allay her fear.

This was the time to choose his words carefully. "I'm not sure. That's definitely a man's footprint by that tree. It's fresh. Could be a hunter. But, Lizzie, I'm going to be honest. I doubt it. We have to get back to the safe house." The radio crackled again. John ripped it from its holder. "Go ahead, Jake. Over."

"Chief. We've got a VIP here. Over."

John knew it would only be a matter of days before she'd come. The Director would want to check out everything herself and give the set-up her personal stamp of approval. He'd have a lot of explaining to do, given the circumstances of what had just occurred. The lady would not be happy. "Copy that. We'll be back in twenty. Set the Eagle up in my office. Over."

"Roger that. Over."

"Did you say the Eagle?" Lizzie asked.

"Yes. The Eagle."

Making their way to the horses, John and Kate mounted up and started down the path at a fast trot. Lizzie turned to John, a cocky grin on her face. "Don't you think we better pick up the pace a bit if the Eagle has landed?"

John stared at her, stunned. "You know about the Eagle?"

"Of course I do. And if you don't get your butt in gear and have your men steep a pot of Earl Grey tea ASAP, you'll all be looking for new jobs." Lizzie winked, kicked her horse in the flanks, and took off at a gallop in the direction of the large barn.

What the bloody hell? John may have discovered some very relevant information to the case out in the meadow. Enough to realize Elizabeth Hallock hadn't filled him in on *every* pertinent detail of this mission. Something didn't quite add up in regards to the Director and Lizzie O'Brien. He'd keep that to himself for a bit longer. But, John Clinton loved a challenge. It was what had drawn him to be an agent. Lizzie O'Brien was an added bonus.

* * *

Kate sat at the harvest table, nestled in the bay window of the farm's kitchen, sipping more lemonade. The cool liquid refreshed her after the heat of the day, and the air-conditioned room had taken the flush from her face. Her ears perked up at the sound of muffled voices coming from behind the office door at the end of the hallway. Someone was most definitely pissed.

When she'd arrived back from the meadow, Kate found Aunt Elizabeth sitting on the wide sofa in the great room, holding court with John's lead team. Kate nodded at the Director and watched as her aunt sipped her cup of tea, chatting amiably with John's crew. Kate knew that was only temporary. When her aunt found out what had transpired in the meadow, Kate felt sorry for all the agents on the farm. She'd wanted a moment with her aunt to tell her she'd pushed for the ride to the meadow to clear her thoughts, but never got the chance.

The door to the office flung open, and Wade came out first. "I'm telling you, it's a bad idea. *Bad idea*." He enunciated the last two words.

Bob followed him, along with Jake and Chuck.

Jake stated firmly, "Listen to me. Lizzie's better off here than anywhere else. We can't take the chance of moving her if someone's poking around." Jake grabbed Wade by his forearm to get his attention. "Are you telling me you don't think can't keep her safe here? If not, you better turn in your resignation and walk away. The Director's right behind us."

Wade countered, "Jake, don't tell me it hasn't crossed your mind, as well. This place is too damn big to monitor. Sure we have the most high-tech equipment in the world, but we need more manpower. It's making me feel like I'm back in Istanbul."

Kate couldn't help but notice the quiet that pervaded the room at the man's comment. Istanbul? Where did Istanbul fit into the equation?

"I've got to agree with Wade on this one." Chuck broke the silence. "This isn't the safest place. Not with what the Director just told us." Kate froze. "I think it would be better to be locked down in a safe house somewhere in Washington or its outskirts. The resources we need would be nearby."

Jake glared at his men. "Well, we don't have much choice. Until the Director is sure the Feds have brought the matter of the Russians to a close, we're staying put. We'll have to make sure we do our jobs, especially now."

"You heard the Director after John briefed her. Or weren't you in the same room?" Usually the calm one of the group, something had set Wade off. "Someone breached the security system. There's been a hit put out on Lizzie—"

Kate gasped, and as she brought her hand to her mouth to silence herself, she inadvertently knocked her glass to the floor. The shattering sound had the team turning to look to where the noise had come from, all reaching for their guns. Surprise was evident on their faces, seeing she'd been sitting in the kitchen, and not in her bedroom where she'd been sent, taking in their conversation.

Jake was at her side. "Lizzie, don't step anywhere." She had forgotten her feet were bare. She'd taken her boots off after the ride to give her sweaty feet some air. "Stay right where you are. Somebody get me a broom!" he called out over his shoulder.

Kate looked up into concerned eyes that confirmed Jake knew she'd heard every word they'd said. Forgetting about the broken glass on the floor, she choked out, "A hit on me? Has this got to do with what's happening at my farm? What's happened to my family?" Kate spit out one question after another. Her breathing became more rapid, her heart raced. Sweat broke out on her brow, and she began to feel faint.

A booming voice spoke over the din of men talking and cleaning up the mess. "What the hell is going on in here? Lizzie, why aren't you upstairs?"

The voice Kate heard faded as did the face that came into her line of sight. "Agent Clinton?" The room grew darker. Everyone and everything began to spin.

"Lizzie!"

Kate tried in vain to keep from falling into the dark hole. But it was no use. Katherine Elizabeth Hallock dropped to the floor, hitting her head on the corner of the kitchen table as her aunt and the lead agent of Operation Hide and Seek stood helplessly by.

CHAPTER NINETEEN

John Clinton was surprised at the rollercoaster of emotions he'd gone through in the past several hours. He prided himself on his professionalism on any job, large or small. He didn't know what to make of his mentor as she sat in an overstuffed club chair at Lizzie's bedside, stroking the younger woman's hand. He'd never seen this side of Elizabeth Hallock before. She'd shown she was human from time to time, not always so pompous and direct, but *never* had he remembered her taking such a personal interest in a case as she was doing now. Once an assignment was passed off, the Director expected only to remain apprised of mission details and the final outcome of the case.

John was pissed. If his agents had been paying closer attention, Lizzie wouldn't be lying in the bed with a large bandage covering her right temple. How could they not have seen her when they'd walked out of the briefing? She'd been sitting at the kitchen table in full view of all of them!

While he'd been briefing the Director and his team about the incident in the meadow, Elizabeth informed them of an important link between the Russian mob and Lizzie's family business. John faced two dilemmas: to find out why the security camera had malfunctioned out in the north meadow and to shield Lizzie from the plan in the works to end her family's involvement with the Russian mafia and the Savorskis.

"This is all *my* fault," Elizabeth muttered out loud. "*My* fault!" She'd been sitting in the same position since the doctor left two hours ago.

Roused from his thoughts and feeling the current situation called for a less formal approach, he tried his best to comfort her. "Elizabeth, you didn't bring this on." John had parked himself in the wooden rocking chair in the corner of the room, his forearms resting on his knees. He eyed both his boss and the woman who lay motionless in the bed. "Lizzie just got so upset she fainted, plain and simple. Some people's bodies react that way from stress. Between the incident in the meadow and then hearing about the hit, her mind and body couldn't take much more."

"But look at her, John." There was a catch in Elizabeth's voice as she dipped a washcloth in a bowl of cool water and dabbed it on Lizzie's forehead. Hidden under the white gauze bandage was a three-inch gash containing ten stitches.

John tried his best to sound reassuring. "You heard Doc. She's going to be fine. Elizabeth, I've only known Lizzie O'Brien for about a month, but she's one of the strongest and most determined women I've ever met. You don't give her enough credit if you think she isn't able to handle what you need to tell her."

Elizabeth, again, took Lizzie's hand in her own. "You're right. I've known her family for a very long time. She comes from good stock. When she came to me for help, I knew she could handle anything."

John sank back in the rocking chair, determined to wait with Elizabeth. He closed his eyes to mask his thoughts. Interesting. He had thought this was a typical domestic assignment. But as he considered both women, he couldn't shake the fact the similarities between the two were remarkable. It was a ridiculous thought on his part, wasn't it? Elizabeth never mixed business with her personal life. It was the cardinal rule of any agent seeking the plum CIA assignments. Once in, no outside life exists. No personal relationships could ever be formed, no lives shared. Oh, some agents had families, but the ones John knew either didn't get the adventurous assignments or were headed for divorce court.

Still, the fact that these two women physically resembled each other was uncanny. He'd heard rumors of a love child many years ago when he worked a job in London, but he and a colleague laughed it off. Elizabeth Hallock? An out of wedlock child born to one of the nation's top operatives? At that point in time, the Agency never would have stood for it. No. Their similarities to each other were coincidental. But the fact that Lizzie knew Elizabeth's code name intrigued him greatly.

"Don't you think we should do that, John?"

John planted his feet firmly on the ground and opened his eyes. She'd caught him daydreaming.

"Not paying attention, Agent Clinton?" John noticed a subtle twinkle in the dark brown eyes that looked him over. "You're tired, John. Go. Get some sleep. We've a long—"

A moan came from Lizzie. John jumped up, hurrying to the side of the bed, opposite where Elizabeth sat.

Placing his hand on the tough, work-hardened hand he'd held earlier in the day, he shook it. He called to her, hoping to rouse her. "Lizzie! Lizzie!" He squeezed her hand, rubbing his fingers back and forth over her knuckles. "Lizzie, wake up!" Her head moved slowly from side to side. John was so focused on Lizzie, he missed the smile that formed on Elizabeth Hallock's face.

* * *

The doors in the vestibule of St. Mark's Church swung open. Katherine could hear the beginning strains of the "Wedding March" played by her cousin on the church organ. The wedding planner smoothed out the cathedral length train of her gown and straightened her veil. The planner nodded the go-ahead signal to her father.

"Let's go Katie-girl."

As Katherine and her father stepped out onto the red carpeted aisle that led up to the nave of the church, Katherine saw Ty, standing erect and tall, looking to make eye contact with her as she moved towards him. God, he was handsome. But more so today in his dark, black Gucci tuxedo. Thomas stood by his side as best man.

Moving slowly down the aisle towards the waiting wedding party, Katherine smiled and nodded at the six hundred guests assembled in the large church. As she approached Ty and the minister, she noticed a sheaf of blue legal papers hidden behind his back. Were those the papers he and her father were yelling about? No, not today! Not again!

"No. Get away from me!" Kate pushed her father from her side. Throwing her bouquet on the ground, she lunged at Ty, trying to grab the legal documents from his hands. But, she was grasping at air.

"No!" Her voice echoed throughout the church." I won't let you do this to me!" The darkness claimed her once more.

* * *

"Katherine! Katherine Elizabeth!" A distant voice she couldn't quite make out called to her. Kate felt her body shake. "Wake up!" The gentle, southern drawl registered at last. Aunt Elizabeth! Kate sighed, feeling a warm, motherly hand smooth away the hair from her brow and caress her cheek.

Kate's eyes drifted open. The reassuring smile looking down at her put her at ease. Trembling from the nightmare, she was relieved to find she wasn't in Hampton Beach. But, oh, what had she done to her head? It ached! She raised her hand to her right temple to find a large lump covered by a bandage. What had happened to her? Why was she lying in bed?

"Aunt Elizabeth?" Kate asked, suddenly frightened.

"Hush, dear. You're fine. Just a small tumble, Katherine. You hit your head on the table when you fainted. The doctor says you'll be good as new in no time."

A man's loud voice boomed and resonated in her brain, making her head ache even more.

"Aunt?" John's voice was the one bellowing by her bedside. "*Aunt* Elizabeth?" There was no doubting the shock in his voice. Her aunt's lead agent had been blindsided. "You're her *aunt?*" John pointed at Kate, his face registering total disbelief.

Kate watched and marveled at her aunt's composure. Elizabeth took in a deep breath and turned to face the man who now stood at the foot of her bed. John Clinton had every right to ask. Kate being Elizabeth's niece would affect his handling of the assignment.

"Yes, John. Katherine is my niece. It's obvious now that I owe you a more detailed explanation. But, I needed to wait for Katherine to be the first to know all of the facts, not just the smaller pieces of a much larger puzzle."

From the moment Kate arrived back at the farmhouse and found her aunt sequestered with the agents, her own instincts told her something serious occurred. Aunt Elizabeth had a curious habit of balling her hands together and scratching her palms whenever something bothered her. She was doing that now as she looked at John.

"Elizabeth, you didn't think you could trust me with the truth?" John truly looked hurt. "It's Istanbul, isn't it? I'm still serving my penance for what happened over there, aren't I?" A serious frown wrinkled his brow.

There it was again - Istanbul. Whatever did that have to do with her?

"No, John. You're mistaken." Elizabeth went to stand by his side, placing her hand on his upper arm. "I know it looks as if my faith was lacking these last few months. You've more than proved yourself since you returned to the States. My hands were tied by powers higher than my own." Elizabeth paused. "I wouldn't trust Katherine to anyone but you. I've broken about every rule of protocol by handing you this op. I may have jeopardized all of your careers, but I know I've surrounded your team with people I can trust."

John suddenly snapped his head up at the compliment and looked directly at Kate. His eyes captured hers. "I won't ever let you down…either of you."

"You won't, John. And you know I won't let you." The look that passed between the two puzzled Kate. What other secrets did they have to tell? "Now, Katherine." Her aunt's demeanor changed. Suddenly, she was all business and her focus was back on the business at hand. "You've got to see if you can get up and dressed. Let's get you a good hot meal. Then we need to talk. You need to be brought up to speed on Hallock Farm. I've got to make sense out of what you heard in the kitchen." Her aunt motioned John to go to the door. "Tell Tim we'll be down in about twenty minutes for supper. Get the team together. I only have a few more hours and I'm needed back in Washington. I want everything settled before I go."

"I'm on it." John moved to the door and turned. "Lizzie… uh, I mean, Katherine…ah, hell, what do most people call you?"

Elizabeth didn't allow Kate the time to respond. "She's Lizzie O'Brien. Until I find out who and where that leak came from, John, I don't want anyone but you knowing her true identity."

John's eyes locked on Kate's. Kate sensed there would be

another conversation, far more private, at another time. "Yes, Madam Director." He nodded and walked out, closing the door behind him.

"Poor boy. He's got it bad." Her aunt purred as she helped Kate sit up on the edge of the bed.

"I know I dinged my head, Aunt Elizabeth. But, now you're the one not making sense. What *are* you talking about?" Kate reached for her aunt's arm and stood up to test her legs. Steady. Good, she had her sea legs.

"Why, John Clinton, of course. I saw the way he looks at you. He thought I didn't notice. An agent's not supposed to have a personal life, but you mark my words." Elizabeth cupped Kate's chin and turned Kate's head so Kate's eyes met hers. "Katherine, that's the man for you."

Kate blushed.

"Not that creature your father decided to hook you up with." Her aunt snorted. "Look where that got you! I kick myself every day that I didn't tell you what I found out about him after I ran a background check."

It was Kate's turn to stand stunned by the side of the bed. "You did *what*?"

"I did what every normal person with contacts would do, dear. I had the Agency check Ty out. What I discovered about him and his father's law firm made my toes curl!"

Kate couldn't move. She was rooted to the floor, staring dumbfounded at the woman beside her.

"And you didn't think to tell me?" Kate tried in vain to yank her arm away from her aunt's firm grasp. "You just blithely let Mother arrange the society wedding of the year and let me think that Ty was the perfect man?" Now that she'd regained her faculties, it was she who was angry. Was it possible this entire mess could have been avoided?

"Now, Katherine." Aunt Elizabeth's soothing tone of voice

was an attempt to calm her. "It wasn't for me to tell you. Ty was part of a life decision, and you were in love with the man. But as soon as you're dressed and fed a good meal, I'm telling you everything. Absolutely everything. No more secrets." Kate saw the tears welling up in the corners of her aunt's eyes. "Come. Let's get a move on and head downstairs for some food. Then, you, John and I will talk. Everything will make sense."

Kate shrugged into her jeans and Cornell tee shirt. She tied her hair up in a ponytail with a rubber band she found on her nightstand, knowing the cap she always wore would irritate her new badge of honor. Just wait until the team of agents saw it. She was sure they'd never let her live it down that she'd fainted dead away.

"I'm ready." Kate pronounced. *Or as ready as I'll ever be*, she thought.

Elizabeth opened the door and ushered Kate out into the hallway. "Follow me, Katherine. There's nothing to be afraid of. You're a Hallock. You can handle anything."

CHAPTER TWENTY

"You idiot!" Zoya emphasized the two words and slapped her brother upside the head as they walked along the street leading to their studio apartment. "What do you think Demetrie is going to do to you when he finds out?"

"The only way he's going to find out is if you tell him, sister."

"Whatever possessed you to go back to the meadow?"

"I wanted to mark out the areas where I could set up my rifle. Demetrie is wrong. There are several good places for my sniper positions if we can draw Clinton out to the north meadow."

"We don't know if someone saw you. If you were seen, Demetrie's contact will tell him. Hell will break loose tonight when he comes home. Besides, did you ever think that you might have left traces of evidence at the scene?"

"What, a few broken leaves? I got out when I saw Clinton coming for me. He didn't see me, Zoya."

"You know nothing about tracking, Stavros. Clinton will go over the area with his CSU unit. Let's pray they don't have any DNA to work with." The smug look on her brother's face showed her he didn't seem to care.

"You forget, Zoya. The mission cannot be done without my expertise. Demetrie's men may be good with their weapons. I am known to be the best. Yes?"

"True. But he has connections. We are expendable. The mission could go on without us. Oh, I'm so mad at what you did! I've waited for over a year to get my revenge. I want John Clinton dead. Just as he thinks I am. Dead at the hands of Elizabeth Hallock and her operatives."

"Demetrie may have connections, but the mission was to enter the States and take out Clinton and Hallock. You and I were given direct orders. We're not to stop until we do so."

In the distance, thunder boomed and a lightning bolt arced through the sky. The heat was stifling. Zoya pointed to the corner café where they'd gone for coffee the other morning. "We need to take cover before the storm hits. Hurry. We'll talk inside."

Stavros nodded and jaywalked across the street. Zoya followed behind. They made it into the café just as the skies opened up. Her brother pointed to a booth in the back corner. Zoya headed for it, sliding in while her brother sat across from her. A waitress took their order and walked away.

"Zoya, I don't like the way Demetrie set up the diversions at the stables. We'll be caught if we proceed as planned."

"You're going to question *him*? Have you got a death wish?"

"We need to get in and get out. Not set off a series of smaller incidents. Clinton's a hardened professional. Elizabeth's best men are there. There's already been one slip up with the inside contact. Doesn't it bother you that we don't know who it is? What if something happens to Demetrie before we finish? You and I will be left to try to enter a staked out compound on our own."

The waitress came back with their drinks. Zoya pondered what her brother said. She thought the boy had no brains except for his skills with a rifle. But he was clearly making sense. What would happen if something didn't go as planned?

Zoya had her doubts, as well. But always one to have a backup plan, unbeknownst to Stavros or Demetrie, she'd planned for an alternative set up. Thunder boomed again, and the windows of the café rattled. Taking a long sip of soda, Zoya eyed her brother thoughtfully. He'd never cared for Demetrie. She tolerated Demetrie simply because he was the means to the end she wanted. She trusted her brother explicitly. She needed a man with a gun, a very well-aimed gun.

The waitress placed their food in front of them. Stavros nodded their thanks and reached for the salt.

Zoya leaned across the table and spoke softly, "For once, I think you're right. But I have one thing to add to your plan. We take down Clinton and the Director together. The girl Demetrie told us Clinton was guarding will be a casualty of doing business. She will be our bait. Elizabeth has her in protective custody for a reason. Clinton is there to do his job." She waited for Stavros to react. Zoya prayed he could keep his mouth shut in front of Demetrie.

Stavros perked up. "When do we go in?"

"Within the week." Zoya hoped she hadn't underestimated Demetrie. She and Stavros would be making a huge mistake if Demetrie became their number one enemy instead of the two she sought the most.

CHAPTER TWENTY-ONE

There were times when Kate's Hampton debutante side loved to be pampered. Today was definitely not one of them. John's team had gone out of their way to make her comfortable since she, oh so gracefully, passed out and injured her head.

When Elizabeth escorted her into the kitchen for something to eat, Wade and Bob jumped up from where they sat to help. Tim heaped a mountain of food on her plate and was ready to pile on more when she waved him off. Jake popped up and down, like a jack-in-the-box, getting drinks. She felt as if she was at a three-ring circus. The agents couldn't do enough to try to please her or the Director.

Now, in the office and out of sight of prying eyes and hearing distance, John Clinton moved an ottoman to place in front of her brown leather chair.

As he reached for her foot, Kate barked, "Stop already! I'm perfectly fine. Really. I can't stand it when people fuss."

"Katherine Elizabeth!" Her aunt admonished Kate sharply as she sat behind John's desk. She took a stack of papers from her infamous briefcase. "John's only trying to be sure you're all right, dear. You've been through a lot. Don't take your frustrations out on the poor man." Her aunt devilishly winked at her.

John settled into a creaking chair. Out of the corner of her eye, she spied the smirk on his face. How she'd so like to smack him! But, how could she even think that when he and his team had treated her well. Her aunt was right. As she'd eaten, she realized she was not only aggravated with her situation, but the lack of control of her life. It wasn't her nature to be foul tempered.

Impatient to hear the news regarding Hallock Farm, Kate pointed to the blotter on the farm desk. "I have a feeling that stack of papers has to do with the briefing you gave the agents."

Her aunt finished reading through a few pages, and then looked up. "Yes. Everyone is up to speed on Operation Hide and Seek. But you and I need to talk so you can understand what's going on. Katherine, I've never liked keeping secrets, but the Hallock family has a unique way of brushing things under the proverbial rug. Several have been buried for years. Unfortunately, you've been adversely affected by them now."

Kate's heart pounded. Please let her be told there was closure in the mess at the farm and she could go home. "If Father's involved, Auntie, I've no doubt there's more than one secret buried in the dunes in Hampton Beach."

"Unfortunately, my dear, you are correct." A stoic demeanor rapidly replaced the mother-like, comforting woman Elizabeth had been an hour before.

"John," Elizabeth instructed, "Tell Jake to make sure every man is at their assigned post. The incident in the meadow may be nothing, but I want to be prepared. Twenty-four seven surveillance in the secure room – two men at the monitors at all times. I want an hourly report sent to me via my secure line."

John rose and moved to the door to do Elizabeth's bidding.

"Yes, ma'am. I'll leave you two to talk."

"When you've briefed the men, come back. You need to hear what I have to say. It will affect the mission's outcome." Elizabeth opened a leather folder she'd pulled from the leather briefcase.

Kate found the silence pervading the room a bit unnerving. The pendulum clock above the mantle in the office ticked loudly as they awaited John's return. It didn't take long before the door opened and John entered. The man carefully balanced a tray of tea and coffee. Placing it on the desk, he poured two mugs of steaming coffee, handing one to Kate and setting one on the side table by his chair. Before sitting down, he placed a blue teapot on the desk in front of Elizabeth, who was sorting through the paperwork before her. Giving Kate a look that said things would be all right, John sat back in the black Windsor rocker. Elizabeth busied herself by steeping a pot of the Earl Grey tea.

Dropping two cubes of sugar into her cup, Elizabeth eyed Kate. "Katherine, I have a long story to tell in a short amount of time. Please don't interrupt. I'll answer your questions when I'm finished. This secret has been with me for the last twenty years, and now, I could kick myself for ever having done what your father asked me to do." She gingerly took a sip from her cup then placed it back onto the saucer. Fumbling through the papers in the leather binder, she found what she needed. She rattled the paper in Kate's direction. "I'm truly sorry for having any part of your father's sordid debacle. But understand, my first thought was to save my family, and I think you know you and your brothers will always be my number one priority."

Kate set aside her mug. John did the same. "What could Father possibly have convinced you to do? I've never known you to do anything you didn't want to."

Her aunt's hand trembled as she held up a very light blue

official document. "Twenty years ago, your father got the farm into a terrible financial mess. Let's leave it that my brother has never had a head for business. Needless to say, we made a pact after I bailed him out." Kate's eyebrows arched. Oh, how she wanted to jump in with questions reeling in her mind. But she had to be patient.

Her aunt continued, "Don't tell me Thomas hasn't come to you over the last several years about your father's business decisions." But before Kate could reply, her aunt jumped in. "I digress and we're wasting time."

As Elizabeth relayed the events that took place twenty years before, she aligned the relationship of that timeline to Kate's current predicament. The pieces of Kate's unknown puzzle began to drop into place. Kate had a vivid visual of her aunt showing up at her father's doorstep to take over Hallock Farm and that of her father's angry reaction. It was obvious her father had no choice but to do as told, especially since saving his precious reputation and standing within the Hampton community meant more than those around him. From Kate's perspective, Aunt Elizabeth had been more than fair. She could have had his ass thrown in jail for abusing her power of attorney. But in all these years, no one in the community had been the wiser, and the Hallock name had been preserved as well as the workings of the farm and its growth since she'd come on board.

"Your mother found out when she stumbled onto the argument in the study. When she heard what your father had done, she picked up her prized Ming vase and heaved it over the desk! After hitting the wood paneling, it crashed into a million pieces all over the floor. Your father cowered in the corner of the room!" Aunt Elizabeth laughed outright and slapped her hand down on the desk. "I never thought your mother had it in her, Katherine. Truly, I didn't. The look on your father's face was priceless!

"But, when all was said and done, your father and I came to a mutual agreement. He gave me his shares in Hallock Farm to replace the ones he'd sold to gain the monies needed for his failed business ventures. At that point, I then became CEO, but allowed him to retain the title, in name only, for reputation's sake."

Kate bolted upright in her chair. "You've been the CEO of the farm all this time? Aunt Elizabeth! Why didn't you tell us?"

"I'm not finished." Elizabeth held up her hand. "The deal almost didn't happen. When it came time to sign the final papers, your father almost reneged. However, my attorney made him see that by the definition of the law, he'd committed fraud. Fraud meant jail. It brought your father around very quickly."

Kate's mind reeled with the new dynamics of her family and the business. She pulled her legs up underneath her, trying to find a more comfortable position. She touched the bandage in hopes it would assuage the pounding within. "I don't get it. Does this somehow relate to what happened with Father and Ty?"

"Yes, it does," her aunt replied. "With the career path I'd chosen to take, I had to make a choice between my country and my family. As CEO of Hallock Farm, I had to ensure the family legacy would live on. I was climbing up the ropes of the Agency and working two serious assignments in Europe. I made a conscious choice, after conferring with your mother, Thomas and my attorney. We hired someone who privately covered the duties as CEO. Several years ago, I rewrote the terms of the Hallock family trust. It was my decision to deed Hallock Farm to *you* on your thirtieth birthday."

John let out a low whistle.

Kate's jaw sagged at the realization of what she'd just found out. "You can't be serious!"

"I most certainly am. Never more so in my life."

Placing both feet on the floor, Kate sat up in the chair, wincing as pain sliced through her head. She grimaced.

Her aunt immediately rose and came around the desk to kneel beside her. "Are you all right? Maybe all this is too much right now. I don't have much time, Katherine. I need to leave. But, I had to tell you in person. I didn't want you to hear it from someone else, especially from your father."

Kate looked into the familiar caring pair of eyes. "I don't understand."

"Understand what?" Elizabeth placed her hand on Kate's knee.

"Why would you give Hallock Farm to me? Why not Thomas? He's the oldest. He's the one most experienced with operating the ins and outs of the business." Her aunt's touch was soothing to her soul.

"Katherine, since you were able to climb up onto your first pony, you showed how much you loved and cared for the farm and the horses. When you came back from college and introduced new techniques, the farm flourished. Hallock Farm came back to life. After I ran the idea by your mother, we agreed it was only right that you be the one to continue to build upon the Hallock legacy and run the thoroughbred facility."

Kate watched as her aunt glanced in John's direction and then trained her eyes on her. Kate knew that signal. She braced for what would come. "There's more, isn't there?"

"Yes. Katherine, think carefully about plans you had for the next six weeks, including your birthday."

Kate's stomach plummeted as her mind focused on the most important day of all. "My birthday was my wedding day!"

Her aunt grabbed for her hand.

The shock of discovering what would have happened had Kate taking a deep breath and exhaling slowly. She did it several times to no avail. Her thoughts spewed out, "And Ty insisted we didn't need to have a pre-nup. Oh, Aunt Elizabeth! How stupid could I have been?" She stopped, the light bulb going off. "Ty was working with Father, wasn't he?"

"I'm afraid so. But in defense of your father, he was a victim of Ty and his family. Ty's father's law firm represents the Savorski family and operates in very powerful circles within New York City."

The reality of leaving her family behind made Kate grip the arms of the leather chair. Her anxiety mounting, she nervously raised her tone of voice. "I have to go home!"

The floorboards creaked as John came to stand beside Elizabeth. He, like her aunt, tried to make her see reason. "Lizzie, you have to stay here until the Feds have finished their investigation and collared the person who put out the hit. Had you stayed at the farm any longer, we're convinced you would have been kidnapped. Let's leave it at that and not let our minds think of 'what ifs.'"

"How much does Father owe?"

John knelt beside her, his sea green eyes level with her own. From the look on his face, she could tell she wasn't going to like what he was about to say. "Lizzie, your father owes the Savorskis two million dollars…plus interest."

Kate stared at him, shocked at the amount. "And the horse and myself would possibly be the interest?"

"We think so," her aunt replied. "So, Katherine, you'll remain here. No arguments. It won't be long. I promise you, we will have you home soon."

Promises. Promises could be broken. Trust was another thing entirely. And the only two people in the world she could trust at that moment were standing in front of her.

CHAPTER TWENTY-TWO

The Director of the CIA headed back to Arlington in the dark of night, accompanied by her bodyguards. Operation Hide and Seek now operated in two arenas, one covered by the CIA, the other the FBI. John knew from Elizabeth's body language she wasn't happy fighting on two fronts.

As the sun broke over the horizon of the west paddock, John whistled under his breath as he leaned on the fence. In disbelief, he couldn't help but shake his head. Lizzie O'Brien was Elizabeth Hallock's niece! If that didn't beat all! And she wasn't just any ordinary equine veterinarian. John had Googled her last night now that he knew her real identity. The woman's resumé was a mile long. Katherine Elizabeth Hallock was born into a famous family on Long Island. And now, given direction of the trust, she was to become the CEO of one of the most prestigious thoroughbred training and rehab facilities on the Eastern seaboard. As he rested his forearms on the newly painted fence, he smiled to himself. He *knew* his instincts had been correct, thinking the two women looked alike. His radar never failed him. However, to be in charge of the protection of the niece of the Director of the CIA in a very covert, secret operation unknown to the Agency itself? John never expected anything like this.

"Chief! Chief!" John turned to the urgent voice calling out. Tim was running up the driveway from the south meadow.

Alarmed, John asked, "What's going on? Where's Wade?"

"Down at the entrance. Something's not kosher." Tim reached him, slightly out of breath.

"You left your partner alone?" John barked out.

"No." Tim leaned up against the fence and tipped his cap back on his head. "Wade and Chuck and a few others are there. We had company again."

"Come again?" Taking off his hat, John ran his fingers through his hair in frustration.

"I didn't bring the truck because we realized it was sitting on top of fresh footprints. We didn't want to disturb the scene until forensics took molds of the tracks.

"There's evidence of at least two people trampling the grass by the post at the turnoff. Some kind of device was set on the ground, like some kind of tripod. Wade thinks from the depths of the holes it was a camera with a powerful zoom lens. Somebody took pictures of the farmhouse and surrounding grounds."

John didn't want to waste another minute. He had to see the tapes. "Come with me. I want to roll back the security footage and see if we can catch a glimpse of who was out there. The tape's time marked."

Tim strode beside John as both men made for the porch. "You took the shift in the secure room after the Director left. Correct?"

"Yeah, but nothing came up on the radar."

The two men entered the kitchen, making their way for the basement stairs. "Well, who was with you during your shift?" Tim asked.

John stopped dead in his tracks. *No. It couldn't happen again,* he thought. Not after Istanbul. He'd found out in his briefing that Mike had betrayed him and the team.

Last night Jake voluntarily showed up out of the blue to give him a chance to rest about four in the morning. And John gladly took him up on his offer.

Damn. John needed to call the Eagle.

* * *

Kate woke to the slam of the screen door below her bedroom window. The sun peeked through the slits in the curtains. She didn't smell breakfast cooking in the kitchen as she usually did. Sitting up slowly, she righted herself on the edge of the bed. Her head still ached, but not as much as the day before. Coffee. She needed a good strong cup to jumpstart her body. She had to check on the horses and do her morning chores.

After a quick shower, she ventured down the stairs. But as she turned the corner to walk into the kitchen, she spied John and his team circled around the table in a heated debate. It was going to be impossible to sneak in and out without being noticed. Curious, Kate backed up, flattening her body against the wall.

"And I'm telling you the lady's got a right to know." Tim spoke up, deep concern in his voice.

"You're entitled to your opinion, but until we know who and what we're dealing with, I think it would be better not to tell Liz. She's got enough on her plate." The loud commanding tone in John's voice startled Kate. She edged closer to the corner of the doorway.

Tim countered, "You're making a huge mistake. It's best if you're honest with her. She's got gumption. Liz is one tough cookie. Give her some credit, John. We need her working with us if anything happens."

Kate walked into the center of the kitchen. Her footsteps on the tile floor caught the huddled team off-guard. Breathe, she thought. In. Out. Look like you're calm. "Well, you all look like you've seen a ghost. I didn't mean to eavesdrop, but from the sound of things I think this is more than a simple briefing." She searched out John, pinning him in his seat with a subtle glare. "I'm a big girl, Agent Clinton. Spill it."

As if he'd read her mind, Chuck rose and went to pour Kate the cup of coffee she'd been seeking, mumbling under his breath as he did so.

"You want to weigh in here, Agent Thomas?" The sharpness in John's tone of voice surprised her.

Chuck turned from the counter with the mug in his hand and handed it to Kate. "Be careful, it's hot."

She readily accepted it, thankful to have something to hold in her hands.

Chuck put the pot of coffee on the table and placed his hands on his hips, a determined look on his face. "Listen, you're the boss, John. What you say goes. I'm just one bodyguard doing his job. But, I think Tim is right. Lizzie needs to know."

Kate could see by the twitch on John's face the man was conflicted. "Let me go on record that we have orders from the Director to handle this differently. Your arguments are logical and sound, but our first priority is protection." John motioned for her to sit at the table. Balancing her full cup of coffee with both hands, Kate sat as instructed. John turned to look at her. "Something went down late last night."

Her knees shook as she gazed into John's eyes.

"Early this morning someone made their way to the entrance by the south paddock. Liz, the evidence supports the fact that one of the people was the same person watching us near the meadow."

Kate grabbed the edge of the table. Common sense told her she trusted these men, but was she really safe? She was trembling both inside and out. "Please tell me, with all your fancy intelligence, you've been able to finally identify somebody."

John's silence answered her question.

"Well, obviously we have a problem, don't we? So what's next?" Kate looked from one face to the other as she glanced around the table, finally landing back on John's.

John drummed his fingers on the table. "For the next several days, we're going to do a thorough reconnaissance on the property. Twenty more Special Ops troops are coming in from Quantico. You won't even know they're here."

Kate felt a tap on her shoulder. Chuck stood there with a fresh pot of coffee. She gingerly reached for her cup, raised it and he topped it off. Taking a sip, she warily eyed the men who excelled in keeping their faces devoid of emotions. "I have a feeling I'm not going to like where I fit into this… plan."

Whispering came from the other end of the table. John glared at Tim and Wade.

John's eyes locked on hers. "Probably not. The Director gave an order that you're to stay in the house for the next two days."

"*What*? I can't possibly… She knows I can…" Kate was flabbergasted.

"You heard me." John's look made her fall silent. "You're going to stay put and keep yourself busy. I've got office work you can do. But on *no* terms are you to venture out into the yard. If someone is poking around, we might still have a chance to draw him out. We don't want you seen. Period. It's too risky."

Kate stewed and countered, "And who will care for the horses? What about the exercise program for Wild Flame? You just can't go and—"

John slammed his hand on the wooden table, causing everyone's mugs to rattle. "Stop! God, don't you have any idea how serious this is? You're not just playing hide and seek. You're living it!"

"Of course, I understand. I'm not going to impede you from

doing your job. But the horses need attention. They need their daily vet check." Kate stood her ground. John's eyes smoldered as she challenged him.

"This team can handle the horses for a few days. You've trained Tim to work Wild Flame and Dark Shadow. But you're going to stay put. Case closed. Got it?"

It wasn't that she didn't understand the dangerous circumstances. She did. But she could take care of herself. How could she make him realize that? Kate was used to being the boss, and his turning the tide on her didn't go over well at all.

"Not being able to be in the barns doesn't make sense. You've had agents glued to my hip since I got here."

John folded his arms and sat unresponsive.

"And what exactly am I supposed to be doing while you're all out being secret agent men?" Kate said haughtily.

John leaned his chair back, balancing it on two legs and looked her in the eye. "I received a brochure from the Peachtree Auction House. There's an auction in a few weeks and I'd like to sink some money into new stock. Given your background, I'd appreciate your taking the time to see if there are any horses I might want to add to Clinton Stables."

"I still don't think—"

A hand came to rest on her shoulder. It was Chuck's. "Lizzie. You've got to help us out here. We can't do our job if we have to worry about you roaming about."

She glanced up, seeing the sincere concern in his eyes. Chuck had treated her with the most kindness and respect since she'd arrived at the safe house.

"Okay. Okay." She threw her hands in the air. "I'll stay in the house. I'll look at the catalog." She paused, thinking. Then, she continued, "I've one condition, or the deal's off." Inwardly, she smiled as she watched John's eyebrow arch.

"You have a *condition*?" His harsh gaze was replaced by a

slight twinkle, which quickly disappeared. She definitely liked to keep this man on his toes for some reason. "This, I've got to hear." The chair legs thumped as John righted his chair.

Kate looked up and down the table, making sure all eyes were on her. Then, she simply stated, "I'll need a gun."

The men stared back, shocked, jaws dropping. Kate inwardly received a small sense of satisfaction, watching John trying to recapture his wits. No doubt about it, she was getting to him. She loved every minute of having the upper hand for once.

"You want a *what?*" John jumped up and placed his hands on the table, leaning towards her.

She stood up and stared him down. "I… want… a… gun, cowboy," Kate said emphatically, poking her finger into his chest. "If you're going to leave me in this house and go about your agent business, I want to be able to protect myself." She motioned to John's silver cell phone on the table. "Go ahead. Call the Director. I'm licensed to carry a firearm."

A chorus of laughter burst out, and John rounded on his men. The room suddenly became quiet.

Kate was determined to win the showdown. "I *can* use one. The Director taught me. Any kind of gun will do just fine by the way. I *can* and *will* defend myself if I have to." Still eyeing the men at the table, she asked, "So what have you got for me to use? I personally prefer a nine millimeter semi-automatic." She'd remember John's stunned facial expression forever. "And if it's not too much to ask, I'd like two rounds of magazines… Just in case." Kate winked at the men.

Chaos broke out around the table. The men were high-fiving each other as they tried to control their merriment at their boss's expense. Oh, John was pissed. Even though he was in charge, he'd pushed the envelope as far as she was going to allow him. It would teach him not to leave her in the dark about matters pertaining to her safety. She might be fearful of the unknown, but she had a right to know any decisions being made on her behalf.

Kate braced for his response. John spoke through gritted teeth. "And would you be wanting a holster for the gun, my lady?"

Hearing the sarcasm in his voice, Kate smiled. *Touché. I hit a nerve.* Kate felt free, in charge of her life for that brief moment. John, however, earned high marks in her book for keeping a lid on his temper. She was so close she could see his pulse throbbing in his neck. Looking down, she realized her hand had come to rest on his chest. She jerked her hand away as if she'd touched a hot stove.

"No, I won't be needing a holster, Agent Clinton. I've been taught by a pro. I'll be just fine without one, thanks. I'll just shove it in the back of my jeans—" Kate caught herself when she realized she almost finished the sentence. "Now, if you men will excuse me, I'll go to the office and search for that catalog." She walked to the kitchen sink, draining the remnants of her coffee and placed her empty cup in it. Glancing back, she called over her shoulder, "Oh, and if you're worried, don't be. My aim is always on the mark. I'm a ranked sharpshooter."

Kate didn't need a mirror to know John was still exactly where she'd left him. No doubt there was astonishment on his face, his eyes dark and glaring at her back as she exited the room.

"You're forgetting I'm in charge, Lizzie. I'll have to give it some thought."

Kate spun on her heels. "There's nothing to think about, *Agent* Clinton. You have to let me protect myself, if necessary. Now, *you* have to trust *me*."

CHAPTER TWENTY-THREE

"Madam Director! This is not some damn Hampton tea party!" John raked his hand through his wavy brown hair. He held his cell phone up to his ear and listened as his mentor gave him instructions, none of which pleased him. "What if she accidentally decides to take matters into her own hands?"

It had been a losing battle trying to convince Elizabeth that Kate didn't need to carry a gun, licensed or not.

He paused as Elizabeth talked in the other end of the secure line. He looked back at Tim and Wade who sat monitoring the view screens, zooming in and out on the property lines as he tried to finish up his conversation.

"Fine. I'll agree to it. But, I want to go on record that this is not my idea. Roger." He turned the phone off. "Shit! That went really well."

"Chief," Wade tried to calm his boss. "I'm not the lead man here, but I have to agree with the Director. If Lizzie knows how to use a gun, I say let her have one."

Tim swiveled in his seat, trying to keep his eye on the screen at the same time. "Ditto here."

John wasn't surprised he was outvoted. In the short time

she'd been at the farm, his team had developed great respect for the woman they protected.

Tim continued, "With all due respect, we can't be in two places at one time. The team needs to be outside, finding out what the hell went down and getting forensics. Add to that we need bodies in the security room. Cut her some slack. Trust her, just like she said. She'll always be in someone's sight."

Walking over to the screens, John stood behind his men. Katherine Hallock frustrated the hell out of him. When she dug in her heels, he felt as if he was talking to a stone wall. And now the woman wanted a gun! He couldn't believe the very thought of Katherine carrying a weapon hadn't fazed the Director. The situation was spinning out of control. He'd told Elizabeth in the planning stages his ranch had too big a perimeter to be fully functional for the success of Operation Hide and Seek. As far as he was concerned at the moment, he was right. And on top of everything, Kate crept into his thoughts a multitude of times when he needed to be a professional – like last night when he tossed and turned half the night. Not being able to keep a handle on his emotions started to alarm him. Lately, he'd become defensive and impatient with her when he had no right. She'd cooperated fully with everything requested of her. Until she'd asked for a gun. She thrown everyone for a loop… except for the one person he thought would have shot the idea down. Interesting.

"John? John!" Tim snapped his fingers trying to break John's deep contemplation. The man was actually laughing. "Got to hand it to you. You've got your hands full. Hell, when Lizzie was in the kitchen telling us she was going to be packing a weapon, I could have sworn I was looking at the Director giving us marching orders. You ever notice the resemblance?"

Tim's comments suddenly made John uncomfortable. The last thing he needed was to make a mistake and blow Kate's cover. He hated keeping secrets from his men. But he'd violate a direct order should he do so.

Wade added, "Tim's got a point. She acts like Elizabeth. All commanding and demanding." Wade elbowed Tim in the side. "We think you might be falling hard for this one."

John sank into the chair behind him, his head in his hands. He heard the two men chortle and glanced up. Tim and Wade were smiling broadly. "Go ahead. You might as well have your laugh now. You're not going to get another chance."

"Ah, Chief…" Wade swiveled his chair around. A wide grin on the man's face was John's clue Wade was about to deliver the final blow. "Just don't go getting shot on this job. We've already picked out our tuxes for the wedding."

Great. Just great, John thought. He'd have to do better to maintain his professional demeanor around Kate. He had to be sure any parallels to Istanbul remained far from his agents' minds. He needed his team focused. John's internal radar told him her father's friends were nearby. It was only a matter of time before they made another move.

* * *

The Special Ops team arrived from Quantico. John assigned Tim to make sure the members of the men already on the ground coordinated what needed to be done with the new highly-trained snipers coming in.

Entering the office and seeing the room empty, John became alarmed. That was until he noticed Kate standing by the corner window, wistfully looking out over the barnyard in plain view of anyone outside.

In a gruff tone, he ordered, "Get away from the window!" Didn't the woman understand? For someone who said she could take care of herself, she sure wasn't thinking with a lick of common sense.

"Judas Priest! You scared the hell out of me!" Kate jumped,

turned away from the window and snapped at him. Normally patient, John had noticed she'd grown less tolerant in the last few days.

"What the hell are you doing? Someone could see in, Kate. You're not thinking!" John moved into the office and shut the door with a bang.

Kate marched to the chair behind the desk and sat down, a sullen look on her face. He didn't mean to treat her as a child, but he was on edge.

"Well, *cowboy*. I can't find that catalog." She motioned to his messy desk. "I've searched this whole office."

John surveyed the piles of papers on the desk and those stacked around the perimeter of the room.

"Got any idea where you put it? I've been waiting for someone to come in to ask. But since I'm *quarantined* to this room, like some horse with a disease…" She spat out the words in disgust.

"Look." John understood her frustration. "I know you're not happy with the turn of events. I'll point out again. You *are* allowed to use the entire house. I only told you not to go outside."

Kate glared at him in stony silence. The lady was one unhappy camper.

Yes, indeed. Kate was definitely related to Elizabeth. He watched as she twiddled her thumbs and glanced up at the ceiling. The same mannerisms, the same looks and as stubborn as the Director, maybe even more. John strode across the room and stood beside her. Reaching across the desk, he accidentally brushed against her body as he searched for the catalog he could have sworn he'd left on the desk the night before. At the mere touch of his arm to hers, a zing of electricity shot up his arm. John gazed down just in time to see a mix of emotions play out across Kate's face, as well. Was it possible she was developing feelings for him? If so, it was time to step back. He was on assignment. John had no right to think of her in any other light.

"Here, it is!" John snatched it from the desk blotter, making sure he avoided her body as he retrieved the thick catalog.

Kate grabbed the red book from his hands. Perusing the front cover, she said, "Wait. I know these people."

His ears perked up. John sat on the edge of the desk by her right side, fully alert. "What do you mean you know the people at the auction?"

"The Watsons." She pointed to the picture of the beautiful home and barns of a glorious estate. "I sent my agent out to this farm last year. The Watsons are known for their Arabians and the bloodlines of their thoroughbreds. Peachtree has quite the reputation up and down the East Coast for their breeding program. Thunderball was their entry in the Kentucky Derby last year."

John felt like a duck out of water. "Explain."

"Thunderball won the Triple Crown – the Kentucky Derby, the Belmont Stakes and the Preakness. The Watsons have made millions by putting him out to stud."

Kate continued to talk, but John's attention was on her, not what she was saying. Her face radiated when she was in her element. Her arms and hands became animated. Lizzie O'Brien aka Katherine Hallock was a downright beauty, a stunning, intelligent woman. And he'd never be able to have her. Not ever.

It was the touch of her hand on his knee that shocked him. The warmth of her hand traveled down a path that went directly from his knee to his groin. His jeans tightened immediately. John swallowed, trying to recall what she'd been talking about.

"I hope you can put your money where your mouth is, cowboy. Based on those plans of yours, you're going to need deep pockets if you want to bid with the big boys." Kate flipped through the pages of the catalog. "Oh, my gosh. Will you look at that!" Her hand squeezed his knee again, and he jerked like a bucking bronco rider. Her eyes traveled up the length of him. Was she eyeing him playfully, or just reading into things? "Boy, I hope you've got what it takes, John. This," Kate slapped the catalog, "is the big leagues."

Yep. He definitely was a big boy and soon to be bigger if she didn't remove her hand from his knee. John cleared his throat and stood up. He had to put some distance between them. He motioned to the auction book.

"I've got a decent cash flow. I don't think I'll have any trouble maintaining the facilities and the operations. I think it's safe to say I can give you carte blanche to buy some thoroughbreds and yearlings to get this place up and running."

Lizzie eyed him thoughtfully. "Can I ask you something?"

"Sure."

"It's sort of personal. I know agents aren't supposed to have lives other than what exist at Langley."

John knew there wasn't any way to stop her, so he might as well find out what she wanted to know. "Fire away."

Kate's eyebrows arched.

"Poor choice of words?"

She nodded. "Listen, I know it's none of my business, but agents don't make millions of dollars. I don't mean to pry, but have you really got that much available cash on hand? After you bring home the horses, the bills to run a place like this will skyrocket. You'll need to keep a vet on call and a farrier to keep the horses healthy. Those are just two items on a very long list. The daily bills for running a place really mount up."

John tried to look like he understood everything she said, but he couldn't take his eyes off her. What had happened here? He was losing his grip on protocol. As she passionately spoke,

John became spellbound, listening to the seductive tone in her voice.

He had been so caught up in her passion and enthusiasm, he hadn't realized she'd risen from her chair and stood in front of him. As she placed her hand on his chest, she glanced up. Her dark brown eyes met his sea green ones. "Your facilities aren't totally ready yet to be bringing in the animals, but they will be up and running in a few weeks."

John prayed she wouldn't feel the rapid hammering of his heart under the palm of her hand.

Suddenly, Kate stopped talking. John watched as her eyes traveled to where her hand lay. It was then John knew guarding Kate had become, for him, more than just another job. *Careful. You can get out of this. It's just hormones and not being with a woman for a really long time.*

"John," Kate whispered his name so softly he bent over to hear her. There was longing in her voice.

"Kate," John placed his hand at her waist. "I don't think this is a good idea."

She glanced back up. Her eyes pleaded with him. The woman didn't want to be denied. Her hand slid up his shirt, caressed his cheek and jaw. By then, both of Kate's hands had snaked around his neck. "One kiss."

"I can't. We can't." John reached up to unlock her fingers, but Kate was persistent. She pulled him to her.

"Katie," he whispered.

"Just one kiss, cowboy."

When she licked her lips, John was a goner. Wrapping his arms around her waist, he drew her closer. John gave in, lightly brushing his lips across hers. She tasted as if she'd just bitten into a fresh strawberry. He bit her lower lip, not prepared for her response. Kate crushed her mouth to his, initiating a more intimate kiss. And he obliged her, their tongues twisting and playing, hinting at what could possibly be between them. She pulled him hard against her, but John broke the kiss and stared down into a pair of dark molten eyes full of desire.

"No," she begged. "More."

"We're taking a big—"

"John!" Jake bellowed from behind the door. "Where are you?" The agent was frantic.

Jake's voice awoke John from the desire induced fog. The man's tone told him something happened.

"In the office!" John shouted, taking several large steps away from Kate as the door opened. She sent a knowing look his way, well aware the last thing he needed was to be found in a compromising position.

Jake barged in. "Chief, you've got to get out to the back training barn!" Jake was panting. "It's Agent Stafford. One of the guys the Director sent for backup."

"What about him?"

"He's dead!"

John heard Kate gasp and spied her face turn ashen with fear.

Jake went on, "He was murdered, Chief. One of the field agents just found his body behind the training barn wrapped in a dark blue tarp. And…" Jake hesitated, carefully watching Kate out of the corner of his eye.

"Murdered? What the hell?" John hadn't had a feeling like this since Istanbul. "There's something else, isn't there? Go ahead. Kate needs to know."

With a somber look, Jake looked at his boss. "His tongue was cut out, mob style. Whoever did this just sent us a message."

* * *

"I overheard you on the phone, Sam. What the hell's gone wrong?" Robert Hallock asked Sam Tanner, seeing Elizabeth's second-in-command standing in the doorway of his study. He eyed Elizabeth's agent from his position by the window where he'd been looking out onto the paddocks. The paddocks, the farm, the horses, everything Katherine had built up over the last seven years. Sam clipped shut the black cell phone he carried and came to stand by Robert's desk.

There was no love lost between the two men. Robert knew Sam thought the same thing he'd thought twenty years ago, when he'd stood with Elizabeth and her attorney at the front door of Hallock Farm.

"There's trouble at the safe house." Sam stated.

An overwhelming sense of panic set in over the Hallock patriarch. "What do you mean there's trouble? Elizabeth assured Helen and me that Katie would be fine. She'd hidden her away until the Feds tied up things here. That special team of agents was supposed to be looking after her."

"Robert, sit down."

Robert paled. From the look on Sam's face the news wasn't good.

Instead of doing as he was asked, Robert headed for the sideboard. He hadn't opened the cupboard when Sam spoke, "I'll have the same thing you're having."

Robert glanced over his shoulder.

Sam said, "Hannah told me you hid some vintage scotch when Doc told you to lay off. She found it when she was dusting."

Robert took two glasses from the top of the cabinet and pulled the bottle out of its secret hiding place. "You haven't answered my question. That look on your face, Sam, tells me my daughter's in serious trouble."

Sam nodded in the affirmative. "Pour me two fingers and we'll talk. By the way, Helen thinks you're dry as a bone. Your secret's safe with me."

Robert poured the liquid into two tumblers, handed one

to Sam, and sat in his black leather chair. He watched as Sam warily eyed him, swirled the contents of the glass around and downed the drink in one large swallow.

"I'll be straight here. No way to be otherwise, Robert. There's been a murder. Elizabeth is afraid from the way it was carried out whoever did it was sending you a message."

Robert choked on the amber liquid as it went down. Placing the glass on his desk, his voice shook. "A murder? What's going on down there?"

Sam held up his hand. "Details aren't important right now. What is important is that you and your security detail keep this from Helen and the boys. Things have to continue around here as usual. If we don't, we'll jeopardize the FBI operation. We'll never make an arrest and end this mess. You want Katie home safe, don't you?"

Robert had known for years that he excelled in manipulation. He wasn't proud of who he was, especially now. He disliked not being the one in control and calling the shots. To Elizabeth, he was nothing more than a pompous ass. But, she'd come to his rescue again. For the first time in his life, he questioned his ability to do anything remotely moral and right. This time he had to do what was best, not for himself, but for his family.

"Of course, I do. But, Sam, the sting? I'm no actor. I have the worst poker face under pressure. I'll be so nervous wearing a wire I'll screw things up. I don't think the plan to invite the Savorskis and their friends to the country club for a party was a good idea. You're putting my family at risk, as well as the other people we invited. People around here know I never conduct actual business in a venue setting of that nature. They'll read me like a book. Script or no script." Robert picked up a pen and started to tap it on his desk.

Sam slid his chair closer to Robert's desk. "Stop! Stay focused. For once in your life, you're finally doing the right thing."

Sam was obviously angry. The man had a right to be. As much as Robert had been estranged from his sister for over twenty years, the man across from him had protected her from the evil in the world. He'd always had her back.

Sam's voice rose in volume. "Helen and the boys are counting on you, and if Katie was here, she'd tell you the same thing." Sam shook his head as he said next, "God knows why, but that girl still loves her daddy."

Robert cleared his throat as his emotions overtook him. Sam was right. He didn't deserve anyone's love and respect. He had to set aside his weaknesses and fears, put away his pride and ego and bring this mess he'd created to an end.

Robert rose, coming around the desk, and paced back and forth on the Oriental rug. "Where did the murder happen?"

Sam got up and walked to where Robert stood, two old enemies eye-to-eye. "The situation is under control. That's all you need to know. Special Agent Clinton and Elizabeth secured the perimeter and more agents were brought in. If need be, they'll fly Katherine back to the compound."

"Thomas told me he has no faith in me, Sam."

Robert had stopped in front of Sam who grabbed both his shoulders and shook him. "You know that old saying 'you can't con a con man'? Well, you're one of the best." Robert tried to shrug out of Sam's grasp. "No! Let me finish. I know you don't want to hear this. We go back a long ways, Robert. But if anyone can pull this off, it's you. And if you're lucky, no one will be the wiser in Hampton Beach."

"I can't believe you and Elizabeth have any faith in me."

Sam's gaze hardened. "You don't deserve them…your family…all this." Sam motioned to the bottle sitting on the desk. "Let's put our differences aside and have one for the road."

Robert thought of what he owed his family - Helen, Thomas, Ethan, Adam, Matthew and most of all, his beloved Katie-girl. He'd con the con man or die trying.

CHAPTER TWENTY-FOUR

John glanced at the clock at his bedside for the fifth time. One thirty. Ever since the murder, he'd slept little. Only catnaps, when time permitted. He could hardly remember when he'd last changed his clothes. Kate's safety, and that of his men, weighed heavily on his mind.

There was no doubt now, in either his or Elizabeth's mind, that there was a leak inside the safe house. John tried his best to fathom how, with the sophisticated monitoring equipment installed in and around the complex, the illicit activities had gone undetected. He had a savvy techno-double agent operative in his midst, and John needed to identify him.

On top of that, Elizabeth was making his job more difficult by thinking irrationally. She was adamant her niece be brought back to her compound or taken to another safe house within Washington. It had taken all the negotiating skills John and his men possessed to convince her that doing so would only place Kate and the entire operation at a terrible risk. It was too dangerous to make a move if the farm was surrounded. Elizabeth had called in a favor to a friend in the tech industry, and his company had done several drone swipes over the safe house landscape, giving John the needed pictures he could use for better surveillance set-up. Asking for satellite imagery would have red flags waving. John was grateful for the former.

As he lay on his bed, the air conditioner hummed in the background. John's mind checked off the chronological timeline of the recent incidents. Studying the evidence gathered, John knew in his gut from past experience, sabotage was becoming more and more a reality. If Istanbul had taught him one thing, it was to trust his instincts. During that fateful operation, John had gone to Elizabeth with suspicions of Zoya being a double agent, but she'd vetted Zoya, telling John his concerns were unfounded. There had been no evidence Zoya had turned… And then hell broke loose.

Shirtless, his jeans riding on his waist, John's thoughts drifted to Kate. During the last few days she'd done as instructed, but not with the same gusto and enthusiasm she'd shown before the murder. Not being able to be with her beloved horses and barricaded in the house sucked the life out of Kate's vibrant personality.

Kate began to overreact to every movement around her since the murder. Every time the kitchen door opened, she jumped. John walked into the office to ask how her research for the auction was going, only to find Liz sitting behind the desk, a gun aimed at his chest. *That* had literally scared the crap out of him.

John glanced at the clock on his nightstand. It was five minutes later than the last time he checked. At the meeting with his team that morning, all agents were in agreement. Something had to be done, a risk had to be taken, and soon. The mood at supper was somber, the conversation stilted. Wade, who rarely commented on anything regarding their charge, noted she'd pecked at her food, sliding the meat and potatoes around her plate. No doubt about it, Lizzie O'Brien, aka Katherine Hallock, was scared. And, as far as John was concerned, she had every right to be. He didn't like the fact he had to keep a secret from his men as to her true identity. However, if there was someone on the team who couldn't be trusted, he couldn't risk the chance of anyone else knowing Elizabeth's niece was here.

John pounded his pillow in frustration as a web of tangled thoughts reeled through his head. A loud, piercing scream broke the silence of the night, echoing down the hallway. John reached for the gun on his bedside table and hit the ground running. The scream belonged to Kate.

Tim and Wade met him in the hallway outside Kate's bedroom door as Chuck bounded up the back staircase, their guns drawn.

"On three…" John commanded. "One-two-three." Both he and Tim threw their weight into the door, breaking the lock. The door swung open and hit the wall. No one was prepared for what they saw on the other side.

Kate sat wide-eyed, propped up on a mass of bed pillows, her body covered in sweat. The room was stifling. Her semi-automatic pistol was pointed at the window. Had someone tried to get in? No, John thought. The Quantico team was on guard duty around the perimeter of the house tonight. The one person whom he suspected was on duty, but being watched by someone he trusted.

From John's PTSD experiences, Kate was coming out of a nightmare. He motioned for his men to stand down.

Approaching the bed, he spoke in a hushed, soothing tone, "Katie…Katie…It's me… John." Kate turned from the window, the dazed look on her face slowly disappearing. However, her hands still firmly gripped the gun. Kate glanced from the window to him and his men and back again, trying to grasp reality. Terror was etched on her face.

"Katie." John cautiously made his way to her. "You're at the ranch." He tried to speak as softly as possible. "You're safe. It's only us. Look. See? Nobody's outside, honey. You've just had a bad dream."

John whispered behind him, "Guys, keep a close eye on Kate. I'm going to get her gun away from her."

"Roger." Three voices spoke out in unison.

With his eye trained on the gun still in her hand, John was within reach in seconds. She gazed up at him as his hand clasped over hers. She flinched, but he could tell by the look in her eyes she wouldn't discharge the weapon. He spoke as she would to Wild Flame, "Let go of the gun, Kate."

Immediately, Kate relinquished it.

"What's going on?" Kate asked, seeing his men standing inside the bedroom door. "What are *they* doing here?" Her eyes flashed back to him. Fear. He saw fear in her dark brown orbs.

Placing her gun in the back of his pants for safekeeping, John sat on the edge of the bed. "It's just the team, Kate. And you've had nothing more than a bad dream. It's over."

Tim had come to stand off to his left, a weird expression on his face. John passed Kate's gun off to his agent. "Here! Lock this damn thing away in the office for safekeeping. I'll give it back to her when she's got her wits about her. Head back to your posts. I'll take things from here."

John didn't need to see the faces on Wade and Chuck to know they shared the same puzzled look as Tim. The moment "Kate" had spilled from his lips, he'd known he'd made a serious tactical error. "I'll explain everything about what you're thinking later. For now, what happened in here stays between the four of us. Understood?"

The three men nodded and stowed away their guns.

"We'll check on the watch, Chief," Tim said. "Don't worry about anything. Just take care of her."

The concern for Kate in their faces mirrored his own. "I

will. I'll get her settled and be down shortly."

The large oak door closed quietly behind the three men, and John turned to face Kate. Again, he wasn't ready for what awaited him. Tears streamed down her cheek, her body shook with sobs. Kate's arms were outstretched, inviting him to comfort her. And he did exactly what he was trained not to do – he walked right into them.

CHAPTER TWENTY-FIVE

Kate's nightshirt was soaking wet. The nightmares had increased since the agent's body was discovered behind the barn. Her enemies were too close. Kate knew she was strong, but she didn't think she could hold it together much longer.

Kate lay on her side on the lumpy mattress. In the dark, she reached for the security of the body beside her. She whispered into the cool night air, "I'm so sorry. It's my mind. I can't seem to put what happened to rest."

John rolled onto his side, his fingertips coming to rest on her lips. "Katie, it's totally normal to have these feelings. Even those of us who are trained to deal with situations like this go through the same thing. We've all been through some sort of trauma. But…uh… you need to change out of your pajamas." He cleared his throat. "You're wet."

Out of the corner of her eye, Kate saw John's eyes fixated on her breasts. Looking down, she could see there was very little left to the imagination.

In a husky voice, he asked, "Where do you keep your clothes?"

"In the dresser. Just get me a tee shirt. Second drawer from the top."

John rolled off the side of the bed and headed to the bureau. Her teeth chattered as the sweat on her body mingled with the coolness of the air in the room. John opened her dresser drawer and quickly slammed it shut.

"What's wrong?" Her eyes adjusting to the lack of light, Kate noticed a strange look on his face. "The tee shirts are right there. Just pull one out. I don't care which one." The man remained motionless, staring at the floor. "What *are* you looking at, cowboy?"

"There are red lace panties in your tee-shirt drawer."

Kate smiled. "And you don't have your shirt on," she sassed back. "Just give me the old blue one. I'm freezing, in case you didn't notice. Well, you did notice. Don't stare at my underwear. I forgot I tossed them in there."

John opened the drawer again, grabbed the requested shirt and tossed it to her. She nabbed it as it flew through the air and tried her best to cover up her body. Her nipples peaked, not only from the cold air, but John's direct gaze. The man did really strange things to her libido every time she was near him. And right now, he seemed bothered by something.

"What is it now, cowboy?"

It was clear to Kate through John's body language he was waging war with his emotions. He barked like a drill sergeant. "You going to change that shirt? I've got to get back to my room and get some sleep. I've been up for thirty-six hours." He twisted the doorknob to make his exit.

"No!" Kate pleaded. "Don't leave!" Where had that come from?

Kate sat on the foot of the bed, her shirt still unchanged. She clenched it in her hands. She felt her body flush with heat. Could she really ask him? "Ah, if you could just wait a minute. Turn your back and don't peek. I need to ask you a question."

"Kate, make it quick. I'm wasted. We've got a long day

tomorrow."

"Please, John? Just turn around. It'll only take a minute." She heard him sigh and watched to be sure he'd turned around.

Kate shimmied out of the wet shirt and into the overly large comfortable navy blue tee, not knowing John watched her every move in the dresser's mirror.

Coming back to stand along side of the double bed, he said, "Out with it, Kate. What's so important I can't get back to bed? What's wrong?"

Would he think her request childish? John promptly sat on the edge of the bed next to her and waited.

"I know you'll think I'm very foolish because I've been touting I can take care of myself since I got here…but…"

"But? Geez, would you look at the clock! I gotta get to bed…tonight."

"The dreams, John. They're so real. I'm scared to go back to sleep." She bit her lip and darted a look at the ceiling.

John took her hand in his and knelt on the floor in front of her. "Maybe I can help." She glanced down when she felt his fingers intertwined with her own. "Kate, I've been where you are many times. The memories go away, but not overnight. Right now, your emotions are raw. There's so much happening. Sometimes it helps to have someone nearby. How about I stay until you fall asleep?"

"You'd really do that?" Kate was stunned he understood. And relieved she didn't have to make a fool out of herself by groveling and risk being turned down.

"Yes. Right now, I'd do anything to get some sleep." But John didn't crawl back into bed beside her.

Perplexed, she asked, "What are you doing?"

She leaned over the side of the bed watching him stretch out on the floor. He'd laid a quilt from the rocker under him, one corner bunched up to form a makeshift pillow. He lay flat on his back, staring up at the beamed ceiling. Feelings she hadn't felt before built up inside her upon seeing her protector shirtless. Her eyes followed the trail of light brown hair that circled his navel and traveled lower to the top of his unsnapped jeans. The sight of him lying there had her heart beating rapidly. Her pulse raced. Why were the thoughts she was having becoming stronger each time she looked at him? Kate couldn't fathom how she, in such a brief period of time, became attracted to this man. She'd told Aunt Elizabeth she was done with men… for good. Ty Bennington had seen to that.

John suddenly surprised Kate by bolting up. His green eyes locked onto hers. "What do you think I'm doing? I'm trying to get some rest, if you'd just stop yapping." Even in a room lit only by moonlight, Kate could see the banked desire in his eyes. "Go to sleep." John enunciated the last three words and lay down again, his back to her.

But, Kate was going to have the last word. "You can't possibly sleep on the floor. It's not comfortable."

"All right. I'll sleep in the rocking chair. Will that make you happy?" John was clearly getting more and more frustrated with her.

As he grabbed the quilt from the floor and went to stand, Kate grabbed onto his forearm. The feel of his bare skin on her fingertips sent a tingle up her arm, making its way into her heart. It was all or nothing. "Lay next to me. Please." There. She said it. "I'll never get to sleep if I can't feel you next me. I promise, I'll go right to sleep." Kate patted the bed, issuing the invitation.

"No, Kate…" John pulled away, but Kate read the "yes" in his eyes.

"Come to bed." The invitation came out in a huskier tone than she intended.

The look that passed across his face told her she wouldn't

need to ask him again. She pulled back the sheets and offered him her hand. John readily grasped it, sliding in next to her, pulling her close. She sighed, snuggling into his side, his shoulder now her pillow. The demons would go away as long as John Clinton could be with her every night, Kate thought to herself. She'd never been a dreamer, but as she looked out the window and saw the stars in the sky, she made a wish.

* * *

Kate stood at the kitchen window, watching the golden globe of light break over the horizon. She felt like a caged animal, yearning to be free after six days inside the house. Her normal world, the one she longed to participate in, was outside the dust-streaked window.

Watching Tim and Wade head to the barn for morning chores made her homesick. Her mind wandered to the previous night. John had made a habit of coming to her room to check on her, ever since that first nightmare. Each time she found herself pulling back the bed covers, John readily accepted the invitation.

Most times, they talked quietly in the dark and drifted off to sleep. Other times, he simply held her. Last night, Kate knew from the soft sounds of snoring near her ear it was the first time, in a long time, John drifted into a deep sleep, not that of a catnapping warrior operative.

As Kate watched Tim and Wade bring two horses out for their daily exercise, she thought how different last night was from all of the others. She'd sensed he needed more from her than any other. Snuggling against the length of him, Kate wrapped her arms about his waist and took in his manly scent. He'd listened to her talk her troubles away night after night. Kate decided it was his turn. She reversed the tables and boldly asked about his life in the Agency, thinking silence would surely follow.

John proved her wrong, much to her surprise. Perhaps it was that he now knew the relationship she shared with the Director. But still, he'd caught her off guard and merely listened. He shared intimate details of his solitary life undercover. Pulling her to him, he spoke in a hushed whisper of his former partner, Zoya. As Kate listened, she was surprised she was jealous of a woman who died on a mission in Istanbul. John explained the unclassified parts of the mission, which explained a lot about the men who protected her.

The opening of the office door drew her attention away from the window.

"Hey, Katie." The warm tone in John's voice, coupled with the hint of a smile in his green eyes, undid her. "I thought you'd still be in bed. What's the matter? Couldn't sleep?"

"No." She returned his warm greeting. "My body clock is still not used to sleeping in. I'm out of sync, locked up in this house." Kate poured a cup off coffee from the pot on the stove and offered it to him. John accepted it readily. "I was supposed to be back out with the horses four days ago."

Kate looked yearningly out the window to where she wanted to be and turned back to him. "I can't go on like this, John. You've got to trust me and cut me some slack. Safe house or not. Just assign me an agent."

John sat at the end of the kitchen table and patted the chair next to him. "Sit."

Sit meant talk in Kate's book, so she refilled her mug and did as requested. After much debate and a phone call from Aunt Elizabeth that left him none too happy, John had given her back her gun. Maybe there was room for more negotiations.

"Your aunt's being irrational She wants you back at the compound. But given the possibilities of what could go wrong, we decided it's in your best interest to stay here."

"And so we do what?"

"The team and the Director decided to wait and let the Feds' sting at the farm play out. If all goes as planned, you'll be home soon." John sipped his coffee.

Her stomach pitched. Why wasn't she jumping with joy over the news?

"You don't look happy."

Kate truly wasn't sure how she felt. She plastered a smile on her face and took a sip from her cup, placing it on the table. "I'll be glad to go home. My biggest regret in all of this is the emotional upheaval it caused my mother. And I left the TEAM in charge of the farm's operation. No doubt, chaos reigns as I speak."

John tipped his head, looking questioningly at her. "The TEAM? Who the hell is that? You have a security detail running your farm, don't you?"

Kate laughed. "Well, yes. But the TEAM is a term I lovingly call my four brothers – Thomas, Ethan, Adam and Matthew." She counted them off on her fingertips. "They always teamed up against me when I was young, hence the moniker. Thomas has been CFO of Hallock Farm for years. He's more than likely up to his ears, involved with the Feds in the op there. Thomas has a good head on his shoulders. He won't do anything stupid. But the others… I'm not so sure."

"So what you're telling me is you left some pretty big shoes to fill when you took off. You're quite the equine vet, Katherine Elizabeth Hallock." John reached over and tucked a stray strand of hair over her ear. As she leaned into his touch, his hand pulled away. "Graduated from Cornell at the top of your class, interned with an Olympic champion equestrian. Need I go on?" Kate blushed, embarrassed by his quoting of her resumé. "And you know this because…?" Kate playfully asked.

John leaned back in his chair, carefully watching her. "Because I work for the CIA. It's my job to know everything

I can about the person I protect and defend, once I know her *real* name."

"I would have remained plain old Lizzie O'Brien if my aunt hadn't let my real name slip. I've been fortunate, John. I've been given some great opportunities in my life. Hampton society has its advantages, and disadvantages."

John scanned the kitchen and pointed toward the window, a frown appearing on his face. "This place must seem like a dump compared to what you're used to. If you'd had anywhere else to run to, I'm sure you would have turned tail and had the Director take you out of here after the first couple of days." John sipped his coffee, then said, "Except that there was the fact that you had nowhere else to run to. And you wound up here."

Hearing the dejection in his voice, Kate's heart melted. She rose from her chair and motioned for him to follow her. When John arrived by her side, Kate hooked her arm through the crook of his elbow and walked him to the kitchen window where she'd been standing earlier.

"John Clinton," she stated firmly like a teacher making a student pay attention. She pointed to what lay outside. The barnyard had sprung to life for the day. "You're so totally wrong about this place. Look out there!"

"What about it, Kate? I'm a small man with big dreams. And a job which might never let them come true."

"You listen to me. I've learned a lot here. *This…*"she emphasized as she hugged him to her side, *"this* is what it's all about. Working hard. Building your dreams from the ground up. Making what you truly want from what you have. I'm actually jealous of what you have here, cowboy."

John stared at her in disbelief. "You're kidding, right? You've got millions, and you think *this* is where it's at?"

"I think we make a pretty good team here, Clinton."

John eyed her cautiously. "Somehow I think you're after something. I have a feeling I'm about to be played."

Kate crossed her heart. "Every word I said is the honest to God's truth, cowboy." She stood on her tiptoes and kissed him on the cheek. His eyes smiled back with definite warmth. "But…"

"I knew it!" John slapped his hand on the counter. "You're up to something."

Kate knew she had him and vice-versa. "I'll explain it all to you later, but right now I've got to get back to work. I've got this boss who's a stickler for getting a day's chores done."

Unlocking her arm from John's, she backed away. Instead of walking into the office to tend to her daily office tasks, she bolted out the kitchen door. Kate jumped from the top step of the porch, landed on the soft ground and took off running for the barn – Freedom!

Had Kate been able to read the mind of the man she'd left behind, she'd knew John was left wondering how she'd managed to best him. Again.

CHAPTER TWENTY-SIX

Zoya eyed the entrance to Café Luna. She and Stavros used the small out-of-the-way espresso bar as a meeting place. She'd taken great pains not to be followed when she'd left the studio apartment by hopping on and off the Metro, first at Metro Center and then at Dupont Circle. She then took a cab and a bus to the neighborhood near the cafe. Stavros had left the studio apartment with Demetrie three hours earlier, and she'd yet to hear from him. Zoya's anxiety level ran high since Stavros made the decision to strike out on his own. And now, he was twenty minutes late.

The doorbell jingled, announcing the arrival of a new customer. Relief swept over her upon seeing Stavros make his way towards her in the back corner. He called to the waitress to bring him a cup of espresso and slid into the booth.

"What took so long? I was beginning to think Demetrie was on to us," Zoya said.

"He wanted me to be sure the plans are set for next week. I don't know if he's testing me. He treats me like I'm some sort of moron, Zoya."

"You don't think he knows about what you've planned for tonight?" Zoya stopped her brother from replying as the waitress placed his cup in front of him. The woman refilled Zoya's mug and left, smiling at Stavros.

"No, I don't." He picked up his cup and took a sip.

"Then what took so long?" Zoya grew impatient.

"I decided to follow him after we met up in the park." Zoya's eyebrows arched. "No. Don't give me that look. I made a good decision. The other day, he made me suspicious when he set off in a different direction than the one I thought he would take after we met up."

Zoya looked out the window of the café and viewed the traffic outside. Cars and cabs, as well as the people, moved along rapidly. Due to what her brother just said, she felt the need to be guarded. Demetrie, or any of his contacts, might be watching the café if Stavros had indeed been followed. But she'd begun to trust her brother's instincts as well as she trusted her own.

"You took a big risk. Whatever made you think, given his status in the hierarchy, you could follow him and not be followed in return? For all we know he has his own personal security detail. He's told us his contacts are close. We just don't know where."

Stavros nodded and signaled for their waitress. When the young girl came to their table, he asked for a slice of apple pie and winked at her as she departed. Zoya slapped his hand with the magazine she'd been reading as she'd waited for him to arrive.

"Fool!"

"No, sister. This time I'm no fool. But, we must work quickly."

Puzzled, she sat still and listened. She'd begun their assignment thinking Stavros would slow down the mission. She'd been surprised at his ability to think through problems that surfaced. Add to that, both had grown more suspicious of

Demetrie's involvement in what they were trying to carry out each day that passed.

"Why?" Zoya asked him.

"I followed him to the Russian Embassy over on Wisconsin Avenue. But…"

Zoya didn't let him finish. "The Russian Embassy? Whatever was he doing there? We were warned to be nowhere in the vicinity of any embassies when we left St. Petersburg for fear of being caught on camera." She stopped when her brother's hand closed over hers.

"Listen to me. He showed some sort of papers and passed through the guard post at the gate and was admitted into the compound. I scouted out the area quickly and went to stand across the street, pretending to buy a hot dog from one of the street vendors. As God is my witness, his visit had a purpose, Zoya. I'm just sure of it. You and I must be careful. I was surprised Demetrie came out roughly five minutes later. He looked up and down the street and hailed a cab. I jumped in another, but mine got tangled in rush hour traffic so I lost him. So now what do you think of my suspicions that the man may not be all he said he was?"

Zoya closed her eyes and willed her heart to stop pounding. She opened them to see her brother's eyes staring directly into her own. "I'm not quite sure. I need to take a few minutes to absorb this. My gut tells me not to go back to the apartment. But to do that would be our death sentence. He's too good an operative. He would know we suspect something. Maybe we're wrong, Stavros. I've known Demetrie since I worked with him in Istanbul. He had my back when things went sour at the warehouse. He spent the same time we did in those dirty cells of isolation. I can't believe what's going through my head right now. Are you thinking the same thing?"

"Yes. But, you know I never liked the man. I'm here for the

job I was sent to do. Things aren't adding up. You and I better take great pains to be sure we are together and, if apart, never followed."

"And tonight?"

"We follow the plan, the final diversion to bring everything into place." Stavros finished up the last of the pie on his plate. "Trust me, it will be all right."

Zoya glanced again out the window. She suddenly stiffened. "Right now, I don't think so. Look. By the front door."

Stavros's eyes widened when he recognized one of the trio standing close together. One was the very man in question - Demetrie.

When they started coming to the espresso shop, Zoya chose the back booth for a reason. It had a view of the street and a waiter's door nearby for a hasty exit. Throwing a twenty-dollar bill on the table, she motioned for Stavros to follow. Zoya and her brother wove their way through the questioning looks from the kitchen staff, making their way out the back door.

Venturing to the end of the alley, Zoya peeked around the corner. She could see the reflection of the front door in the window of the store across the busy street. The three men still stood there, deep in conversation.

"They're still there. Come. We'll get around the corner and take the metro. We need to get back. If he's there when we get back, we'll just pretend we've been out sightseeing. Get that camera out. Keep your eyes on anyone who could be watching for us."

Running as if their lives depended on it, the two made it to the metro car just as it readied to take off. They couldn't have timed it more perfectly.

A chill ran down Zoya's spine as she sat in an open seat. Stavros must have sensed her nervousness and touched her trembling hand. "Zoya. I am no fool. It's just you and me now.

We must be wary of anything we say around him and how we respond to his commands. Let's finish the job and go home."

Zoya shook her head in disbelief. For once, she had to admit her brother was dead on. Clean up the operation. But now, there were three bodies on her list instead of two.

CHAPTER TWENTY-SEVEN

"I can't believe it's been two days in a row." Kate stared down at him, propped up on her elbow, her hand rested over his rapidly beating heart. The room was dark due to the impending storm. Thunder rumbled off in the distance. Every time lightning flashed, the room lit up and John could see her as if it was daylight. She was stunning, her auburn hair drawn up in a ponytail, her face freshly cleaned and tan. In those brief moments of light, he read the wistful longing in her eyes. She, like him, wanted what she couldn't have.

"What's been two days?" John was puzzled.

"Since you let go of my reins. Let me outdoors - with my agent, of course." Another flash lit the sky. Pure excitement showed on her face. Two days of tending to the farm and the animals had done Kate's spirit and outlook a world of good.

John gently brushed a stray wisp of hair back behind her ear. "Kate, you really didn't give me much choice. You took off for that barn as if you were headed for the finish line." He laughed, remembering the scene outside the kitchen window, agents running in every direction trying to corner her. Could the lady leap a fence, or what? By the time John realized she was no longer anywhere near the back porch, he'd surrendered.

He had no choice but to do as she requested. Trust her – with an agent to monitor her every move. Wade had been more than happy to volunteer. Even accompanied by a bodyguard, Katherine Hallock could more than take care of herself. Placing his hand over hers, he laughed, "You were running like a prize filly at the Kentucky Derby."

Kate laughed, but then solemnly said, "John, I couldn't take it. My place was with those animals. Surely you know by now who and what I am."

John understood perfectly. Kate was a proud, intelligent and determined woman. She possessed a strength of character and sense of integrity like no other woman he'd ever met. And she was stubborn and demanding. Like someone else he knew. "I know you couldn't, Kate. That's why the Director and I decided it would be best to let you stay within the confines of the farmyard and the training pens - with your gun, of course."

"What am I going to do, John?" Kate drew her body closer, her voice whispered in the dark near his ear.

"You're just going to have to be patient. We explained this all to you. The Feds are—"

Her calloused fingertips touched his lips to silence him as her knee slid up and over his thigh, pinning him to the mattress. "No, you're not following me, cowboy."

John's body hummed. "Kate, we're taking a big chance here. I shouldn't be lying in this bed. Period. I've violated every rule of protocol these past few nights." John swallowed hard as Kate's finger seductively drew a path from his lips, down his chest and circled his navel. His jeans grew tight. "Katie," he growled. "We *can't.*" He bit his lip and groaned as she slid her hand over the bulge in his pants.

A man could only take so much. Oh, to have the memory of one night with Kate. That one spellbinding night that would be with him forever. When he looked into her smoldering dark eyes, John gave into the desire he'd tamped for so long. John wanted her. He needed her. With one swoop, he whisked her up in the air until she straddled him.

"There! Satisfied, now? Can you feel what you do to me?" At that moment, a flash of light and a boom of thunder rang out simultaneously. The room illuminated Kate's silhouette. He picked up her hand and kissed her palm, then placed it over his heart. "Feel what you do to me every time I'm near you."

Kate pulled her hand away and in the semi-darkness, with the lightning flashing more and more frequently, John watched, fascinated, as she slowly slid her tee shirt up and over her head. She pulled the clip from her ponytail and shook out her mane of auburn hair.

"Like what you see, cowboy?" Kate's husky tone only made the blood rush to his groin faster.

John's mouth went dry. He had to touch her. Reaching between her legs, he felt lace. He swallowed hard. "You've got them on." The image of Kate wearing nothing but red lace panties raced through his mind.

"Just for you. But, I don't think I'll need them tonight. Do you?"

Kate lifted one leg, then the other as John slowly slid them off, his hand gliding down her thigh as he released first one leg then the other. He flung the panties to the floor and with his forefinger circled her most sensitive spot. She was wet and slick. And ready.

As Kate arched her back and tossed her mane of long hair over her shoulders, a moan escaped her lips. John couldn't wait to unleash her passion. Her body was bare for him to see in its natural state. She was all he'd fantasized her to be. But John desperately needed to be free of his jeans, feel their bodies skin to skin. Kate surprised him by taking control. She positioned herself more comfortably on his lap.

"Cowboy, I can't take this ride all by myself." Kate leaned down to whisper in his ear. She started to ride the ridge of his jeans.

John trailed his wet fingertips up through the triangle of her feminine hair. In the semi-darkness, Kate's eyes darkened with desire.

"You're the most beautiful thing I've ever seen, Katie."

Kate sat up and placed her hands on his shoulders. She looked down at him. "Then don't stop, cowboy."

John squeezed her nipples. Her breasts were perfection. Hell, her whole body was just as he'd imagined. Rising up, John brought her closer to his mouth, licking first one breast then the other. He flicked his tongue around her pert, pink nipple and then gave the other equal treatment.

Kate groaned. "More." John obliged her.

Suddenly he found himself flat on his back pinned to the mattress. John understood her meaning all too well. She meant business and she wanted him as much as he wanted her. He heard the snap of his jeans and the sound of his zipper being opened. He groaned, coming to the realization their loving would be fast and quick.

John gritted his teeth. "Slide my jeans off, honey. I need you to touch me." Kate did as he asked. At the touch of her warm hand sliding up and down the length of him, John's hips bucked off the bed.

"Katie, honey. I'm not going to last. I need to be inside…"

A loud knock pounded on the door. "Boss! Boss!" Tim was yelling at the top of his lungs from the other side. "Boss, you in there?"

This couldn't be happening now. Not again!

"What is it?" John ground out. He shoved Kate to the side and rolled off the bed. He reached around in the dark for his pants, hopping into them one leg at a time. In a vexed voice, he called out, "This better be good!" *Because you're interrupting me in the middle of the best sex I'll ever have.*

"There's a fire!" John heard clothes rustling behind him. Kate was getting dressed as fast as she could.

John flung open the door, not caring that Tim could see into the room. "Where? Who? What?" he barked out.

Tim stood in the hall, silent, eyeing his shirtless boss.

"Tim! Where's the fire?" John punched his agent in the shoulder to get his attention.

"The training barn. Jake just spotted it. Chuck and Wade are in the security room checking the tapes. Come on!"

John took off behind Tim, but stopped abruptly. "Wait!" There was one thing he had to do. Tim turned and looked at him in disbelief. John ran back into the bedroom only to collide with Kate who was running out.

"Oh, no. You're not going anywhere." John pushed her back through the doorway. "Get back in the room and take that gun out of the nightstand. Stay right here. You wait until I give the all clear. Do you read me?"

"You're going to need help with the horses."

"For once in your life, Katherine Elizabeth, do as you're told!"

John left Kate standing in the doorway as he ran to catch up with his partner. But he had a sneaking suspicion, as he ran down the stairs two at a time, the woman wouldn't stay put. When Kate went to make her move to help, John prayed she'd take the damn gun with her. If she was as good a shot as she claimed to be, maybe the damn mission would end that night!

CHAPTER TWENTY-EIGHT

Do this. Don't do that. If John Clinton thought she was going to sit on her rear while the barn burned to the ground around the animals she'd lovingly cared for, he was sorely mistaken. Not knowing what was at stake in regards to the horses reacting to the fire, he would need his head vet to care for them. Kate's mind whirled with the possibilities of what could be happening. The horses could be burned or even worse, dead. Kate dealt with the fallout of barn fires when she interned during college, and the sights and sounds were gruesome. Putting down an animal was the worse thing she'd ever done, and to this day she remembered each one. Twiddling her thumbs would accomplish nothing. No, she was most certainly not going to stay put.

Kate tugged on her riding boots and rose to look out the window. She detected the faint orange glow of the fire off in the distance.

Kate yanked open the drawer of the oak nightstand and drew out the semi-automatic pistol. Before she slid it in the back of her pants, she checked the magazine. Loaded. Now, all she had to do was make her way out without being noticed. From her vantage point, she scanned the perimeter of the yard surrounding the house guarded by agents. She noted a slight opening by the hedge. If she could make it to the porch stairs undetected and into the garden, there was a path that would lead her down to the side of the large barn and where she wanted to be.

Treading cautiously down the back staircase, she reached the last step by the kitchen and paused. Peeking around the corner, Kate double-checked to be sure no one was still in the kitchen, given the circumstances. The room was empty.

She flicked off the light and made her way to the window. Listening for signs of life on the first floor and hearing nothing, Kate slowly opened the wooden screen door that led out to the porch. Ducking below the railing, she tip-toed down the side stairs, using the rose hedge as her shield. Her eyes darted in every direction, seeking the best way to get across to the muddy path. If she could just make it down the side of that barn, she'd be in the vicinity of the training barn that was thoroughly engulfed in flames.

With time of the essence, she stepped out from her position only to be dragged down from behind against a bulky body. A large, gloved hand covered her mouth. She froze.

"Kate! It's me." A familiar voice murmured in her ear.

Kate sighed in relief.

"I'll let go as long as you stay silent. Don't talk. Just nod."

Kate did as instructed, but didn't remain silent. In a hushed tone, she rounded on the man and countered, "What the hell are you doing here? Aren't you supposed to be downstairs with Chuck?"

Wade's eyes darted around in all directions as he spoke to her. "The boss knew you'd head for the burning barn no matter what he said. So, I'm assigned to get you there in one piece."

Kate went to stand and was jerked down to ground level.

"Jesus, Kate." Wade's voice was barely a whisper. "We don't

know if anyone's infiltrated the yard. This hedge is the only shield we have at the moment."

Kate hunkered down. "What do we do now?"

"I told the agents over to our left to cover us. Once we're at the end of the barn, there's open territory. Stay close. I'll get you to those horses. Ready?"

The sweat on Kate's brow wasn't just from the heat of the night but from the adrenaline rushing through her. "I'm right behind you."

"On three."

Wade counted out the numbers on the fingers of his left hand, pushed her behind him and moved forward. Wade turned to give her thumbs up. Kate signaled back with the appropriate response. She could see the surprised look hidden under the dark face paint he wore.

Their footing was precarious at times, but it didn't take long to travel the path and arrive at the back end of the barn. Wade put his arm over Kate's chest, pushing her back against the barn wall. An inferno raged before them. Kate felt the heat burn her cheeks from the flames that shot into the night sky.

Kate signaled to move farther out, but Wade shook his head, pointing to the open area. The wide expanse leading up to the training barn was filled with men running in every direction with hoses. Two agents struggled to bring one horse from the barn, but it reared up. Dark Shadow. Kate's vet eye immediately spotted the horse was injured as it whinnied in pain. It pained Kate greatly not to be allowed to see to its comfort and care.

As smoke filled the clearing and drifted over them, it became more difficult to clearly make out who moved about. Kate drew a bandana from her pocket and covered her nose. Kate noticed that Wade finally was carrying on a conversation and breaking his silence with the team. She prayed John was giving directions for what to do from that point on. Wade's brow furrowed.

"What's wrong?" Kate nudged her bodyguard with her shoulder, but he didn't move, just eyed the area once more as if he was looking for something or someone.

"John said not to venture any farther. Said to tell you the horses need medical attention. Dark Shadow has the worst wound. The men will bring the horses to us. The training barn has to be seen by CSU. I know that's not what you wanted to hear, but we have to wait here. Where's your vet bag?"

Kate pointed inside the barn they'd been using as a shield. "There are minor supplies in the bag. And another I can use that contains some meds. I certainly didn't come prepared for major injuries."

Wade and Kate turned to look and take in the scene in front of them, hearing more screams and commands coming from John and his men. Kate shook her head. It was a waste of precious time. No one had to tell her the barn was a total loss. But the horses? She needed to assess them ASAP.

She pulled her bandana away from her nose and sniffed. "Do you smell that?" A pungent aroma drifted in the night air.

Wade nodded. "Something with a kerosene base. Smells strong, too. As if someone just dumped some nearby. You wait here. I'm going to check out the back of the barn before I let you go in and get the bag."

Kate made a move to follow, but the look Wade sent her way had her backing up against the barn wall. Wade's disappearance around the corner left Kate with an uneasy feeling. For security, she drew her gun from her jeans. The hair rose on the back of her neck and chills ran down her spine as the minutes ticked by and Wade didn't return. It shouldn't have taken this long to check over the barn. Kate readied her gun and took up a defensive stance. Wade was taking too long and from Wade's message, John's team should have started bringing the horses for her to take a look at. Her eyes searched the smoky dark terrain in front of her, but she saw only outlines of people moving about.

She decided she had no recourse but to look for Wade. With the butt of her gun, Kate dug an "X" on the sidewall of the barn, marking where she'd been. Aunt Elizabeth trained her well. Praying John's men were not far behind, Kate peered around the corner, her gun drawn, held firmly with both hands. Looking in all possible directions in the dimly lit building and still not seeing Wade, she cautiously paused near the opening. The whiff of kerosene she and Wade smelled earlier was definitely stronger now as she moved inside.

However, she wasn't prepared for what she saw. Kate stopped, her eyes dropping to a pair of combat boots lying twisted on the floor. Wade lay unconscious, blood gushing from a cut on his temple.

Her guard momentarily down, she was taken by surprise when an arm snaked out of the darkness and locked around her neck. Kate was immobilized. She struggled, but the more she tried to release her assailant's grip, the tighter he tugged on her windpipe. At that moment, her captor had the upper hand. With one swift move, whoever it was yanked her farther down the barn's corridor. She lost her footing, as well as the firm grip on the pistol in her hand, when she stumbled. The gun clattered to the floor, much to Kate's dismay.

When her gun hit the cement, the grip around her neck loosened. Stunned at the turn of events, Kate barely could speak. She needed answers, but wondered if she would get them.

In a raspy voice, she asked, "Who are you?" She wrenched her head from side to side, trying to identify her assailant. She drew in a deep breath, feeling faint. "What do you want?"

"Don't make a move, Miss O'Brien!" Kate was surprised by

the hint of a Russian accent in the deep male voice hissing in her ear as he released the grip he had on her. However, the barrel of a gun still dug into her lower back. "Go where I tell you. Make one sound and I'll put a bullet through that agent's head back there. Right now, he's knocked out cold. My job is to take care of you first. Then, I'll come back and finish him if you don't cooperate. Move! You hear me?"

All Kate could do was bob her head up and down. She had to follow the man's instructions and try to get as much information from him as she could. Perhaps he would slip with intel.

"Okay. I'll do what you want. Just leave him alone," Kate's replied as a sharp pain shot down her shoulder and arm. With her senses on high alert, she smelled dust, grime and kerosene. Her captor was taller than she was. Kate approximated by six inches in that the top of her head came to rest just under his chin. Had Ty sent him? Or the Savorskis? How had the agents manning the secure room missed seeing him? There were so many cameras within the barn. Kate needed to think and react with speed. And she had to develop a plan to warn the others without getting herself and Wade killed in the process.

She wished she could somehow see his face as he shoved her. The position of his grip and the gun in her back steered her every move. He had her angled so she couldn't even throw an elbow to his gut.

"We're going to make for that ladder and hide in the loft until I get the signal. Then, you come with us."

He was kidnapping her! Her heart pounded in her ears, the adrenaline already coursing through her body on overload. Kate's first instinct was to do exactly what he told her to. If this man really worked for the Russian mob, she knew what would happen once the ransom was paid. She was a dead woman. The mob didn't stand on principles; they only did for themselves and their kind.

Bypassing empty stalls, they came to the center of the barn. The open area gave her the only chance to make a move. She had one chance and she was going to take it. Shifting her weight, she stepped back hard, down on the top of her assailant's foot. The pain that ensued had the man bending his elbow, bringing his arm and the gun up near Kate's face. Kate took her opportunity and bit him. Hard. She sank her teeth into his wrist, tasting fabric, skin and blood.

"Bitch!" he cried out, his voice echoing down the dark chamber.

Kate's elusive move was enough to allow her to turn to face her attacker. A mask over his face hid his identity. But the man, even with his injury, was fast. He raised his hand with the gun to strike her. Kate flinched, protecting her face with her hands.

"You little bitch! I told you if you did anything …"

Kate scanned the area for something to use as a weapon. She'd heard her gun skip across the cement. It had to be close by.

"What?" Kate spat back. She forged on, fueled from the anger within. "You'll kill me? Go right ahead. Every agent remotely near here will be on you in seconds." She didn't know where she got the courage to dare him, but she had him looking about. Even though his face was hidden from view, he looked temporarily disoriented. "Take your best shot. It's what your boss wants anyway, isn't it? Do away with the daughter so he'll have more leverage with the father?"

Her captor stood with his gun aimed at her heart, his chest heaving. "What are you talking about? I will drop you where you stand if you don't do what I tell you to." His demand was terse.

He was playing with her in his denial of why he was after her. She needed a stall tactic. Keep him talking. "You know exactly what I'm talking about."

"Give me your gun."

"I don't have my gun. It's on the floor over there." Kate pointed to the hay pile. "I dropped it when you grabbed me." She raised her hands, devoid of any gun. "See? No gun."

Unfortunately, height had its advantage when he suddenly reached for her. Successfully grasping her ponytail in his fist, the stranger wrenched her head so that she could see his dark eyes. Pain shot through her forehead.

"You've a gun in your boot," he snarled. Mumbling in Russian under his breath, he then said in English, "You placed it there this morning when you checked the horses."

Kate stood, stunned at his revelation. Only someone in the barn would have known she'd snuck the derringer into her boot. "You'll have to take it, Einstein, because, I'm not…"

Kate lay sprawled on the cement floor before she knew what hit her. She tasted blood at the corner of her mouth. Dazed, she looked into the eyes of her captor, the only part of his face she could see. They were the wild eyes of someone with a score to settle. She felt him draw the derringer from its hiding place.

"Now, get up!" When she didn't move, he kicked Kate in her ribs as she lay on the cold concrete. A piercing pain shot up her side. "We go up that ladder. Get up off the floor!"

Struggling to roll to her side and rise, she spied a shadowy movement farther down the corridor. Kate wasn't going to give in to whoever this man was or what he wanted from her. Every muscle ached as she slowly rose to her feet. He moved forward.

"Wait!" Kate yelled out. "I'm coming. Just give me a moment to catch my breath."

"Nyet. No time." The man almost ripped her arm out of its socket as he dragged her to the ladder that led to the hayloft. "You come now!" He shoved her forward. "You go, Lizzie O'Brien. Up. Quick!"

Pain exploded in her ribcage as she tried to raise her arm to climb the ladder. As she placed her boot on the first rung, a voice rang out, "Kate? Kate? Are you in here?"

She froze. If she could just bring her leg up with enough force she could catch her captor off-guard and divert his attention. But, her legs felt like jelly. As she looked over her shoulder, she watched in horror as the man raised his gun in the direction of the voices coming towards them. John and Jake stood squarely in range of the gunman's aim. But John was at a disadvantage, blinded by the darkness of the corridor, while the gunman could see John's silhouette clearly from the spotlights that had been installed out by the door's opening. There was only one tactic to take.

"Gun! Gun!" Kate screamed out. She lunged, pushing the stranger off-balance. The man's gun flew across the cement. Even in the darkness of the stable, Kate saw its shiny barrel. Her pain aside, she crouched and rolled across the cold floor, while she alerted John and his men. But she wasn't fast enough.

The heel of the man's boot crashed down on her wrist. "You're just another stupid—"

Two shots rang out in rapid succession. The Russian dropped to the floor by her side, eyes wide open, one bullet through his temple and the other lodged dead center in his chest.

"Katie!"

"Liz!"

"Miss Hallock?"

Dazed, Kate looked up from the floor to see four men hovering over her. It was over, but she couldn't move. John knelt by her side, his hands gently roaming her body to assess the damage done by the intruder. She grimaced and cried out when he touched her ribcage.

"Kate, we're going to patch you up real quick, okay?" John's voice was soft and soothing.

Kate wished she could reach up and wipe away the concern she saw on his face. He was there with her. Alive. That was all that mattered.

She winced as she slowly got up from the floor. "I'm okay. Really." She tried to make a joke. "Didn't even need my gun." She tried to smile up at John, but burst into tears instead. "Where's Wade? How bad is he?"

"Doc's tending to him. Knocked out. He's got a bit of a bad gash on the back of his head. He'll need a few stitches." Tim was standing beside John, also with a worried look on his face.

John looked over to his agent. "Tim, get the medic. We'll bring Kate up to the house." John lifted her gently into his arms as if she was a broken doll. She felt like one. Kate snuggled into the warmth of his body. "Katie, we'll have the doc take a good look at you."

Kate had nothing left in her. She began to shake and tremble. "John…" Kate stammered. "Who?"

"Shush, honey. We're going to figure this all out."

As John carried her to the door of the barn, Kate could smell the acrid smell of the remainder of the barn fire. Jake met them at the doorway.

"Jake, be sure no one touches that son of a bitch. Get the Director on the phone. As soon as I've tended to Kate, I'll be back. Tape off the crime scene. Start finding out what you can. Run his fingerprints through the database search on Interpol. And make sure no one lights a match. There's kerosene all over."

Moving out the barn door and down the side path, John kissed the top of Kate's head. "Don't worry. *Nothing* like this is *ever* going to happen again. I'm going to kill the son of a bitch who set out to get you."

CHAPTER TWENTY-NINE

It took longer than expected for the Quantico medic to bandage up Kate's wounds. The doctor had grown frustrated that John wouldn't leave Kate's side, interfering on more than one occasion to assess her injuries for himself. The more John took in of the beating she'd taken, the better he felt about his team taking out the unknown suspect. When he added the lengthy conversation with the Director regarding Kate's condition and the time it took to relay the events that played out, John was impatient to hurry back to the scene of two crimes: the arson and his unidentified dead body.

As he approached the front entrance of the barn, the spiteful edge in Jake's voice could be heard clearly echoing throughout the barn, taking him by surprise.

"Can you believe this? The son of a bitch deserved it. Now we've got to find out how he got here." Not only was Jake angry, but the man's voice brought John back to a year ago. Jake sounded as if he were in shock. What the hell was that all about?

Eyeing the group of agents gathered around the body, John quickened his pace. Jake knelt over the man and stripped a pair of standard issued blue forensic gloves from his hands.

Wade, now fully conscious and seemingly alert, assisted Jake. He placed the dead man's ski mask in an evidence bag. As John drew closer, he watched Wade shake his head in disbelief. "I don't know about you, but I want answers. The damn man's risen from the dead!"

There was silence all around as each man on John's team stepped in for a closer look.

"If I'd known who it was, I'd have put more rounds into him," Tim replied, staring down at the dead body.

John pushed through the circle of agents to see for himself what had his men disturbed, but Jake stood in his way. John reached out and touched Jake's shoulder.

Jake rounded on him. "What?"

"Get me up to speed. What's all the commotion about?"

"We've got one hell of a mess here, boss."

John looked about to see his agents waiting for a response. "What are you talking about? I left you running a check with Interpol. You should have something by now. I've been gone long enough."

"We don't need Interpol, Chief," Tim said.

A sense of dread crept over John as he saw the sober faces. He looked down onto the blood-soaked concrete and did a double-take. He stumbled backwards at the shock of who he saw lying in a pool of blood on the floor. Knowing full well the identity of the man who had been shot dead, John stood speechless. He crouched down to get a better look and shook his head in denial.

"What the hell's going on here, boss?" Jake asked.

John was just as stunned as his men who, if he was correct, were back in the throes of what went down in Istanbul. Their pasts had come full-circle.

Wade held the side of his head, glaring down at John. "When we were debriefed, didn't the Director tell us he was shot dead during our rescue operation?"

John rose as Wade walked to where John stood by the body, his hands on his hips.

Every man standing at John's side had shared in the horrific torture of captivity. The man lying dead on the ground was evidence their past was not behind them. The Director had a lot to answer for.

John took a deep breath to steady the feeling of anger he felt so that he could deal with the crisis at hand. He had to set an example and keep his men calm, given what had just happened so that they could do their jobs without mental distractions. He radioed instructions to the Ops team. Turning to his crew, he said, "Has the barn been checked for any trace of an accomplice?"

Tim nodded. "We went over it with a fine toothed comb. No sign of anyone else. Why?"

"Kate insists the man said his friends were here."

A cold feeling of dread had passed over John. His gut now told him Kate had stumbled into a trap meant for him. He couldn't shake the feeling there was more. Stavros Stalinski was a sharpshooter, but an underling. What had he been doing trying to get to John by himself? No, there had to be others. And, more alarming, why, again, wasn't John warned of an intruder? Bile rose in his throat as he took in the sight before him. John stared into the blank, lifeless eyes of the man who'd beat him to within an inch of his life. John shivered as his gut told him the possibility that Zoya might be near as well.

* * *

Upon seeing the Eagle emerge from the Black Hawk helicopter an hour ago, accompanied by members of her staff, John breathed a small sigh of relief. But he was surprised to see Sam Tanner along for the ride. He naturally assumed the man was overseeing the Feds' sting in the Hamptons. However, due to the serious issues that had arisen at Clinton Stables, it made perfect sense Sam be called in. He'd been on board the operation in Istanbul from its planning stages to its failed implementation. And for now, John reasoned Sam was the perfect man to bring calm and rational thought to his ops team and, above all, keep the Director focused. She'd let her guard down during his call the previous night, again trying to insist that Kate be brought to the compound. John had heard a muffled conversation between her and Sam. It was then she announced she was headed for his farm with her own team. During the past twelve hours, John had plenty of hours to meditate on whether or not he'd have his job when the mission was done.

Jake and Tim stood next to him, leaning over a map on the table, deeply engrossed in studying the pattern of the recent incidents boldly circled in red. John didn't need to take a survey. Everyone, the pros that they are, were on edge, knowing the perpetrators were getting closer to base camp.

"Stavros was dead, Madam Director. You said so yourself. It was a confirmed kill. Zoya, as well." John sat opposite his boss, his eyes locking on hers.

Elizabeth sat at the head of the table, a bit flustered as far as John could tell. He spied her pulling out one classified file after another from her briefcase. "Yes, John. The President and I were shown *pictures* as evidence of his demise when we freed you and your men. Zoya, also. I just can't believe that we all were played."

John tried his best to hold his tongue. He counted to five and said, "With all due respect, Madam Director. What explanation did the NSA give you when you contacted them earlier?"

Elizabeth looked up and placed her glasses on the top of her head. A mix of emotions played across her wrinkled brow. She shuffled through several files and, finding the one she'd been searching for, pulled out what looked like to John at a distance, blurred photographs.

"I've been on the phone with every possible agency since you phoned. You know it hasn't been easy for me to access Istanbul information. I made a few enemies in Washington by the way I handled the incident. That file was sealed and locked away, but I managed to get a hold of these last night from a friend who thought I should see them." Elizabeth laid out the two eight by ten pictures on the table. "Look at them very, very carefully."

John, Tim and Jake picked up the photos and passed the pictures back and forth. John expected to view the autopsy photos of Zoya and Stavros. Instead, John's eyes saw the photos taken at the border patrol crossing in Canada.

"Last night, my contact in Homeland uncovered video footage of Zoya and Stavros entering the States. He made me the photos when he recognized her. See the time stamp? He was up all night diving into the archives of recent DC photos and stumbled across a meeting with an unknown contact at Mount Vernon several weeks after that date."

John held onto the Mount Vernon photo longer than he should have. The image of Zoya was crystal clear. His heart pounded in his chest as memories and images came rushing back. Yale. Her decision to return to her native Russia. And the woman's sudden appearance as an agent on the stage in Istanbul, followed by her ultimate deceit.

"The contact in D.C." John pointed to the face in the photo. "Have we run any facial recognition?"

Sam spoke up. "That photo was only discovered this morning. However, all within our inner circle are now operating in classified mode. We hope to know by tomorrow at the latest if he's in the system."

"For what it's worth, I've got to believe there's a record somewhere. He's got to show up on the Interpol database." John was restless, disgusted. Full of anger that he'd placed Kate in the middle of God knows what. And here they'd all been thinking of a simple operation of keeping her safe until the mob in the Hamptons could be contained. The clock was ticking. Zoya, if alive, and John's gut told him she was, was closing in: on him, his team and most of all his beloved Kate. Zoya was a ruthless individual and he surmised at this point, full of revenge. Nothing would stand in her way to take him or anyone surrounding him down. Hell, if she and her operatives made her move now, she'd have full aim at the Agency's elite ops team and both the Director and number two man in her sights.

John caught Sam eyeing Elizabeth as if there was a hidden signal between the two.

Elizabeth spoke calmly to the crowded room. "People. You all now know why Kate was brought here. With my niece inadvertently involved, we have to have a solid plan to protect her and once again, bring down one or more of the world's most dangerous operatives." Her eyes pierced John's. "I ask you all to trust me. Katherine can handle what comes her way. Also, I can assure you as we speak, agents are flushing out known neighborhoods where the three had frequented."

John saw his men shaking their heads in disbelief. He didn't blame them. He felt sucker-punched. He was reeling in disbelief. He'd lived the past year thinking the horrors of what he'd been enforced to endure were behind him. With therapy, life had returned to some form of normalcy, especially with the assignment to Operation Hide and Seek.

John tapped the map and motioned for the members of his team to circle around the table. "Before you start issuing orders, Madam Director, I believe we have a major problem.

There are several of us who are convinced there's a breach in security. Our monitor tapes were convincingly doctored. But what boggles my mind is the speed at which the tapes were spliced and changed."

Everyone at the table looked their counterparts up and down. John would feel the wariness setting in, but all the men stood stoic, waiting for directions.

The Director tapped her pencil on the pad of paper in front of her. "I hand picked every man on your team myself, John." She turned to Sam. "You've been awfully quiet. I've noticed you've been taking copious notes. What do you think?"

Leafing through his legal pad, Sam looked up, his eyes circling the table. "First, let me point out that the kinds of diversions set up by Zoya and Stavros certainly made it possible for us to think the Russian mob had found Kate. All the diversions were well-paced and set to keep everyone off-balance and focused on Kate, not John and his team. I am one hundred percent certain Zoya had no idea why Kate was here. But now, with Stavros dead, we need to be prepared that she and her contact will make their final move. Once she finds out her brother is dead, she'll go all in. She'll be a maniac. That could work to our advantage. She'll get sloppy. But…"

"But?" John saw a look he'd never seen on the man's face before.

With his pen, Sam drew a large box at the bottom of the pad of paper as if to emphasize an idea. "Well, John, I'm bothered that if she's working within a cell here in D.C., perhaps they've recruited more people. Their location is a big question in my mind. I believe we've covered ourselves here to handle what comes down. But my biggest concern is the possible infiltration not just here, but within the Agency."

John watched the Director's head snap up.

Sam swiveled to look in Elizabeth's direction. "I suspect

we've got a double agent among us, Madam Director."

"And what do you propose? Anyone?" Elizabeth looked over her glasses at the men around her and locked eyes with the leader of Operation Hide and Seek.

John knew it fell on his shoulders to make the final move to end his team's mission. To flush out the one woman who deserved to be lying on the cold concrete floor alongside her brother.

"I have a plan." All heads turned towards John. "But this time, *you* have to trust *me*, Director. And you're going to have to trust Kate. I can only pull it off with her working with us."

Elizabeth's eyebrows shot up. John could tell that disapproval was on the tip of her tongue, but Sam laid a hand on hers.

Sam shoved the map in his direction saying, "Keep us informed every step of the way. I trust you to call the right shots. Isn't that so, Madam Director?"

The Director nodded, but added, "You owe me, John Clinton. Don't you ever forget what we discussed on D deck."

John folded up the map and rose to leave, knowing he had a lot to do. "Yes, ma'am. I made you a promise and I fully intend to keep it. The plan will be on your desk by morning. If you'll excuse us, my team and I have work to do."

The panel leading into the security room slid open and all heads turned to the doorway. Wade walked in, his face pale as if he'd seen a ghost.

John's heart plummeted. He'd been through hell and back on missions in foreign lands, but he seemed more invested emotionally in this case than in any other.

"Director?" Wade asked as if he was wary of her answer. "We have another issue."

John saw Elizabeth eye Sam. He braced for what could be worse than what they'd experienced over the last several hours.

Wade cleared his throat and stood tall. "We were making

rounds and checked in on Kate. She's not in her room. We checked the whole house, the grounds around the perimeter of the house, too."

Oh no, John thought. The accomplice. He looked to the Director for guidance but she was leaning on Sam for support.

"Kate's missing."

CHAPTER THIRTY

Kate knew it was only a matter of time before her disappearance would be discovered. Too many agents prowled the grounds for her to go unnoticed for long. Battered and bruised emotionally and physically, Kate's mind had demanded a quiet place to think. Making her way into the small barn off to the side of the house, she spied a hay mound on the floor behind the first stall door. She grimaced in agony as she lowered herself onto the pile. Leaning back against the jagged barn siding, Kate rested her wounded right arm in her lap. She closed her eyes and let the tears she'd held back flow like a river down her cheeks.

Tonight had showed her what she'd run from originally seemed like a walk in the park. When compared to the issues she'd faced at the safe house during the last six weeks, she couldn't be angry with anyone involved. She'd come to the right place at the wrong time. Now embroiled in John's web of international espionage, she shook her head in denial of the scale of events.

Kate didn't want John to be angry, although he was. She'd heard him talking to her aunt on the phone. How could his team, given their intelligence, know the diversions set were not that of Ty's doing? There were too many parallels.

Sniffling, Kate took a deep cleansing breath. She wiped the tears onto the sleeve of her shirt. As she looked around, she'd known she'd come to one very important decision. No way was she returning home until Ty and her father's business was dealt with once and for all. And she had to see for herself that her aunt and John came out on the right side of the Russians who'd been after them. No one could force her to do otherwise.

Trying to turn toward the window to take in the peaceful, starry sky, pain shot down her right shoulder and into her arm. Kate closed her eyes, willing the ache away. Her thoughts drifted to the gift Aunt Elizabeth bestowed upon her. She was in awe of the woman's generosity and still shocked at the role she was to take on come her thirtieth birthday.

The question that popped into her mind over and over surprised her, given all that she had put into Hallock Farm since her graduation from vet school. Did she really *want* to be CEO? What would Aunt Elizabeth think if Kate told her there was a possibility she didn't want that life in Hampton Beach any longer?

Lying in bed night after night with John's arm wrapped securely around her, Kate knew Clinton Stables had become more of a home to her than her prestigious life in the glorious Hamptons. But Kate wanted the man beside her to come with it. And John's life didn't allow for her to have a place beside him.

Ty Bennington was history. The feelings she'd had for the man she thought she'd loved with every fiber of her being disappeared the day she walked down the staircase and into her father's study. How was that possible? How does someone love a man so fervently one day, then be done with him the next, never wanting to look back? Ty hadn't entered her thoughts since she'd arrived at the compound in DC, romantically or otherwise.

Seven weeks ago, Kate didn't have a care in the world, not a worry in sight. She'd achieved the career she so longed for by working in the family business. The wedding to her perfect man was to be the society event of the summer.

On closer examination, given time to think as she worked these past few weeks, she'd been in denial of her true feelings. Kate realized she'd been on the run from Ty and had begun to turn away emotionally since the onset of summer.

The better part of the last month they'd been together, they'd barely been in each other's company. When she questioned him on why he didn't actively participate in their wedding plans, he had an excuse - for everything. Hell, she'd gone to three engagement parties by *herself*. While her mother and Mrs. Bennington had been beside themselves, Kate had done her duty and made the appropriate excuses for her fiancé, as one does in Hampton society.

Putting her thoughts of Hampton Beach behind her temporarily, she concentrated on her mixed emotions about remaining at the farmhouse. Kate no longer felt the safety and security it offered. She couldn't fault the men who were sworn to protect her. She felt trapped between her own need to answer the call of family duty and the happiness she so desperately wanted – with the man she could never have. John Clinton had a different call to his country.

Aunt Elizabeth's arrival worsened Kate's emotional state. One look at her aunt and the dam burst. The women hugged each other. Kate tried to apologize for what had gone wrong. Had Kate known what was in store for her when she'd run that fateful day, she would have stayed behind and taken what her father and his cronies had to dish out. One phone call to her aunt would have sufficed. With her brothers' help, and her aunt's contacts, they'd have handled her father's sordid business dealings by bringing in the Feds and seeing that the Savorskis were somehow caught dealing illegally with the farm's business.

But had she not flown the coop to Arlington, John Clinton wouldn't have entered her life. The image of the tall, handsome man flashed through her mind. She'd spoken the truth to him that night out at the paddock. She envied everything he had at Clinton Stables…and more. Here she was, seven weeks from a broken engagement and she couldn't get enough of him. She craved every minute spent with this proud man, knowing she'd have to walk away when his job was over. Whenever John praised what she'd done at the stables, she basked in his glowing words, knowing there would never be another person who would appreciate and accept her for who she was. He'd let her find herself and discover who she was truly meant to be.

Moving slowly to sit on the edge of the hay bale, Kate allowed a wave of dizziness to abate. She shook her head to clear her muddled mind from the side effects of the painkillers the medic had given her.

The sound of boots stepping on pavement caught her by surprise. No one called out. What if her assailant was telling the truth? What if he did have an accomplice who'd managed to wait in some secluded area to pick up the pieces should he fail in his mission to capture her? She held her breath, listening as the footsteps of the intruder came closer.

Even though she'd been looking for peace and quiet, Kate came prepared. A sense of urgency empowered her to reach for the pistol lying at her right side. She picked it up, her arm still shaking from her injuries.

The footsteps halted just outside the stall door. Kate raised the gun and cocked it.

Before Kate could counter the unsteadiness of her hand, mixed with the effects of the pain meds, the gun accidentally fired. The bullet ricocheted off the hinge of the door and splintered the top of the wood railing.

"Jesus, Kate!" It was John. "Put that gun down, I'm coming in. You okay in there?"

"I think so." Kate's voice slurred as the room began to spin.

Two sea green eyes locked on hers as John knelt beside the bale, a frown deepening across his brow. "Katie, what's going on? You scared the hell out of all of us. Your aunt included. We've been searching this farm for a half an hour. What are you doing hiding in here? You need to be in bed. The doctor told you to rest."

Kate stood up, but winced and clutched her ribs. "You don't understand. None of you do. I need to go home, John. I can't stay here anymore. I *have* to go home! Tonight!"

John rushed to support her as she stumbled. "Kate, you know you can't go. It's too dangerous."

The floodgates gave way. Kate sobbed and held her aching side as John supported her, nudging her to the barn door. Her knees buckled, but she was saved from hitting the hard floor as John scooped her up into his powerful arms. She mumbled incoherently as he kissed her brow and took her back to the farmhouse. How was it that she felt more at home at Clinton Stables, in his arms, than she would ever feel again at her very own Hallock Farm?

CHAPTER THIRTY-ONE

"You better brew up some more coffee, Tim," Wade called out from where he sat at the kitchen table.

Tim was putting the roast into the oven and stopped, placing the pan on the kitchen counter. He turned to look at the team assembled. "You're right. It feels like they've been going at it forever, and it doesn't seem to be letting up. From the sounds of things, the Director doesn't sound happy."

John's men weren't used to sitting in the kitchen. Neither were John and Sam. But that's where Elizabeth told them to stay when Kate demanded to speak with her aunt. Alone.

John looked at Sam, who sat at the table, sipping the last remnants of the coffee in his mug. John had known the man for over ten years, and yet, there was a mysterious side to him that always intrigued him as an agent. "What do you think they're talking about, Sam? The Director wasn't pleased when Kate just took off. And from reading her body language, I'd venture a guess she didn't like being put on the spot by Kate."

Sam placed his cup down and tipped his chair back. "I don't need to tell you boys that Katie's got a mind of her own. I think you knew that from the second she set foot here. But I know her. She's not leaving that office until the Director tells her what's going on at home and how we're going to get out of the situation here. She's scared, but she won't show it. But, she's also angry. I've seen that look before."

John looked at the man who seemed unnerved by everything happening about them. "What look?"

"The one that says Katie's cooked up something none of us, including the Director, is going to like. Why do you think she demanded to see Elizabeth alone? Yes, sir. I've got twenty dollars in my pocket that says that Kate's trying to convince Elizabeth *she* can help flush out Zoya." The mere thought of Kate remotely participating in their operation made John's stomach lurch. "Katie's emotions are fried. She came here looking for a way to sort things out. And look what she's involved in. We were supposed to be settling things at home while she figured out how to deal with the fallout of the betrayal of her father and Ty. She's pretty private, except when she's with Elizabeth."

Sam read her right. Kate didn't openly show her emotions, John thought. But she had to him. At least until last night. He'd gone to check on her to find her door locked. He banged on the door afraid she might have bolted out the window or worse, that someone had penetrated the now even tighter perimeter.

He was relieved but somewhat perturbed when she answered through the closed door, "Not tonight, cowboy. Don't worry. I've got my gun. If you're thinking of breaking down the door to check on me, I'll shoot first."

John knew Sam was baiting him, waiting for a reply, but Wade spoke up first.

"Sam, I didn't mean to eavesdrop on my watch in the secure room last night. You and the Director weren't pleased with the operation in Hampton Beach. Things didn't go as planned?"

"No."

Sam got up from his chair and strode to the kitchen window,

glancing at the office as he walked by. The voices behind the door became progressively louder and the conversation more distinguishable.

Sam said, "You all know about the planned sting at the country club. Robert and Thomas were wired to tape their conversations, but the main characters pulled a no-show. By the time the Feds could track down their whereabouts, they'd left the country. A fake flight manifest was uncovered at Gabreski Airport. There were a few leads, but they're a dead end. And the money Robert owed them—"

The door to the office flung open, and Kate stormed out. Elizabeth's anger was only slightly masked as she followed her niece out into the kitchen. John never saw Elizabeth so flustered and out of control. She never allowed her staff to see her as other than the professional she was. Ever.

"Katherine Elizabeth, you're out of your mind. Where did you come up with this idea?"

Kate stopped at the counter and turned to look at her aunt trailing on her heels. They were nose to nose, like two fighters readying for a match. Kate showed no sign of backing down. "From you, of course."

"I will *not* agree to your insane idea. It's not going to happen under my watch." Elizabeth defiantly crossed her arms over her breasts and stared from her niece to John and Sam and back to Kate. "*Absolutely, positively, no.* I simply will not allow it."

Kate glanced around at the people gathered. "Did you not just tell me your agents found the apartment where Stavros hid with a woman and another man?" Elizabeth made no comment. "So, let's put the pieces together. Zoya is here. Somewhere. With an accomplice." John gripped the edge of the table. "*He* got me into this mess." Kate pointed to John, who slowly rose from his chair.

"Kate, if you're thinking of doing what my gut tells me you

are, I'm siding with your aunt. My answer is no."

Over Kate's shoulder John saw Sam waving a twenty-dollar bill.

Kate merely shrugged, apparently not caring about their opinions. Hadn't the woman given any thought to the fact her aunt and his ops team were professionals and knew exactly what they were doing? He could see Kate hadn't given one thought to how much danger she'd be in.

Kate grinned from eye to ear. Yeah, he had her pegged. She had something up her sleeve. He'd be paying Sam before too long.

"The answer, cowboy, is yes. *We* most certainly are." Kate's hands encompassed the men sitting in the kitchen. "With *my* help we're going to bring that Russian filly out into the open."

"Kate," John's voice growled back at her.

"Cowboy, *you* gave me the idea." John stared blankly at the woman, who stood calmly pouring a cup of coffee from the pot on the counter. "Oh, for God's sake, John. The auction house! *You* gave me that catalog, remember? I knew that catalog would be good for something sooner or later. Aunt Elizabeth knows what I want to do. I'll leave to all of you to strategize how to get it done. That's what you're best at."

Kate took a long swallow and placed the cup back on the counter. "Aunt Elizabeth will explain. I'm a bit rusty on the nuances of updated strategic details. And I need to clean my gun. Just in case." She winked at the crowded kitchen, turned and walked up the back staircase, leaving everyone to stare at each other.

Oh no, John thought. Where the hell is this going?

* * *

"*Are you out of your ever loving mind, Elizabeth?*" John slammed his hand on the table and knew when her eyebrows arched that he'd crossed the line when he'd called her by name.

But he'd reached the point where things were out of control. And, besides, John wasn't going to let the woman he'd fallen in love with come into harm's way. There. He'd finally admitted it. He'd been fighting the attraction he had for Kate since the day she walked into the barn. "Zoya's brother is a trained gunman. Obviously, some people on their side thought he was dispensable, if need be. Apparently, there's more than one person on their team out there who may be able to do his job. Whatever possessed you to let her talk you into this?"

"Are you finished, Special Agent Clinton?" Elizabeth asked, placing her hands on the other end of the table. The piercing look she sent his way was his clue that he was in for the set down of his life.

"Am, I happy about this? No. Can I control what I never knew about? No. Do I trust Katherine to help us complete the mission once and for all? As mad as I am about her grand idea, I most certainly do think she's fully capable of being an asset to you. And why is that you must be thinking? Sit down!" Elizabeth's commanding tone had John and the others taking their places in the chairs around the long rectangular table.

Sam came to stand at her side. Elizabeth's eyes fell on each man individually as if she was taking the temperature of the room. His men never experienced this side of the Director. They inched forward in their seats, hanging on her every word, not wanting to miss what she had to tell them. John sat ready for fireworks, though what kind he didn't know. Silence pervaded every corner of the room as his agents watched and waited.

Elizabeth took a deep breath and began, "Katherine Hallock is not just my niece. I trained her. Six years ago, she worked for us as an operative in Vienna. Katherine was instrumental in breaking a breeding scandal at the Spanish Riding School."

John shook his head, not quite sure he'd heard Elizabeth

correctly and took in the faces around him, who were equally as astounded as he was. It wasn't the first time since he'd met Kate that he was speechless. The woman was full of surprises.

Elizabeth continued, "Don't look so surprised. Don't tell me you all haven't wondered. Her mannerisms. Her demeanor. Jake, you even told me Katherine reminded you of me. And don't forget, she requested a weapon." The corners of her mouth tipped up in a smile. "She's really, really good at what she does. Graduated number one in her class at the Farm." Elizabeth paused, her eyes roaming the table, stopping at John. She was baiting him. "Cat got your tongue, Agent Clinton?"

John felt as if he was the bird about to be eaten by the Cheshire cat. His mind flashed over events of the past weeks. How Kate had stepped up to handle herself. Strong, Determined. Pigheaded. "Director, I want it noted that I think this is the stupidest idea…"

Elizabeth balled her fists as they rested on the table. She and Kate were going to have their way.

"Okay. Okay. We'll have Kate's back. We'll bring Zoya in. But then, with your permission, we're going hunting for the SOBs we left in Istanbul."

Heads nodded in agreement with the option John had laid on the table.

"If you bring me Zoya, I'm sure I won't have any problems convincing my superiors to let your team go hunting, Agent Clinton. Sam? Could you go in the office and gather the maps Kate used to plot out what will be done. There's also the intel she gathered about the auction house." Elizabeth's right hand man walked away without saying one word. "Gather round. Agent Clinton and Agent Hallock will partner the new operation."

John had tipped his chair back, contemplating the state of Operation Hide and Seek. The mention of Kate being assigned to be his partner sent the chair flying backwards. He and his head landed with a thud on the kitchen floor.

CHAPTER THIRTY-TWO

"You couldn't tell me you're an *agent*?" John firmly gripped the steering wheel of the truck with the attached horse trailer as he drove down the road leading to the Peachtree City Auction House. "I've been with you night in and night out. You've told me some of your deepest secrets, and yet, you omitted one very important fact. It would have been very helpful to know you worked for the CIA."

"The operative word is 'worked.' Past tense. Besides, you know the rules of protocol, cowboy. No one, no one, is to know what you really do when you work for the Agency." Kate turned the knob on the dashboard and cranked up the air-conditioning. "God, it's hot in here. Must be all the hot air."

Kate gave him that cheeky grin he loved so much. At any other time, he'd return the smile, considering the irony of everything. But right now, all he could think of was throttling the woman beside him. He was not only mad at Elizabeth, but also with Kate, and with the whole damn situation.

"Let it rest, will you? We've got a job to do."

"Don't take this the wrong way, but thanks to your brilliant idea, I think the Director will be writing my ticket out of the Agency." John stared straight ahead. Even though the cab of the truck was cool, he took a bandana from the console and wiped the sweat that had beaded up on his brow.

Kate turned to him, eyes wide in shock. "What do you mean you could be finished?"

"Kate, the Director gave me one last opportunity to prove myself worthy of resuming my life in the CIA after what happened overseas. She was adamant I follow the rules. I got the 'Don't break protocol' speech. This operation was, I mean is, my last chance."

"So we spent some nights together and let our emotions get entangled a bit. Aunt Elizabeth doesn't know you slept in my bed." John took his eyes off the road. His sea green eyes stared at her, not sure he'd heard her correctly. "I did the research. You didn't break any rules. Technically, the manual says you're not supposed to become involved with your *partner*. We weren't teamed up until two days ago. You were *protecting* me before everything hit the fan."

John hit the brake to slow down as they approached a line of traffic entering the grounds of the auction house. No doubt about it, there was going to be an extremely large crowd and grounds to be monitored. Kate was convinced her plan was going to work. Zoya was going to take the bait, but while John didn't want Kate in harm's way, he and his team were in agreement it was the only way to go. And an agent didn't deviate from orders given.

John negotiated a wide turn with the truck and trailer and headed to the designated parking lot. "You had every chance to tell me. I bared my soul to you. You could have done the same."

John drove through a crowd of trucks and cars.

Kate's eyes took in the sights around them, especially the people. She reached for his knee, and he flinched at her touch. "I was *retired*. R-e-t-i-r-e-d. Finished. Have been since I did that job in Vienna. For God's sake, I went underground *once* only because Aunt Elizabeth needed my skills as a horse trainer and breeder. For the record, when this mess is over, I'm out of here."

Kate took her hand away from his knee and looked out the windshield. John sat stunned. *What the hell are you thinking? Your career's going to be a wash. And the woman just stated she's going back to the Hamptons. Get the job done and let her go.*

Kate wants a better life than what you have to offer no matter what she'd said.

* * *

Kate saw a stunned, pained expression cross John's face. Her last comment didn't come out quite the way she planned. But it was true. She and John both knew it. They were fooling themselves to think otherwise. After today, if the mission was successful, she'd be going home. A sudden overwhelming sadness swept over her that matched the look on his face.

John's voice broke into her thoughts. "Signal to Wade and Tim to follow us into the right lot."

Their truck halted behind a line of other trucks and horse trailers, waiting for the parking attendant to wave them into a space. Kate watched John, cautiously eyeing the people exiting their vehicles.

"Kate, let's talk about the auction strategy. We agreed to bid on the broodmares and the two stallions being offered by Dudley Farms, yes?"

John had a unique ability to keep her on her toes. One minute, he was talking about breaking rules and the possibility of losing his job. Now, he focused on the roles they needed to play. Kate had insisted the two of them needed to stand out, keep bidding on prize animals so they would be seen and heard. A map of the auction grounds had been found in a studio apartment yesterday when the FBI had done a sweep, based on a tip. Zoya and her contacts would definitely be there.

Kate once again reiterated what they'd gone over. "Yes. The research said the horses are worth the money. And if we're lucky to get them, they should pay you good dividends in the long run." Kate watched as John checked his rearview mirror again. "What's the matter?"

"Nothing. Just checking to be sure Tim and Wade are parking nearby. They're a couple of trailers back." He patted her knee. "We're going to do this right, Kate."

Kate stiffened. "I know we are. My aunt and her team set up a security perimeter. Before you park, can we get back to this?" She patted the catalog in her lap.

"Yes, ma'am." John saluted. "I love it when you go all cowgirl on me."

She laughed at his playfulness, knowing full well he was trying to steady her nerves, which had been on overdrive since breakfast. As much as she'd participated in the Vienna sting six years ago, it had been a long time since she'd brushed up on her skill sets. Kate felt as if the odds were stacked against them today, given the number of people. Her aunt had had to break her silence with her superiors and confirm the fact Zoya had infiltrated the States. Running a personal covert op had her aunt called into the Oval Office and hadn't set well. But the President and his chain of command didn't question the request for manpower to work today's assignment.

"Kate! Kate! Where are you?"

Kate left her musings behind and concentrated on finishing what she was saying. "The bloodlines are as solid as you'll ever find. When I faxed them our request, the Jockey Club confirmed the necessary papers and history of ownership." Kate thumbed through the catalog, looking at the notes she wrote in the margin. "Remember, you agreed to my recommendations of sticking to the sales catalog rankings, especially based on the horses' pedigrees." She stopped talking. "What? Why are you looking at me like that?"

"You're amazing. How does anyone keep up with you?"

Kate beamed and sighed. "It's my job, cowboy. My passion. It's what I do best. Why do you think I walked away from Vienna and a career with the Agency?" Suddenly the truck screeched to a halt, almost bumping into the trailer hitch of the rig in front of them. "Hey! You better watch out."

"I'd rather be watching you." John wiggled his eyebrows. Quickly waved into a parking place, John parked the truck and shut off the ignition. "Got anything else you want to tell me before we head out to the check-in tent?"

"As a matter of fact, I do. You have to make me a promise." Kate's voice took on a serious tone.

"And what would that be?"

Kate stared out the window at the wide expanse of barns, pens and people. "First, you're not going to buy a horse just because you think it looks good."

John reached across the seat and placed his hand inside her thigh. "So, should I feel if she's got good bones, like this?" John slid his hand up her leg and into the juncture between her thighs. Kate gasped, squeezing his hand tightly in place. "And secondly?" He leaned forward and kissed her lightly on the lips.

The heat of the day had nothing to do with the heat she felt between her thighs. Kate sucked in her breath. "Always have my back, cowboy."

"Always, cowgirl." John took her in his arms again and kissed her as if the kiss would be their last.

* * *

For the first time in weeks, the nightmare of Istanbul played over and over in his mind last night. He believed that led to the uneasiness he couldn't seem to shake. Getting out of the truck,

John and Kate walked over to where Tim and Wade waited.

John checked in with the security team via his earpiece. "Dark Shadow to Night Owl. Wild Flame in place. Over."

"Roger that, Dark Shadow."

Chuck and Bob had assumed their assigned positions around the auction pens earlier in the day. Elizabeth put them in charge of commanding the remainder of the field agents on the premises while Jake and Sam stayed back at the farmhouse controlling the safe house operation. She had planned on arriving at Clinton Stables by early afternoon.

Kate stumbled, and John grabbed for her arm. He shook his head. The woman was trying to walk and read at the same time. That damn catalog hadn't left her side since she found out they were really going to implement her plan and come to Peachtree. Hell, she'd practically gone to sleep with the books and maps last night, like some kid with her precious teddy bear.

"Kate, come on. You told me I've got to get in line for a number." John tugged at her sleeve, realizing her mind was elsewhere. Zoya was to be her number one priority and the purchasing of the horses second. She needed to be sharp and on task.

"You with us, Kate?" Even Tim noticed Kate's distraction. "Or lusting after those horses you want to buy."

Kate blushed, then laughed outright at Tim's joke. His men knew how much she loved her work and how thrilled she was to be entrusted with the job of setting up the mainstay of the Clinton Stables.

It didn't stop John from noticing that she tugged an old cowboy hat lower on her brow. John shared Kate's concern at being recognized. They were supposed to find Zoya before she spotted them. "I'm fine. Sorry to hold you all up. I've got horses and a Russian on my mind. We better get moving. John needs to get over to the tent." Kate sped up, leaving the three men to follow in her wake.

John gave a nod to Tim and Wade to watch their charge and headed under the huge white awning that housed the auction registration booth. Within minutes, he had signed the appropriate paperwork and had his bidding number.

When he walked outside, Kate and his men were where he'd left them. Waving the large white card, John remarked, "Well, lady and gents, number twenty-one. I think it may be our lucky day." It had been a long hot ride from Clinton Stables. Since the auction wouldn't start for another hour, John scanned the area for the beverage tent, along with a place to sit in the shade and out of sight. "Anyone thirsty?"

Heads nodded in unison. After taking drink orders, he walked over to the beverage bar and returned with two cups of iced black coffee and lemonade for Kate.

"John, let's go over and sit under that tree." Kate pointed in the direction of a large shady area. Tim and Wade took their cups from John and made for a stretch of grass under a large dogwood tree fifty feet from where Kate plopped down. The two men constantly scanned the crowd as the throngs of people made their way to the auction pens and barns.

"So, how about our chances, Kate? We don't see this many when we buy cattle up in Montana." John leaned his back against the trunk of the tree, one eye on Kate and the other scoping out the layout of the area even though, from Kate's drawings, he and his men knew it from memory.

Kate sat cross-legged and replied, "We came with a solid buying plan." She took a long sip of the cold lemonade. "If we don't make out as well as I predict, I'll owe you a dinner. Relax, cowboy. Auctions are always like this."

John saw her take in the people around them at the tables. She seemed to jump when somebody got too close. "The crowd bothering you? If so, you say the word and we're out of here."

"No. You promised me you'd have my back." She stood and brushed the dust from her jeans. "Come on." She motioned for him and the others to follow. "They're calling for the people who sit in the VIP section. That's us." Her enthusiasm, considering the danger, was contagious. "Remember, we buy the stallions and the four broodmares first."

"Yes, ma'am."

"Oh, and don't forget the mantra." Kate's eyes twinkled.

"And that would be?"

"You get what you pay for. We have a saying at Hallock Farm before every race."

John had to bite. "And what would that be, Miss Hallock?"

"Keep your eye on the prize." Kate smiled and cocked her head in the direction of the pens.

He was in love with Katherine Elizabeth Hallock! She was the real deal. She wasn't false. She stood for what she believed in.

"Well, are you ready, cowboy?"

By then, Tim and Wade had joined them.

"I'm ready…And, I've got your back. Let's get going. But you better be right or…"

"Or what?" Kate glanced at him with a puzzled look.

"Or you're going to owe me a whole lot more than just a dinner." He hoped her flushed face was from thinking of the possibilities of what dessert might entail.

When John stretched out his hand, Kate slapped the catalog she held in it. She winked at him, then signaled the two men trailing behind them. As he walked along, he longed to pull her up against his body. He had to make her realize they were a perfect fit.

CHAPTER THIRTY-THREE

"Sold!" The auctioneer yelled out. "And the winning bid for the two Arabians goes to number twenty-one. Come sign for your horses."

Kate practically jumped out of her bleacher seat when the gavel went down. John tugged her along behind him as they made their way through the crowd of people. Those nearby clapped him on the back, offering congratulations. Hell, this was the part he wanted to avoid. Cameras from the local newspapers clicked away. Pictures in the papers were the last thing he wanted, and there wasn't a damn thing he could do to stop it without making a scene. Any picture of Kate would be recognized by the national media, and given social media, picked up within the seconds. John had to figure out a plausible way to get her back to the farm. He'd had no acknowledgement from his agents about any sightings of Zoya or her Russian agents, identified by Interpol.

Kate threw her arm around his waist. "Yes! We did it! John, we struck gold! And the horses! God, they're worth every penny you spent. I can't believe you bought them."

John whipped his signature over some paperwork he'd been handed and turned to her. "I bought them for you." His finger flicked the end of her nose. How could he tell her everything he'd done today had been only for her? And when she was gone, and the job permitted him time to return to the farm, she'd always be there with him in spirit? Always.

"For me? You did this for me?" Her eyes sparkled with delight, and the beaming smile she sent his way melted his heart.

"Excuse me," a voice interrupted their conversation. "Tom Davis, *Equestrian Magazine*."

Oh no, John thought. His biggest fear came to fruition. He immediately felt Kate let go of his shirtsleeve to stand behind him out of sight of the reporter. John tried his best to shield her.

"Isn't she *the* Katherine Hallock of Hallock Farm in Hampton Beach?" The reporter tried to get a better view of Kate by maneuvering around the burly hulk of the agent's body.

John placed his hand on the man's shoulder to stop him. "The lady's not taking any questions right now."

"I guess you're right. She's not going to be making any comments."

John looked at the reporter with a puzzled expression, watching as the man motioned behind him. "If you'd take a minute to look, Miss Hallock has gone MIA."

John whirled. Kate was gone. No. While his eyes searched the crowd in the immediate vicinity, he called for back up. "Wild Flame is out of the corral." He looked for the black, straw cowboy hat he'd given her that morning. With its silver sparkling ribbon, it would stand out in the crowd. Kate wasn't a short woman, and he was a tall man. But he came up empty. Panic slowly set in. Where the hell had she gone?

"Dark Shadow, I've got a visual." It was Chuck. "We have problems, boss. Over."

John began to move. "Status report. Over."

"There's a man and a blond woman escorting Kate to the south parking lot. Over."

"All agents converge immediately. Over."

"Chief, there's one more thing. Over."

"Continue. Over."

"The lady's got a gun in Kate's back."

"Copy that." John reached for his gun and ran like he'd never run before. He didn't need any kind of description to tell him the identity of the woman. It had to be the woman who'd risen from the dead: Zoya Stalinski.

* * *

"Just move along and do as you're told."

Kate couldn't believe one minute she'd been standing behind John seeking protection from the probing eyes of the reporter, the next a .45 mm pistol was shoved in her back. A blond woman with a sultry, Russian accent whispered to remain quiet as she pulled Kate away from where she'd stood behind John to be out of the way of the reporter. This was perfect. Kate would do as she was asked. John wouldn't be happy, but the trap had been sprung.

"Who are you?" Kate feigned ignorance, knowing full well who held her captive. But it was the man with the woman who surprised her most of all.

"You know exactly who I am," the woman sneered as she ushered Kate swiftly to the parking lot. "Don't play dumb."

Kate slowed her gait, leveraging for time, but the woman jammed the gun deeper between her shoulder blades. Praying John and his team had spotted her and her companions, Kate kept pace as the trio made their way to a small, black truck parked between a large semi and a horse van of the same color. Smart. Camouflage. Out of sight. The semi was positioned with its back doors open and gate down, easy access for the truck to drive up and in. Close the doors and drive away. *That* was not in Kate's plan. She'd intended to remain out in the open. Lead John's enemies to the team. Inside that semi, Kate's tracking device would be blocked. She was sure of it. She'd need to improvise.

"She's too quiet, Zoya. I don't like it." Stopping abruptly, the man wrenched her around so she could clearly see her captors. So *this* was the infamous Zoya Stalinski, and the man at her side was none other than the infamous Demetrie Sarkov.

Zoya baited her with sarcasm. "You surprise me. I thought you'd be screaming for help, Miss Hallock. What a coup for us that we've taken the Director's niece hostage in the process of hunting down the two we sought most."

"Where are you taking me?" Kate enunciated every word.

But, it wasn't Zoya who answered. Demetrie did. "Where this will end once and for all. But, this time, it will be in our favor." Kate eyed the Russian spy cautiously.

"Get her in the truck, Demetrie. We've wasted too much time already."

As the woman opened the door to give the man access to the backseat of the cab, Kate rounded on her. She shot her leg up and connected with the woman's wrist, taking Zoya by surprise. The gun flew into the nearby tall grass.

Zoya called out, "Demetrie, the gun!"

But Demetrie didn't obey her, his dark, hairy arms tightly circled Kate's waist instead. Kate jerked her head back as she'd been taught, making contact with his chin. As she was doing damage to Demetrie, Zoya recovered her balance and now held the gun securely in her hand. She pointed the gun directly at Kate's chest.

Within minutes, Kate was bound and gagged. She lay behind the driver's seat, hidden from view. The engine of the truck started, and her heart hammered with anticipation of what was to come. The rumble of tires on tin told her Demetrie was driving the pickup into the semi just as she predicted. The engine stopped, doors opened and closed, throwing her into utter darkness. Damn. What trick did she have up her sleeve to get of this mess?

* * *

John, Wade and Chuck climbed aboard the chopper that landed in the paddock near the auction house. The place was a hum of activity as agents swarmed out onto the grounds to find Kate, as well as those who left in pursuit of the semi in their vehicles, in case she was hidden on the grounds.

"Dark Shadow to Base. Over."

"Base. Over."

"Give me the Eagle."

"Copy that."

The Director's voice came through in an authoritative manner. Kate may be her niece, but an operation was going down. John was grateful she'd put her emotions aside and taken the lead. "What's the status of the semi?"

"Made the turn for the highway to Clinton Stables two minutes ago." John looked back out the open door of the chopper to see the second chopper following behind.

"Make sure they turn in the lane. Then land. Let's take them on the ground. I want this done on our terms."

"Roger. Coming in. Over."

"Will be ready and waiting, Dark Shadow. Over."

There was no doubt the Eagle had his back as John gave the chopper pilot the headings to land in the field on the eastside of Clinton Farm. There were plenty of trees and scrub pines that could be used for camouflage. He couldn't fathom why Zoya would roll right into the farm. The woman had always been a major risk taker. But why converge on an area surrounded with Special Ops teams? The only thing that made sense was perhaps their plan to use Kate as a bargaining chip to get to him and Elizabeth. But how could Zoya have known Elizabeth had deployed from her office to the farm? John had an eerie feeling the mole was about to show his face.

As the chopper and its occupants banked to the right, leaving the semi behind in the sights of the second helicopter, John's anxiety level rose with the knowledge that Kate, though trained, was within the confines of the truck and held by two Eastern European terrorists. Kate had proved she was tough. She was right. He had to trust she would know what to do and when to do it.

CHAPTER THIRTY-FOUR

Elizabeth gave the order for all members of John's team to check their positions as the semi crashed through the barricaded gate at the entrance. No one was prepared for what came next. The truck, seemingly out of control, rolled up the driveway and rammed through the sidewall of the large barn, its cab now hidden from view of the monitors in the secure room.

"Roll out." Elizabeth, eying the multitude of screens, gave the command to surround the barn. "John, you and Jake post yourselves just inside the small barn. Wade and Chuck will remain in here with me. I want updates every five minutes."

John and Jake moved quickly, seeing the others do so as well.

The dust was settling and allowing for better visibility from the collision of the semi with the barn.

"What do you think?" Jake asked.

"We wait. The Eagle's in control of the op."

Both men waited behind the barrels set up inside the doorway of the small barn. Even though there had been a tremendous boom on impact, the yard was now eerily quiet. Popping up for a better look, John raised his gun and pointed it, hoping Zoya would make her exit from the interior of the barn. His biggest concern was that no one knew if Kate had been injured on impact.

"Eagle, we spy no movement. Over."

Silence.

"Eagle, do you copy? Over." John adjusted his earpiece. Why didn't Elizabeth respond?

"Eagle! We have no visual. Permission to go forward? Over."

No chatter came through his earpiece. His mind quickly flashed back to a similar scenario in Istanbul, but he recovered when Jake shook him on the shoulder.

"What's happening?" Jake inquired, his eyes darting around the yard.

John spotted movement, not in the area of the barn, but from the vicinity of the back porch. The door was opening, the barrel of a rifle poking its way out. John nudged Jake to see what he couldn't believe he was viewing. He gripped the butt of his Glock, pointing it towards the door as Jake set his rifle on the barrel beside him. He couldn't have been more shocked as Elizabeth and Wade were marched slowly down the steps, arms raised, their hands behind their heads.

"Shit!" John and Jake spoke in unison. Their eyes were glued on the man who ushered the Director and Wade to where they stood in front of the hedge. Chuck. The easy going, "I care about Kate", "Let me handle that, boss" was the traitor. At the beginning, John couldn't shake off the fact that Jake, his co-leader, had betrayed him, as Mike had in Istanbul. But when he started to chart out the incidents with Chuck's whereabouts, he knew after taking Sam Tanner into his confidence, they'd have to set a trap. But not like this. This hadn't been how John had wanted it to go down.

John strained to hear what Chuck mumbled to his hostages as they moved out into the yard. A team of agents scrambled to form a semi-circle around the trio, while others remained in position with their rifles trained on the large barn.

Chuck called out, "John, I can't see you, but I know you're there. Tell your agents to stand down or I'll be putting bullets into the skulls of the Director and Wade." Chuck carried a large rifle, capable of leveling a decent number of people in a short amount of time.

"Do as he says," Elizabeth ordered, cranking her head slightly to get a view of her captor. "I want proof of life that Katherine is all right."

Jake tapped John on the shoulder and pointed to the large barn. Trying to keep one eye trained on Chuck, John watched as Zoya made her way from the barn. Her gun was strategically placed against Kate's temple. Kate was smart, not struggling, but trying to stumble along and slow down Zoya's progress. Before too long, the two had made their way behind a yellow pick up truck parked strategically in front of them. *Chuck's doing, no doubt.* The orders were to keep the yard clear.

A tall man followed several paces behind Kate, taking up a position at Zoya's side.

"Who the hell is that?" Jake whispered.

John pulled out his binoculars for a closer look. He swore he knew all the operatives within Zoya's inner circle, but he'd never seen this guy before.

John was about to answer Jake when Zoya's voice rang out. "Chuck, bring those two closer to me. Slowly. I want to see the look on the Director's face when I pull the trigger on her beloved niece. This has been a long time coming, Elizabeth Hallock. You've no idea what pleasure this brings me."

Chuck pushed his captives forward as instructed, his eyes and gun trained on the agents as he moved himself and Wade and the Director towards Zoya.

"Where's Stavros?" Zoya yelled. "He was supposed to be

here."

John had waited for Chuck to relay the death of her brother and let the ramifications fall where they may. John wasn't willing to let things spiral into utter chaos.

Chuck sneered, "This is going to be good, John. Let's hope all hell doesn't break loose when she hears the news." Chuck placed his finger more securely on the trigger of his gun. Even from where he hid, John could see the sweat pouring down Chuck's brow. Taut nerves made for a tricky trigger finger. And that made John nervous. This had to come to an end. He knew just how to get things rolling. His men were trained well.

Stepping out from behind the barrel into plain sight, his Glock still aimed at Zoya, he spat out, "He's dead, Zoya. We killed the SOB."

"No! You lie! Stavros! Come out! We have them at last, brother!" She tightened her grip on Kate. Zoya's eyes darted around the yard, as if she thought her brother would magically appear.

"I can show you the body. But first, you have to let Kate go. The Director and Wade, too."

Her dazed stare told John she was shaken to her very core, but she was a highly trained operative and she wouldn't be swayed from what she'd come there to do. From there on out, he had to be careful in baiting her. Lives were at stake.

The rock solid belief in her cause told John she wouldn't back down.

"You are messing with me. I'm in charge here, as you can see. You've made my day now that I have both of you. And her niece is a bonus. It is just as we planned, eh, Demetrie?"

The man beside her remained silent for some reason. His radar went on high alert. Why hadn't the man answered Zoya? He watched as Demetrie slowly raised a small pistol, which up until that point must have been hidden in the palm of his hand.

Before John could make sense and process everything going on around him, Kate shouted, "Now!" Her words echoed throughout the yard. Two shots rang out. One dropped Chuck in his tracks, and the other came from Demetrie Sarkov's pistol. He'd taken Zoya out with one bullet to her head. With Kate in such close proximity, blood spattered her shirt as the spy slumped to the ground in front of her.

There was a mad scramble in the barn's yard. Jake left his side, running to help out. He was so into the moment of being reunited with Kate, he didn't see his team and the other agents grab their weapons and take up positions, looking for the possibility of other shooters. John had eyes for only one person. And she was running hell-bent into his outstretched arms. He tightly scooped her up, swinging her around, sighing in relief. He knew one thing. There was no way he was *ever* going to let her get away from him.

"Nice shot on Chuck, Jake. Stand down. All clear." The Director's voice came through his earpiece. She was commanding as ever. John was in awe that it was over. Who was that man who dropped Zoya where she stood?

Elizabeth walked to where Kate and John stood, their arms linked together. "Katherine, are you all right?"

"I'm fine. Once I knew Demetrie was with me in the truck, I knew you'd made the contact."

The man in question walked up to the trio. Elizabeth made the introductions. "John, meet Demetrie Sarkov. Demetrie works our European theatre and stumbled across Zoya hiding in St. Petersburg last year. That was after we'd been told she was dead. He decided to follow her and set up false contacts to get her into the States. He knew she came to find us. I found out he was working a lead for the Feds when he showed up at Hallock Farm, and Kate made him."

"What do you mean she made him?" John asked.

"Demetrie and I worked on that Vienna case." The corners of Kate's mouth turned into a wide grin upon seeing the newcomer. "Glad to know you still got it, old man."

"Well, I've been trained by the best." Demetrie bowed playfully and nodded to the Eagle. "If you'll excuse me, there's a mountain of paperwork to fill out. I'm short on time. I'm due back in Russia in two days, Director."

"I'll meet you at Langley tomorrow morning and debrief you."

"I will tell you again you missed your calling, Miss Kate," Demetrie said, kissing her hand. "Until next time."

"No." Kate said firmly. "There won't be a next time. I want to go home. And yes, Director, I know the protocol. I, too, will be at Langley in the morning." She promptly walked away, a wistful look on her face, staring back at John over her shoulder.

"You're going to let her walk away, John Clinton? Just like that?"

"I have no choice."

"Then you're a bigger fool than I thought you were." And with that comment, Elizabeth Hallock left him standing alone in the dusty yard.

CHAPTER THIRTY-FIVE

"He's a beauty, isn't he?"

Kate spun around.

"Fine lines, great coat, good bones. How am I doing?"

Kate gave him a sly smile. "You're learning, cowboy."

John moved next to her. They stood in silence for a few minutes, watching the horse nibble from his mash bucket, his tail flicking the flies away.

"Thunderbolt will be the mainstay of your stable with his bloodlines. He's going to make you a *lot* of money." Kate looked up at him, a pleased smile on her face. "He cost you a small fortune, but you'll have a chance to race him in the not too distant future." She crossed her fingers over her heart. "Scout's promise. My professional opinion is that I don't think he's peaked on the circuit yet, from what I've been able to research."

John took a chance, putting his arm around her. Her reaction was just what he hoped for. She nestled her head into his shoulder and wrapped her arms around his waist.

Looking down into her deep dark eyes, his feelings for her hit him deep in his gut. His thoughts were more than attraction and lust. He'd lost his objectivity a long time ago. And he knew exactly when. The day she'd walked into his life, pushed him out of the way and taken control of birthing Wild Flame. At that point, she'd become the center of his being, and he'd fought it every step of the way, to no avail. They were meant to be together. But she was leaving.

All John could think about at that moment was loving her, having the memory of one last night in her arms. He wished she could remain at his side for the rest of his life. Kate had become his reason to get up every day. In his profession, he'd made the choice to walk life's journey alone. But things had changed. This woman had made him want more from life than the simple the thrill of the hunt.

John tried to read her emotions as she gazed up at him, her eyes dark and mysterious. Did she reciprocate his feelings? With all she'd been through, she had a right to be guarded, having been deceived by her father and her fiancé. She'd loved and lost, not only in life, but also in love. If only he could convince her what they had was unique. It could work. He was willing to throw his duty of love of country to the wind, if only Kate would walk the remainder of life's journey with him and not her beloved Hallock Farm.

An elbow nudged his side, rousing him from his musings. "Hey, cowboy! Where'd you go? Penny for your thoughts?"

"I've got some thinking to do."

"What do you mean?" Kate took a step back to look up at him, her brow etched in concern. "Is something wrong? Did I do something? What…?"

John placed his fingertips on her pink, puckered lips. "Stop. Nothing's wrong." How did he tell her that in the nights he lay next to her, the quiet had him thinking of Elizabeth's talk before Operation Hide and Seek began. Elizabeth thought the time had come for him to retire from field work, use his skill sets to train new operatives. Elizabeth informed him, although he was once again being put in charge of an ops assignment, she was testing his abilities to perform. Why? Because, in order for her to sign off on his overall return to the field, she needed confirmation he could refrain from acting recklessly in a foreign country and that his days in therapy had worked, the PTSD was truly gone. He had to prove to her he was fully functional and rational on all counts. Coming from his mentor, that had stung.

Kate bit the tip of his finger, a smile playing across her face. "Don't placate me. I can read you like a book. I've gotten to know you better than you think I have, John Clinton. Give! Is it the job? Has Aunt Elizabeth threatened to dismantle your team? I'll pick up that phone in a heartbeat, if she has."

God, he loved her. The way she came to his defense surprised him. "No, it's not that. After the briefings, the team and I have some job decisions to make." John decided not to elaborate, but Kate wouldn't let the matter drop.

"What would you do if you weren't running around playing secret agent man?"

John reached down and brought her hand up to rest on his chest, knowing she was trying to make light of a serious conversation.

"You've got a great life ahead of you. You have your dream. Look around at what we've done, John." When she placed her other hand over his, and looked into his eyes, he was a goner. "Aunt Elizabeth told me always to let my heart lead me in making my decisions. There are times when thinking with your head doesn't help."

"And did your heart guide you here, Kate?" His dark eyes pierced hers.

"In some manner, yes. I think I knew for quite awhile that Ty didn't love me. I was too busy and too much in denial to accept it. And being chased by the mob can get the old heart pumping, too." They both laughed at her attempt at her joke.

"How'd you get to be so smart, Katie?" With his finger, John brushed her hair behind her ear. He then cupped his hand behind her neck. He longed to kiss her.

Kate hugged him tightly to her as their eyes met.

"John…"

"Katie…" The two spoke in unison.

John melded his lips to hers, so sweet and soft. Deepening the kiss, he brushed his tongue back and forth gently in hopes that Kate opened her mouth, allowing him access. She didn't disappoint him. Their tongues joined together, the kiss grew passionate. John felt what she did to him at the slightest touch, his jeans growing tighter. Kate had to stand on her toes in order to raise her arms and lock them around his neck. Could she not feel how they were a perfect fit, their bodies molding together?

John slid his hands under her sweatshirt, feeling the warmth of her skin. He glided his hands seductively over her stomach, stopping to brush his thumbs on the undersides of her breasts. He felt her shiver at his touch. Delighted at discovering she'd not worn a bra, his fingers trailed their way to her peaked nipples. He pinched them, hearing a gasp escape from her lips. He wasn't sure which of them groaned. They were two kindred spirits bound by passion, and he hoped, love.

Kate released her hands from around his neck and moved them ever so slowly until they lay on the front of his shirt. Her fingertips left a tingling trail. John pulled her close, rubbing his manhood against her belly to show her exactly how she made him feel.

Not wanting to waste another minute, John scooped her up in his arms and said, "Stop me now, Katie. I don't want to turn back. I want you. All of you."

In a loving caress, Kate cradled his face, her eyes smoldering with desire. "Just love me, cowboy," she whispered.

Entering the open stall across from Thunderbolt, John lay Kate down on the fresh mound of hay. Neither one of them could peel their clothes off fast enough. Kate was his hidden treasure, and John couldn't wait to find the secrets she had buried within her. The very thought made his blood rush to his penis. Peeling off the last layer of his clothes, John turned to find her lying naked on the yellow straw bed, beckoning him to come to her. Kate was as beautiful as he'd fantasized. Perfectly proportioned, her skin lightly tanned with a small amount of freckles sprinkled across her body. Lying alongside her, he feasted his eyes upon her. He slid his fingers over her feminine mound and watched as she licked her lips in anticipation of the pleasure he would give her. Her body gave him a clue she was ready to be his. Sliding one finger inside her, he found her wet and slick.

Ever so slowly, they intimately explored each other's bodies, touching and trading kisses in the most intimate places. Kate's hands roamed over his sinewy muscles and rock hard abdomen. Her fingers twirled in the hairs around his navel and when she glided her finger up the ridge of his penis, John moaned out loud. He reveled in the power they had over each other.

Kate's body glistened and smelled of jasmine. "Please, love me, John."

"Just let me touch you for a little bit longer, honey. I've dreamed of this." As Kate writhed below him, he kissed and licked a path up and down her body. He knew he wouldn't last, but he had to hold on. He had to have her his way, brand her, and make her his own.

John parted her thighs and let his tongue lick the outer rim of her womanhood. John rolled his tongue around her clit. Kate's hips bolted off the floor. She tried to reach out for him, to bring him to her, but he needed to finish what he started.

Again, he slid two fingers deep within her. It was Kate's turn to groan with pleasure, her voice echoing in the dark barn. John knew she was spiraling out of control as he felt her tighten around his fingertips. She rocked herself against them, desperately seeking the release he wanted her to have. Kate grabbed for him as she climaxed. She shuddered, crying out his name.

"John, I've never felt—" John stopped her with a prolonged kiss. It was his turn.

Sliding his leg between her thighs, he parted her legs wide and positioned himself to enter her. As if planned, moonlight broke through the skylight and beamed down on the two lovers.

"I love you, Katherine Hallock," he whispered softly in her ear as he spread kisses down her neck. He felt her hands pull at his waist.

"And I you. Come let me love you, John."

Her raspy, husky voice was his undoing. John plunged into the very depths of her. As he pumped his cock into her body, he rested his forehead on hers. He felt tears on her cheeks. Rising to take a look at the pleasure on her face, he braced his arms on either side of her and started to stroke in and out. The faster he plunged, the slicker and wetter Kate became. From his head to his toes, he felt like a volcano ready to erupt. His body was hot. He sizzled as sweat dripped from his body onto the woman below him. A groan escaped Kate's lips, a sign that she was on the brink of coming again. Kate locked her legs around his hips and rode him, stroke for stroke, drawing him into her deeper and deeper.

With one final thrust, John's world spun and shattered into a climax unlike any he had ever experienced. He felt his seed spilling over and over. This woman was his world. And after what they'd experienced, John knew without asking that he was hers.

Savoring in the glow of their lovemaking, John pulled Kate to his side. "Spend the night with me, Katie."

Reaching up, she lovingly stroked his chin with her fingertips, replying, "I won't leave you."

The most romantic moment of John's life was broken by Kate's giggle. What the hell? They'd just made the most passionate love and she was laughing? Glancing down, he saw devilish eyes and a cheeky grin. The best part of Kate was her spontaneity. He never knew what to expect.

She tried her best to keep a serious face, but failed miserably. Her laughter was contagious. He started to chuckle as well. "What the hell is so funny, cowgirl?"

"If this is what you meant about 'hitting the hay', cowboy, I, for one would like to unionize for better working conditions. Personally, I'd like a bed written into my contract."

John kissed her lightly on the tip of her nose, taking her face in his hands. "God, I love you! And yes, you'll get your bed, but I hope you don't have plans on getting much sleep tonight."

Kate sat up and reached for her clothing. "Well, come on then! The clock is ticking. And for the record?"

John was lost. Where was her mind going now? He, too, stood up and pulled on his jeans, throwing his shirt over his shoulder. He had to cool down. The sight of her standing in the barn with the moonlight behind her, dressed only in her tee shirt and no panties made his heart race and groin harden again. "The record?"

As she bent to put on her pants, she looked back at him and winked, "Next time, I'll do the riding. On top, if you don't mind."

CHAPTER THIRTY-SIX

One month later

John Clinton couldn't hear the woman trying to talk to him, due to the fact he was wearing the required noise protectors at the firing range. He walked along, watched as the trainees fired their weapons, pulled in their targets to assess their aim and fired again. He knew he was frustrating the Director in that he ignored her, but he had a job to do. The woman was forever on some kind of timetable. Suddenly, a substantial tug on the sleeve of his black suit spun him to face one hundred and eighty degrees, in her direction. She crooked her finger in the direction of his office. Since she was still his boss, John had to follow the command.

Entering the inner sanctum, he threw the orange ear protectors onto his desk and faced the woman who had marched in behind him without closing the door. He stood still, waiting for whatever was on her mind.

"You hate it here," Elizabeth stated bluntly.

"How did you know?" John motioned for her to sit at his desk in the more comfortable chair, which she promptly did. He picked up the phone. "June? Some tea for the Director, please. Yes, yes, Earl Grey. Make my coffee black and strong. I think I'm going to need it."

Elizabeth didn't even wait for him to sit down. "Your men. I got a call this morning from Jake."

John smirked then merely shrugged. "Jake, huh? He says I hate the job? Well, Madam Director, I'm working."

"But it's not the same, is it?"

John had to admit the woman always got right to the point. "No. I can honestly say being in the field had its mental challenges and advantages. I loved the thrill of the hunt. But you were right. I lost my perspective and became reckless. It was time to give it up and move on."

"You didn't answer my question, John Clinton. You've missed the point."

The door opened. John's secretary set a tray down on his desk and walked out the door. John poured Elizabeth her cup of afternoon tea. He grabbed for his cup and sat in the chair on the other side of the desk.

"And exactly, what point am I missing?"

"This job is not the same." She emphasized each word.

"You've lost me. I'm here. I'm doing the training you thought I should do for my career. I don't have all day to play games. Class is about to start. What the hell do you mean by 'the job is not the same'?"

"Katherine's not on this job with you."

John choked on the liquid he'd just swallowed. Kate. How he'd missed her. Every time he thought of watching her get into the Black Hawk helicopter the morning after the shooting and flying to Langley for a debriefing, his heart hurt. They'd said their goodbyes. Kate cried and held him. But, she let go and boarded the chopper. It tore him to pieces, but they both knew they owed their duty to two very different worlds - family and country.

"John!"

John snapped to attention. "Madam Director…"

"If I'm going to say what's on my mind, let's dispense with formality. Call me Elizabeth. I think you earned the right to do so when you saved Kate's life."

John frowned, not wanting to discuss what, he was sure, was going to be put on the table.

"Face it, John. You fell in love with my niece. Oh, don't give me that shocked look. I knew what was going on. And I've seen her. She's as miserable as you are. I think more so. Sense of duty is a crappy excuse for why the two of you can't be together."

John's eyebrows arched at the mere thought that the Director was directing him to break the rules. "How is she? Really?" John had to know.

"She's wasting away. Throwing herself into a job she hates. But she's bringing Hallock Farm back from the brink of destruction. Of course, she won't talk to her father. But she's doing her *duty*. Let me tell you about love, John. You only get one chance. And sometimes it's on the run." Elizabeth stopped, her gaze drifting off to a place on the wall behind him. John noticed how deep in thought she became.

"You sound like you've had some experience." Now it was John's turn to snap Elizabeth back to reality.

"I've had a wonderful run, John. But to get here, I sacrificed family and love for duty and country. I gave up the one true gift that came from the love of a wonderful man. The Black Swan."

Suddenly, it clicked. John sat forward, eyeing Elizabeth, taking in the resemblance. "Does Kate know she's your daughter?"

"No! And if I'm lucky, she never will. It's a secret we all promised we'd carry to our graves. She's grown up happy and loved. Why do you think I gave her the farm? Don't make the same mistake I did. Don't sacrifice your chance to have love and a family." Tears welled up in his mentor's eyes.

John rose from his chair, walked around the desk and engulfed the woman he admired for so long in a loving hug. The woman's sniffling ceased, but Elizabeth still held him tight to her.

Regaining control of her emotions, she instructed John one more time. "Do your job, Agent Clinton. Go get your woman."

* * *

Kate had never felt so worn out in her life. Between dealing with the financial fallout, loss of customers who had heard about her father's shady business dealings and birthing two foals that morning, she didn't know if she could make it to her own bed in the main house that night. Maybe she'd just sleep on the cot in her office as she'd done the last four nights.

She looked around the office in disgust. Her secretary had given her notice because Matthew made a pass at her. Kate was left to discover that the woman had no office skills whatsoever. Hallock Farm was slowly rising from the ashes, but it would be a few months before all was righted - if she didn't lose her sanity first.

Kate promised herself she would have the top of the desk cleaned up by lunch. An important client was coming in to look over some stock, and the money would go a long way into helping Hallock Farm out of its woes. Plus, she was needed back at the training pen by three for a time check of two horses Hallock Farm was thinking of racing the following year.

The door to the office swung open.

"Kate!" It was Hugo Tedesco, one of the younger trainers she'd hired upon her return.

"What? You can't enter like a normal person and knock? I could have clients in here."

"Kate, there's some guy down at the paddock. He's got a really big horse. Says you're the only person he'll let ride or train him. You got to come quick!"

"I can't leave right now. Have Joe Jansen take care of him."

"Ah, no can do. You see…the man…he's also got a really big gun. And says if you don't get your rear in gear—"

Kate bolted out the door leaving a stunned Hugo in her wake.

Jumping in the Jeep parked outside, Kate took off like a rocket. As she rounded the bend and the paddock came into view, she saw a large horse trailer. Her heart raced. She put the Jeep in park and ran for the paddock, leaving the engine running.

He was really here! John Clinton. Standing in *her* paddock. At Hallock Farm. And the man was smiling. He held the reins of a horse in one hand and a gun in the other.

"What are you doing here, Agent Clinton?" Kate could hardly speak.

"I think I like the name 'Cowboy' if it's all the same to you. And just so you know, there's no more Agent in my title." He was grinning from ear to ear. "As you can see, I've got a horse that needs training. Someone once told me she thought he might be Derby material."

Kate moved closer to be sure he wasn't just some vision she conjured up. She patted the horse's neck and looked up into the sea green eyes that had haunted her every night in her dreams for the last month. "I'm sure Hallock Farm can do this fine steed justice. Did you have a particular trainer in mind?"

"As a matter of fact, I drove all this way to bring him to *you*."

Kate tried her best to keep a poker face. "Well, I'm sorry to disappoint you, *cowboy*, but I won't be working here much longer. As of Monday, Hallock Farm will have a new CEO. If you want, you can talk with him."

Kate would remember the stunned look on John's face forever.

Growling, he said, "Where the hell will you be working? I came all this way—"

"I'm going to be taking a job as a head vet at a very fine breeding facility. In Virginia." John's eyes lit up just as she hoped they would. "It will have a very fine reputation when I'm done with it. Perhaps, you've heard of it? Clinton Stables?"

John handed the horse off to the young boy who stood next to him and stuck the gun in the back of his jeans. He swept her off her feet so fast he took her by surprise.

"God, Katie. I almost lost you. I love you."

She looked into his eyes. Her secret agent man. "I love you, too, John Clinton. I'm just glad you went on one last mission to find me."

EPILOGUE

One year later

The sounds of the trumpets heralded the arrival of the horses to the track. "My Old Kentucky Home" played over the loud speaker. The excitement of the crowd invigorated the couple as they found their box seats in the owners' section of the sprawling complex.

John and Kate sat surrounded by their invited guests. There to witness the big day for Clinton Stables were Aunt Elizabeth and Sam Tanner, as well as the rest of the Hallock clan. Even Robert Hallock was present. It had taken some convincing, but John pointed out to Kate the importance to show the unity of the family. It would be sometime before she forgave her father for what he'd done.

"John, I don't know if I can take all this excitement." Kate patted her rounded belly.

John Clinton laughed at his very pregnant wife, hugging her to him.

"And they're off!" The announcer yelled through the speaker. Kate shot to her feet with John by her side.

"Easy, boy." Kate never gave up shouting instructions from

the stands, as if the horse could hear her.

How many times had she and the trainer gone through the course and the timing and jockeying for position? John shook his head.

The crowd's enthusiasm was electric and exciting. John seized hold of Kate's hand as Thunderbolt came into the final turn.

"Thunderbolt is coming in from the outside, John! Just as I planned it! He may win!"

"Easy, Kate. The race isn't over yet."

The crowd in the family box was standing and cheering as Thunderbolt approached the home stretch. He passed the favorite, Night Song, and made for the rail, hugging it close. Down to the finish, the jockey pushed him towards the finish line.

"Run! Yes!" Kate yelled, jumping up and down. John heard the family behind him, cheering on the winner. He'd chosen two winners, the one on the track and the lady at his side.

Thunderbolt streaked across the finish line. His horse had won the Kentucky Derby!

John hugged Kate to him while trying to shake hands with Sam at the same time. The trainer, who'd been standing on his left side, slapped him on the back.

Kate was beside herself, delighted, euphoric. "Oh, my God! Oh, my God!"

"We did it, Katie! You told me we picked a winner that day at Peachtree. God, I love you!"

"Oh, my God!" Kate repeated herself. This time John saw a stunned look on his wife's face.

"Kate, what is it?"

"John...my water just broke." Kate's remark silenced the crowd surrounding them.

"Well, Mrs. Clinton, we have a problem." John smiled down

into the dark eyes of the woman he'd fallen in love with the day they met. "Because I know nothin' about birthin' babies!"

THE END

Enjoy the **LOVE ON THE RUN**? Read more of the exploits of the Hallock family in Book 2 of the series, **HAMPTON THOROUGHBREDS**: **HURRICANE MEGAN**.

Matthew Hallock is known in Hampton beach for two passions – one-night-stands and his stake in the Sunfish Beach Club. When Megan Spears lands a job as his chief lifeguard, he is drawn to her from the minute she blows her whistle. But Megan has no time for men. She's on a mission – literally! And even if she did have time, in her book opposites don't attract.

Can two people from totally different walks of life find the common ground they need to walk hand-in-hand into the future under a Hampton sunset?

Coming Soon: Book 3 – **THE ROMANCE EQUATION**

ABOUT THE AUTHOR

Growing up in the Hamptons in the 60's and 70's, there was no such thing as *People* magazine or paparazzi. It was an honor to work for many of the rich and famous. Diane was a "townie," but her personal interactions with the people of Hampton society helped fuel the fire that, one day, she'd write a series of books based in the small hamlets hugging the southern shore of Long Island.

However, the dream of writing went down the drain one day in tenth grade English class when the teacher announced, "Miss Culver, I've a drawer full of red pens, and they are all for you!" But she was not to be dissuaded. Following the sage words of her favorite poet, Robert Frost, she followed the "Road Not Taken" and became an award-winning mathematics teacher.

When a health crisis forced her into retirement, writing a book was on the top of her bucket list. LOVE ON THE RUN was born. Readers began asking for more tales of the Hallock clan. The series started to take shape and, when completed, will have, at this moment a total of ten books.

In her downtime, she loves to play golf and travel. London tops her list of places she's been, especially if she can antique Saturdays on Portobello Road. Her favorite author is Jane Austen. She's even had to put herself on a budget when it comes to reading all the variations and sequels to *Pride and Prejudice*. She devours books on the Revolutionary War. Boston, Washington, D.C. and Williamsburg are her preferred historical places to visit.

Diane now resides on the outskirts of Syracuse with her own romance hero. When winter rears its ugly head she curls up by the fire, writing or reading and sipping Earl Grey tea. Knowing she can head home to the Hamptons to family and Jetty Four come spring and summer makes winter pass quickly. There's just something about walking along the shore, squishing the sand between her toes and breathing in the salt sea air that brings peace to her soul.

A SPECIAL THANK YOU

The author would like to extend a very special thank you to the following people: Gayle Callen, (www.gaylecallen.com or www.emmacane.com), who introduced her to a writing community called CNYRW (Central New York Romance Writers – a chapter of the RWA). She was down and out when Gayle told her to pull out a dusty manuscript and come meet a group of supportive writers, published and unpublished. The group opened her eyes to a whole new world. She never looked back.

Diane is deeply grateful to Gina Ardito, her editor, and also an award winning international romance author. Her books are the best! (www.ginaardito.com)

The series would not have been possible had it not been for her assistant, Jessica Lewis (www.authorslifesaver.com). Jessica designed the covers and helped the author navigate through the world of e-pubbing and launching the book in large print. She has indeed, the past five years, had the author's back and been a true "lifesaver".

Finally, Diane would like to pay homage to her friends of the Long Island Romance Writers (www.lirw.org) who keep her in touch with what was is happening in the Hamptons when she can't be "home" to enjoy the sand, surf and long walks on the beach at Jetty Four.

Made in the USA
Middletown, DE
13 May 2019